The Something
Borrowed
Sisters

The Something Borrowed Sisters

SHIRLEY JUMP

FOREVER

New York   Boston

Forever
Hachette Book Group
1290 Avenue of the Americas, New York, NY 10104
read-forever.com
twitter.com/readforeverpub

First Edition: December 2023

Forever is an imprint of Grand Central Publishing. The Forever name and logo are trademarks of Hachette Book Group, Inc.

The publisher is not responsible for websites (or their content) that are not owned by the publisher.

Forever books may be purchased in bulk for business, educational, or promotional use. For information, please contact your local bookseller or the Hachette Book Group Special Markets Department at special.markets@hbgusa.com.

Library of Congress Cataloging-in-Publication Data
Names: Jump, Shirley, 1968- author.
Title: The something borrowed sisters / Shirley Jump.
Description: First edition. | New York : Forever, 2023. | Series: Harbor Cove
Identifiers: LCCN 2023031147 | ISBN 9781538720264 (trade paperback) |
    ISBN 9781538720691 (ebook)
Subjects: LCSH: Sisters—Fiction. | LCGFT: Novels.
Classification: LCC PS3611.A87 S66 2023 | DDC 813/.6—dc23/eng/20230711
LC record available at https://lccn.loc.gov/2023031147

ISBNs: 978-1-5387-2026-4 (trade paperback), 978-1-5387-2069-1 (ebook)

Printed in the United States of America

LSC-C

Printing 1, 2023

To my family. They are, by blood and by love, an awesome group of people who love me despite the fact that I talk too fast, usually burn at least one thing at dinner, and can only sing off-key.

CHAPTER 1

Twinkling lights strung between the trees provided a star-lit sky, the perfect backdrop to the early Saturday evening setting, dotted with a white tent, tables, and chairs. Margaret Monroe had to admit that it looked...magical. Like someone had lifted a picture of a wedding off of Pinterest and plopped it down right here in the town of Harbor Cove, Massachusetts.

Grandma's two-story Victorian house on Bayberry Lane had been positively smothered with pink and white balloons—every single one Emma's idea. They were tied to the porch, the lamppost, the shutters—everywhere. Her little sister's passion for balloons was almost as great as her middle sister's love of the color pink. A sprinkling of pink rose petals led down the wide back steps and created a trail in the lawn leading to an elaborate wood arch, hewn by the groom himself.

The Monroe family had spent several days creating a fairy-tale wedding setting in the backyard of Grandma Eleanor's house. Everyone had pitched in except for Gabby, who had been ordered to stay away so that it could all be a big surprise on her wedding day. When she'd snuck over and seen the setting earlier that night, she'd cried with joy, which was exactly their intent. Margaret's middle sister, Gabby, was marrying her best friend, Jake, and everything, from the clear early evening sky to the violinist playing romantic instrumentals, was exactly as it should be.

And yet, Margaret could barely bring herself to smile. She'd struggled all day to put on a happy face while the girls hung out in Gabby's old room to get their hair and makeup done, while helping Gabby into her dress, and then while they had one final glass of champagne before Gabby became a married woman.

The violinist began playing a modern, peppy version of the classic processional music. The groom's father and the bride's grandmother went down the aisle first, arm in arm. Grandma sat on the left side of the aisle, Jake's father on the groom's side. The girls' father, Davis, walked down the aisle with his second wife, Joanna, and took a seat in the front row. There was a hush in the crowd as the violinist shifted gears to a slower version of the song, signaling that the bridal party was next.

The officiant nodded and bridesmaid Emma began her stroll down the aisle with a happy little sashay of her hips. Margaret waited a moment and then followed after her sister. Margaret's steps were more measured, less dancing and more formality. She clasped the small bouquet of fresh flowers so tightly she was afraid she'd break the stems. Margaret hated the pale pink dress she was wearing, hated the cheery, ridiculous balloons, and most of all, hated her tight, uncomfortable shoes. She was overjoyed for her middle sister, Gabby, and Jake, who had been a friend of the family for as long as Margaret could remember, but she could have done without the Pepto-Bismol reminder of true love and all that crap.

Maybe Gabby and Jake would be the case that proved her wrong. Emma and Luke seemed happy together, but their marriage was like a brand-new seedling. Give it some room to grow in funky directions and pair that with the challenges of years rooted with the same person, and things could change.

You're just being bitter. It's Gabby's wedding day. Stop.

So, Margaret kept a smile on her face and pretended she believed happily-ever-after existed. But inside, she knew the truth: Even the best of marriages with the best of intentions could fall apart, ebbing away bit by bit when you weren't looking.

Margaret gave Jake a smile when she reached the end of the aisle and then stepped to the left, in front of Emma. Four-year-old Scout skip-walked down the aisle, scattering pink rose petals onto the runner before darting shyly into the seat by Grandma. Emma gave Scout a little wave from under her bouquet that Scout returned, and the people in the audience *awed.*

The violinist switched gears into a rousing rendition of the wedding processional, and Gabby began walking. Gabby clearly didn't believe the same things Margaret did about marriage. She was positively glowing with joy as she came down the aisle and met her groom. As Grandma would say, one bad apple didn't mean the whole tree was spoiled. Margaret's two sisters could very well be happy forever with their husbands. Just because Margaret's marriage was teetering on the brink didn't mean theirs ever would.

Margaret went through the motions—taking Gabby's bouquet, fixing the train of Gabby's dress—and avoided looking at her own husband, Mike, who was sitting in the front row with Grandma, her not-official-yet-boyfriend, Harry, and Luke's daughter, Scout. Luke and another friend of Jake's were serving as ushers, while Jake's best friend and boss at the newspaper, Leroy Walker, held the position of best man. The officiant, a customer of Gabby's who apparently did wedding gigs whenever he wasn't working as an engineer, greeted the crowd, introduced Gabby and Jake, and made a couple of dorky jokes that made everyone laugh except for Margaret.

Thank goodness Gabby was the center of attention in her vintage dress, worn by their mother three decades ago. From the side, she looked almost exactly like Margaret's favorite picture of their late mother, a candid shot from Momma's own wedding. Her brown hair had been swept into a messy bun and she was wearing their mother's pearl earrings. The resemblance was so close that it caused a burst of nostalgia to tighten in Margaret's chest.

"Jacob Theodore Maddox," the officiant said to Jake, "please take Gabriella's hands and repeat after me."

Jake grinned as he captured Gabby's hands in his. From where Margaret was standing behind her middle sister, she could literally feel the love emanating out of Jake's every pore. The feeling was like a tidal wave, powerful and deep. Had Mike ever looked at Margaret that way? Had he ever felt that kind of all-consuming love?

Had she? Those days seemed so far in the past. It was as if it had all happened to someone else.

There was a moment back then when it seemed nothing in the world existed but Mike and Margaret—the M&M's, Grandma used to say. Margaret's gaze drifted to him and darted back when she realized he was looking at her, too. Was he thinking of those days, too? Or was his mind wandering to whether the Patriots were winning their game tonight? Margaret decided she didn't want to know.

The officiant adjusted his tie, smiled at both of them, and then dropped his gaze to the binder in his hands. "Jacob, do you take Gabriella to be your wife—"

"I do!" Jake said.

The officiant chuckled. "I wasn't done yet, but I love your enthusiasm." The people in the audience laughed and *awed* again. Grandma dabbed at her eyes with a handkerchief, and Scout looked around as if she was trying to figure out what everyone found so funny.

Jake leaned into Gabby. "Sorry. I guess I can't wait to marry you," he whispered. Gabby giggled and gave Jake's hand a squeeze.

"Same here," she said.

"Okay, then I'll make this quick," the officiant cut in. "Do you take Gabriella to be your wife, to have and to hold, to love and to cherish, forsaking all others, for as long as you both shall live?"

Jake was practically bouncing in place with excitement and joy, and his smile stretched from ear to ear. "I sure do."

Several people in the audience wiped away tears. Even Margaret felt a swell of emotions, but it was a weird combination of happiness for her sister and Jake mixed with a little bit of something that felt a lot like envy.

She'd been married for ten years and honestly couldn't remember the time when she and Mike had had that same kind of…magic. Granted, her wedding had been far less conventional, almost an outrage at the time. If Margaret Monroe had a rebellious streak, it had started and ended with the day she married Mike Brentwood.

Her gaze drifted back to her husband. Once upon a time, she'd seen his broad shoulders and thought she could lean on them forever. She'd seen that familiar look in his eyes and read it as true love. She'd seen every smile as an endearing piece of the man she'd fallen in love with, back when she was too young to truly know what love was.

In those days, he'd been everything she wasn't—daring and spontaneous, outgoing and adventurous. Their first date had been a long, winding motorcycle ride through picturesque valleys of fall colors, Margaret's arms wrapped tightly around Mike's waist so she wouldn't fall off the back of the bike or let go of this boy who intrigued her like no other.

Mike was going places, he'd told her. Leaving this town and taking his chances on making it big as an author, doing anything other than getting the accounting degree his father wanted. The day after graduating college, she hopped on the back of Mike's bike, and they ran off to New Hampshire and got married. It was the single most spontaneous thing Margaret had ever done.

He still had the same mop of dark hair that he'd had in his late teens, only it was shorter now, less wind-ruffled bad boy and more straight-and-narrow office worker. When his brown eyes met hers, she still felt, for a second, like she could lose herself in their dark depths. Then Scout tugged on Mike's sleeve. He looked away, and the fleeting connection disappeared. If it had ever been there to begin with.

Around her, the wedding had been moving along while Margaret had been daydreaming about things that should have been and never were. She realized she'd missed Gabby's vows. Gabby was staring at her and mouthing *ring*.

Crap. Margaret slid Jake's thick wedding band off her thumb and handed it to Gabby. A moment later, Leroy handed Jake a ring to put on Gabby's hand. A few more words and it was over, with the officiant pronouncing them husband and wife.

"About time," Jake said as he swept Gabby into his arms and dipped her down for a sweet and tender kiss. She laughed and kissed him back, a hand on her head to hold her veil in place until he swept her back onto her feet. Then he took her hand in his, the violinist changed gears, and the two of them literally danced down the aisle to a Matchbox Twenty song while well-wishers clapped along.

"Almost makes you cry, doesn't it?" Emma whispered to Margaret as they watched the newlyweds sashay away. She had brought her chin so close to Margaret's shoulder that Margaret caught the scent of Emma's light floral perfume. "They look so happy."

"Yeah," Margaret said. "Or something like that."

Emma flashed her a look of concern. "What's up with you? It's Gabby's wedding day, and you sound like Scrooge on Christmas."

"I..." This wasn't the time or the place to talk about the ten million things revolving in Margaret's mind or the decision she had yet to make. Emotions rioted in her gut, too many to capture in words, much less share, something Margaret tried never to do. Emma was the spontaneous one, the one who wore her emotions on her sleeve. Gabby was more cautious but open with her heart and full of words when she was happy, sad, or angry. Margaret, however, kept her emotional cards close to her chest. Maybe it was because she was the oldest or maybe because she'd had to grow up so quickly when their mother died, but either way, she wasn't about to spill her guts about what was going on inside her, not now, and probably not ever. So, she latched on to the most obvious excuse for her funk and let that take the place of the truth. "It's just a lot, seeing Gabby in Mom's wedding dress."

Gabby had tailored their late mother's wedding dress to fit her, adding a long tulle and lace veil and attaching a matching train that skipped across the lawn behind her. She looked beautiful and so happy it should be illegal.

As Margaret and Emma started following down the aisle, Luke came up beside them, slipping his arm around his wife. Scout scrambled up to take Emma's opposite hand and the three of them took the lead with Margaret trailing behind, a party of one.

"I almost burst into tears when she came down the aisle," Emma said over her shoulder. "She looks so much like Momma. It was incredible. And the whole wedding was just…"

Emma kept talking, but Margaret had stopped listening, her mind already drifting back to the same question she had yet to answer for herself. It was the question that had been haunting her for weeks, after she woke up one day and realized that even with Mike sleeping beside her, she had never felt more lonely in her life. *What am I going to do?*

Margaret couldn't just sit at this crossroads forever, waiting for the life she'd wanted to come sailing back by or for joy to suddenly fill Mike's eyes and their home. The status quo had become untenable for both of them. Which meant Margaret had to decide.

She watched the guests leave the wedding site and stroll toward the big tent set up with more twinkling lights, pink linen–covered tables, and a parquet dance floor. The band, a local four-piece group called Winging It, was tuning up, and soon everyone would be eating, drinking, and celebrating love. Margaret had heard the band several times and loved their music, but still she lingered, delaying for as long as she could.

"You okay?" Mike said as he approached Margaret. He put a hand on the small of her back, a momentary touch that felt more like an obligation than love because it was gone in a blink.

A part of her ached to lean into Mike's touch before it disappeared. To grab him and say, *Where have you gone? Where has our marriage gone?* They'd had the same argument last year and the year before, and his answer was always the same: *I'm still here, aren't I?*

He was here—physically. Emotionally, he had left her years ago. Or maybe she had left him. Either way, the fun, happy marriage they'd once had seemed like a mirage.

"I, uh, need to help Gabby with her train." Margaret spun away and headed for her sister. Action, that was what would take her mind off all of this. Anything that could keep her from thinking too much and wondering about things that were never going to change. She saw Mike head toward the cash bar. Even from here, she could sense the unhappiness radiating off of him.

Gabby was talking to their grandmother, who looked absolutely adorable today in a light blue lacy dress that came to her knees. Eleanor Whitmore had put on a pair of low heels, maybe because her date—and sort-of boyfriend—Harry

Erlich was several inches taller. He had his arm around her waist, protective and tender, and reminding Margaret yet again of all the things she was avoiding. Was everyone at this wedding in love, for Pete's sake?

"Gabby, we need to fasten your train before you trip over it and break your nose." Margaret took her sister's hand and pulled her toward the area around the back of the tent. Away from the view of Harry mooning over Grandma and Luke and Emma giving each other a little kiss.

"Ow." Gabby tugged her hand out of Margaret's grip. "I'm not five, you know. I'm fully capable of walking over there on my own."

"There's a lot to do at the reception, and you can't do any of it if you're tripping all over yourself. Turn around."

Gabby didn't move. She put a fist on her hip and glared at Margaret. "Meggy, what is your problem?"

Ugh. She hated that nickname her sister insisted on using. It didn't help Margaret's mood one bit. "I don't have a problem, Gabby. Work with me, will you?" Margaret shifted around Gabby and tried to slip one of the thread loops on the train over the tiny transparent buttons on the dress.

Gabby turned out of her reach. The loop slid out of Margaret's grasp. "This is my wedding day. Can you at least try not to be your usual grumpy self?"

"I am not—" Margaret stopped herself. She thought of her grandmother's quirky wisdom and how she had a saying for almost any situation. In this moment, she'd probably say: *If one person says something to you, they're a lone voice in the wilderness. If two do, it's a crowd shouting at you to notice.* Both Emma and Gabby had remarked on Margaret's sourness today.

Heck, even Margaret could feel the storm clouds hanging over her head. It wasn't fair to her sister to darken the wedding with her own problems. "You're right. I'm sorry."

"It's cool. Weddings are stressful, no matter how you slice it." Gabby turned back to the front again, and Margaret bent down to pin up the train. She had made it through two of the twelve loops when Gabby said, "Do you want to talk about it?"

"Not here in Pepto-Bismol land." Margaret put up a hand to cut off Gabby's objection. Yet again, Margaret had let her own irritation spoil Gabby's happy moment. "Sorry. You know how I feel about pink. Like you said, it's your wedding day. And this is nothing, really. I'm just in a weird mood."

"Are you sure that's all it is?"

"Of course." But it was a lie, one that she'd told many, many times over the years. Margaret had spent most of her life hiding the truth from her sisters, shielding them from the darker parts of life. They'd been through enough when their mother died. Emma had only been five, Gabby slightly older at eight, when their world imploded. Even though she was only a touch older at nine, Margaret had vowed that day to make sure nothing ever hurt her sisters again.

It had been a lofty goal. And almost impossible, she realized when they were teenagers and boys came along to break their hearts. Even though she knew her sisters were now full-grown adults, the part of her that had watched them crumple on the love seat that day their father delivered the devastating news had never quite gone away. As she got older, she learned to feign happiness while inside her stomach churned with doubt and stress, and she controlled the narrative to protect her sisters from pain.

"There," Margaret said as she fastened the last loop and fluffed the fabric to help the pinned train fall perfectly into place. "You're all set. And if I haven't told you already, you look wonderful in Momma's dress. She'd be so proud of you, Gabby. So, so proud."

Gabby's eyes filled with tears. "Do you really think so?"

"Of course. And not that it matters as much, but I'm wicked proud of you, too." She chucked Gabby under the chin and wondered when her sister got so grown-up. It seemed like yesterday when they were all little girls, playing Barbies on Grandma's living room carpet. "You turned out okay for a younger sister."

Gabby laughed, erasing the tears from her eyes. "Thank you for my something borrowed, by the way." She fingered the necklace Margaret had loaned her that morning.

Seeing the necklace on Gabby's neck brought back a thousand memories in a rush. It was a simple design and nothing terribly expensive. Mike had bought it for her in a shop in Portsmouth the morning after they got married. They'd been walking to breakfast from the inn they had stayed at for their wedding night, and she'd seen it in the window. Two intertwined hearts, each punctuated by a colored gem that screamed "meant to be." An aquamarine for his birthday in March, and a diamond for her birthday in April.

Whenever Margaret looked at that necklace, she thought of all the hopes and joy that had been in the air that day. Then time passed, the necklace got tucked away in Margaret's jewelry box, and the dreams they'd once had settled into a humdrum, painfully silent reality.

"It's adorable," she'd said that day on the sidewalk.

"Just like us." He'd kissed her temple and squeezed her against him.

"You are such a dork. An adorable dork, but still." Margaret laughed as she rose onto her toes and kissed Mike.

"I have an idea," Mike said. "I'll be back in a second." He'd darted into the store. The next thing she knew, the shopkeeper was lifting the necklace out of the window while Mike made goofy faces through the glass. A moment later, he was behind her, fastening the necklace and whispering how much he loved her.

"You are everything to me," he'd said. "You're the only future I want. Forever."

Now the necklace was part of another wedding, another potential happily-ever-after. Maybe it would create more joy for Gabby than it had for Margaret. She lifted the pendant. The lights strung in the tent danced off the stones. Once upon a time, she'd worn this necklace every day, almost superstitious about taking it off and breaking the magical spell of that day in New Hampshire. Over the years, she'd realized there was no such thing as magic and this necklace was just a necklace, not a talisman. "You know, this necklace is the whole reason I took over the jewelry store and made it my own."

"Really?"

"Mike told the owner we had just gotten married, and he came outside to congratulate us." She remembered standing on that sunny sidewalk, holding Mike's hand, giddy with happiness, thinking that life could surely only get better from this moment forward. "He and I started talking and I told him how fascinated I was by jewelry. How unique it can be, how special it can make someone feel. The owner of that store is the one who gave me my first job in the industry."

When she'd told the owner she lived in Harbor Cove, he'd told her he was in the middle of opening a second store, and if she wanted a job, he'd hire her. Margaret had started working there a few weeks later and eventually bought Carats in the Cove when the owner and his wife retired. All that from a single piece of jewelry.

"Serendipity, huh?" Gabby smiled. "Well, that makes the necklace all the more special." She gave Margaret a kiss on the cheek. "And now I must grab my new husband for a dance. Thanks, Margaret. For everything."

The band launched into a cover of a Katy Perry song, perfect for setting a mood of fun and celebration. Gabby danced away, hips moving with the beat. Jake crossed the dance floor, caught her hand, spun her around, and then drew her against his chest for a long, tender kiss.

Margaret looked away from the image of wedded bliss and tried to ignore the growing surge of envy in her stomach. She prayed that her sisters' marriages always remained that happy. That they would never know what it was like to feel like a soloist in a union that was supposed to be a forever duo.

God, she was really getting maudlin, wasn't she? Margaret shook off the thoughts as she crossed to the table of appetizers and fixed herself a plate she didn't really want. There was no official head table, just a sweetheart table for two at the front of the room, which left Margaret free to sit wherever she wanted. She opted for a table in the corner, hoping no one would bother her or try to make small talk.

The rest of the guests were busy mingling, getting drinks,

or congratulating the new couple. Margaret fiddled with the food on her plate and selfishly wished the reception would hurry up and end so she could go home, climb into bed, and put on something mindless like *Chopped* until she fell asleep.

Mike ambled across the space and sat down next to her. He set his nonalcoholic beer on the table and then handed her a glass of Chardonnay. "Got you a drink at the bar."

"Thank you. That was thoughtful of you." And a nice distraction for Margaret. She took a sip. A bright pink ring of her lipstick smudged across the rim of the glass like half a kiss.

"Every once in a while, I get it right." Mike sipped at his drink and watched the guests moving across the large space under the tent. The hum of conversation wove in and out of the music. "They look happy."

"Yeah." Margaret sipped at her wine and ignored her food. The stress in her stomach kept her perpetually nauseous. She'd lost ten pounds in the last couple months, undoubtedly because she had no appetite and spent any free time she had logging punishing runs along the trails that ran through Harbor Cove. "Hopefully it'll work out for them."

"There's the pessimist I know and love." Mike tipped his bottle and clinked with her glass. He took a long sip of the Heineken and went back to watching the crowd. Silence became the uncomfortable weight between them.

Margaret traced the pink ring on her glass, swooping semicircles in the condensation. "Do you, Mike?"

"Do I what?" His words were half-hearted, his attention drifting with the crowd.

"Do you love me?" There. She'd said it. The question she had danced around for months, maybe years. The one answer she wasn't so sure she wanted because it would force her to make a choice.

Mike swiveled back to face her. His dark brown eyes met hers. The gaze she looked into was older now, wiser, less full of the fire that had been part and parcel of the Mike she had married. The ten years of their marriage had changed both of them, taking away some of the spontaneity and rebelliousness that she had fallen in love with and quieting her own temporary moment of wanderlust. They'd become, for all intents and purposes, a cardboard couple that clocked in and out of work, rotated through the same handful of dinners week after week, and slept or read when they were in bed together. "What kind of question is that?"

"You can't answer a question with a question, Mike."

"I'm not, Meg." He ran a hand through his hair and let out a sigh. "Why are you doing this today, of all days, at Gabby's wedding?"

"Again, answering a question with a question." She shook her head. "Forget I even asked."

"Are we seriously fighting about whether I love you or not?"

Yes, they were, and Margaret could read what was underneath the answers Mike refused to give. She'd known the truth for a long time. Why was she so surprised? And why did it sting so much? Instead of showing those emotions or saying any of those pointless words, she became the stoic, practical Margaret who never got ruffled. "Questions: three. Answers: zero. I think your nonanswer tells me all I need to know, Mike."

"Can we have one day, no—" he put up a hand "—one

hour where we don't argue about grammar or dishes or what color the new roof should be?"

She took a long drink of wine, waiting for the smooth, oaky Chardonnay to slide down her throat and begin to shave a little of the edge off the stress. To keep her from thinking about the conversations she had never had with Mike and all the things he didn't know. It was too late, she realized. Ten years was too long to wait for something like that. "Maybe we shouldn't talk at all. That ensures we don't argue."

"Right? That's worked for us for ten years. What's another ten years of silence?" He grabbed his bottle and got to his feet. "I'm going to the bar."

"You just—" But he was already gone, leaving Margaret alone with a now-cold plate of chicken wings and Swedish meatballs.

There was a manila envelope in her tote bag inside Grandma's house. All she had to do was open the envelope, add her signature, and just like that, she could put a period on a sentence that had trailed off years ago.

They had settled into a life that was the opposite of that motorcycle ride, the impetuous eloping in New Hampshire. She went to bed at 9:30 every night, falling asleep with the TV on before Mike climbed in an hour later. Her alarm dragged her out of bed at 5:30 a.m. to go for a three-mile run before work while Mike headed off at seven for the gym to play racquetball or swim some laps. They passed each other in the kitchen on their way out the door to work and texted once at lunchtime to discuss what to make for dinner. On the weekends, he mowed and trimmed, and she vacuumed and dusted. They lived parallel lives that rarely intersected.

As month after month, then year after year, passed by, a resentment had begun to build in Margaret. Slowly, grain by grain, the hourglass of optimistic hope she'd started out with when she'd eloped began to drop into a deep bottom of pessimistic reality: There was no hope of resurrecting her marriage. Not anymore. She'd thought that finally accepting that truth would give her some kind of relief, but if anything, all it did was make her want to fall apart.

CHAPTER 2

Mike stared at the envelope on his desk while a Styrofoam cup of crappy break room coffee grew cold and the noisy clock on the wall ticked away the morning. He didn't have to open it to know what it contained. Rumors had been in the wind for months and now the day he'd been dreading had come.

The envelope wasn't even sealed, a small touch that said HR hadn't even cared enough to keep the contents under wraps. Half the people on Mike's floor had received one of these envelopes this morning, little slim white packages waiting on their desks when they arrived Monday morning. No one-on-one meetings, no warning, nothing but a cold, impersonal, one-page letter.

A month ago, Henry Cavite had sold his accounting firm, which had grown into one of the biggest firms in Massachusetts. The giant national firm that bought it had assured everyone there would be no cutbacks, but the axe had been hanging in the background. Anyone could do the math and see the redundancy between the new ownership and Cavite's employee base. Now that axe had fallen, taking 50 percent of the people at Cavite CPA with it.

Mike slid the letter out of the envelope and unfolded it. In three short paragraphs, he was told that he was being laid off, effective immediately, and receiving one week of severance pay per year of service. He'd spent a little over nine years here, nine years of punching in and punching out, then taking work home and putting in unpaid hours just to keep up with the steady flow of client accounts. Doing what his father had wanted him to do, stepping into the same job—and eventually the same office—as Nathan Brentwood had once occupied.

All because he'd made a promise to his dying father to clean up the mess his father had left in his wake and then dumped in Mike's lap. Gambling debts, hospital bills, and broken promises that had left Mike's mother in massive debt and a twenty-one-year-old Mike as the only answer.

There was a knock on his open door. Larry, a friend since day one, poked his head inside. "You get one, too?"

Mike fiddled with his envelope. "Puts a real dent in my plans to buy a Maserati this fall."

Larry laughed as he entered the room and dropped his lanky body into one of the visitor chairs. At six-foot-four, Larry was too tall and too gangly for the chair. He looked like a parent squeezed into a kindergartener's seat at a parent-teacher conference. "Like you were ever going to buy anything more practical than a Honda. Your life is work, Mike. Hell, you've barely taken a sick day in all the years I've known you."

"Not anymore." Mike folded the letter into thirds before sliding it back into the envelope. "I don't know what I'm going to do."

"Get another job." Larry shrugged. "There are a ton of CPA jobs out there. I know that because I've been on ZipRecruiter ever since people started whispering about layoffs. I applied for several positions and have three interviews lined up for this week." Larry crossed one knee over the other and leaned back in the chair. "Dust off the old résumé, and you'll have another position in a heartbeat. And probably with a company who appreciates their workforce a lot more than this place does. Who lays you off with an envelope on your desk? Cowards. They couldn't even have the decency to tell us in person?"

"What if…" Mike shook his head and let the sentence hang in the air, unfinished. He had a mortgage and a car payment, along with utility bills and a new roof they had just financed. Getting any other job but the one he'd been trained to do would be foolish and completely impractical. "Yeah, you're right."

"What's with the *what if*? This is your career, and you're damned good at it. Cavite recruited you before you even graduated college. What were you, a freshman when you started out on the help desk? Then one of the busier CPAs from the day you passed the exam? You've been one of the top guys here for as long as I can remember. The one everyone goes to for answers to questions these baby CPAs can barely formulate."

Mike chuckled. "I don't think I'm that good."

Larry popped forward and leaned his elbows on Mike's desk. "See? That's the problem. We both know the new owners are too dumb to see how great you—and me, I might add—are at our jobs. But you should know, man. You're smart as hell. Everyone knows that."

Mike arched a brow.

"Everyone but the idiots who run this place. Obviously." Larry got to his feet. "A bunch of us are going down to the Corner Pint for a beer and sympathy party. You in?"

Mike tapped the envelope against the smooth wood of his desk. He had work he could—and should—do because the clients were counting on him. Then he thought of the callous way he'd been laid off, the pittance of a severance after nine years of sixty-hour work weeks, and decided, for the first time in a long time, to say the hell with it.

Mike rarely drank. His father had done enough drinking for Mike and half the state of Massachusetts when Mike was a kid, so he avoided the hard stuff entirely, and every once in a while had a beer or maybe a glass of wine. It was Monday morning, certainly not the right time to start drinking. But he'd had a hell of a bad day, and for the next few hours, he didn't want to think about the future or next steps. He got to his feet, leaving the envelope on his desk. "It's almost five o'clock in Montenegro, so why not?"

Larry draped an arm over Mike's shoulder. "A piece of advice. When you go on these interviews for a job way better than this sweatshop, leave your inner geek at home."

❧❧❧

Margaret paced the tiled kitchen floor, tidying countertops that were already pristine and counting the minutes until Mike got home. The manila envelope sat on the smooth granite surface of the kitchen island with a pen beside it. She'd signed her name a few minutes ago, two words that had taken her years to write.

Headlights swung across the kitchen windows. The car sat in the driveway for a few minutes. Then someone got out of the rear, and a few seconds later, the garage door lifted. The car left—probably a taxi or rideshare, but Margaret didn't have the bandwidth to worry about where Mike's car was—and the door chugged down again.

Margaret stood on the far side of the counter, shifting her weight from foot to foot. She didn't want to look too zealous or too nervous. This whole thing should be calm, peaceful, and civil. There was no need for drama, even if her stomach was rioting and her heart was racing. Just then, she noticed she had left her other checkbook out on the counter. She grabbed it and shoved it into her purse just before Mike came inside.

The door between the garage and the kitchen opened and Mike walked in, carrying his briefcase in one hand and his car keys in the other. He dropped his keys in the dish on the small table beside the door and took two more steps before he lifted his head and realized Margaret was there. "Oh. You're home."

The words had a tone of disappointment, and Margaret told herself that didn't hurt, not one bit. "I left work a little early today. I wanted to talk to you."

He set his briefcase on one of the island stools before sinking into another. He unbuttoned his suit jacket, slid it off, and draped it carefully over the leather case. Then he took his phone and placed it face down on the counter, square with the edge. It was all a ritual with Mike, an ordering and straightening that seemed to allow him to disconnect from his workday. "I need to talk to you, too."

The manila envelope contrasted against the pale granite

like a stop sign in the middle of the desert. She couldn't avoid it or ignore it. She had to face it and deal with it before she lost her nerve.

Mike took off his glasses and rubbed at his eyes. "Today, I—"

"I filed for divorce." She slid the envelope across the counter. Four words and their lives were irrevocably changed. It only took two words to marry him, twice as many to erase that marriage.

"What?" He stared down at the package and then back up at her. "A divorce? Now?"

"Is there a better time, Mike? Because I'll be sure to send you a calendar invite." She cursed under her breath and shook her head. "I'm sorry. I want this to be a civil thing, not the two of us barking at each other."

He put a hand on the envelope but didn't open it yet. "I've had a really crappy day. Can we have this conversation later?"

"There is no conversation to be had. I'm just finally addressing the elephant in the room. You and I haven't been happy for years. Why prolong the agony? You deserve a life that is happy." Her voice broke a little on the last word, and her throat caught. "We both do."

"You're telling me you're unhappy." Flat words, unemotional, like he didn't care.

She arched a brow. "Neither one of us has been happy for a long time. That's not a news flash."

"But I thought—" He shook his head and picked up the envelope. "I guess it doesn't matter now." Mike pulled out the documents, scanned the pages, and then set the petition down. "I'm not signing this now."

"What? Why? We're roommates, Mike, not husband and wife. Let's just get this done and move on."

He cursed under his breath. "That is so Margaret of you."

"What's that supposed to mean?"

"The Margaret side of you doesn't like to deal with the hard conversations. So, you write up a little to-do list, cross off each thing, and never stop to think about whether what you are doing is the right choice."

"I *am* dealing with the hard stuff. I'm the one who went to the lawyer and got the petition drawn up."

"Which is a hell of a lot easier than actually sitting down and working on our marriage." He got to his feet, taking his time to gather up his suit jacket and his briefcase. "And actually talking about the things we don't talk about. Ever."

She held out the pen. "Mike, come on; let's just get it over with."

"Get it over with?" His voice had the high pitch of incredulity. "Our marriage is not a malaria shot. We aren't just going to do this quick so it doesn't hurt. Because you know what? This does hurt, and it will hurt for a long time."

For a second, she wondered if she'd made a mistake, if Mike truly did love her and wanted this marriage to work. She started to come around the counter, closing the granite divide between them. She stopped. His eyes were glassy, his cheeks flushed. The faint scent of hops floated between them. What the hell? "Are you *drunk*?"

He dropped his gaze. "I had a bad day."

Instead of coming home and talking to her about whatever had happened, Mike had opted to go out drinking with his friends. On a Monday. Was he heading down the same path as his father?

It didn't matter. This wasn't her problem anymore. She shook her head before the tears in her eyes spilled over. "Just when I thought you cared, Mike. That this marriage meant something to you." She tossed the pen onto the counter. It skittered across the envelope and came to a rest against the paperwork. "I'm going to bed. In the guest room."

CHAPTER 3

Mike woke up the next morning to the droning of the lawn service next door, a nice little punctuation mark on his massive, roaring hangover. His stomach was angry, his head even angrier. He stumbled into the bathroom, grabbed a bottle of ibuprofen, and swallowed two of them dry before he crawled back into bed.

This was exactly why he didn't like to drink too much. The aftermath. Not to mention the guilt he felt for literally rushing down the very road that had destroyed his childhood. Getting sucked in with his friends to have *just one more*, like his father had time and time again. He could see how easily his father had slipped down this slope, and in some ways, it made him understand and forgive his father a little more. Nathan Brentwood's gambling habits certainly hadn't helped. Every time he lost big, it set off another bender. Dad and his best friend, DJ, had spent more time in bars than they had with their families.

Mike refused to be that man. Yesterday was an anomaly that he would not repeat. Even if the memory of Meg saying *I filed for divorce* made him want to live inside a bottle of tequila.

The rest of the house was quiet. He didn't hear Meg stirring in the next room or the water running in the hall bath. No smells of coffee coming from the kitchen or pots clanging for breakfast. It was already after eight, which meant she had probably left for work before he got up. He wasn't sure if he was relieved or disappointed about that.

He heaved himself back out of bed, grabbed a T-shirt, and then made his way down the stairs and into the too-bright kitchen. The room looked exactly the same as it had last night, except for a single coffee cup sitting in the sink. Meg's purse wasn't in its usual place on the table by the garage door, and her keys weren't in the dish. Had he really expected her to be standing here, telling him it was all a big mistake?

Mike knew his wife well, and the one thing she didn't do was retrace her steps. She made a decision and forged forward like a horse with blinders. Once she did that, there were no other paths to take, no detours to consider. They'd once made a road trip to Chicago, driving throughout the night and stopping only for gas because Meg didn't want to be one minute late for the 3:00 p.m. check-in at the hotel. He'd told her a hundred times that the concierge didn't care when they got there, but Meg would not deviate from her plan. She'd made 6:00 p.m. dinner reservations at Spiaggia, regardless of whether the both of them were dog-tired from the drive, the first of many planned to-dos during that weekend away. It had felt more like a museum tour than a vacation.

When had she changed and become this regimented, controlled woman who rarely laughed? Was it when they were struggling to make ends meet in the early days? When she bought the jewelry store and spent a few months in the red as she carved out her own path as a businesswoman? Or had something else happened—maybe someone else—while he wasn't looking?

No. Meg wasn't a cheater. Yet for years, he had had the feeling that there was something she was hiding from him, a sentence left out of their conversations. Could he be wrong about his wife?

He filled the coffeepot and set it to brew. Then he dropped onto one of the kitchen stools. God, his head hurt. He couldn't remember the last time he'd had that much to drink. Five of them had ended up down at the Corner Pint, wallowing in their misery and spending part of their sever-ance on a sizeable bar tab. He had hazy memories of a lot of beer, too many shots, and calling an Uber to get home.

Never again. This wasn't the way to solve what was going on in his life. It hadn't worked for his father, and it wouldn't work for Mike. If anything, that decision to get plastered had made it worse. Much worse.

The divorce petition was still sitting on the countertop. Meg had folded back the pages and left the pen—clicked and ready to write—beside a yellow, arrow-shaped sticky note that said *Sign Here*. He could see the tight loops of her signature above where his name should go.

Mike picked up the pen and hovered over the line. He stared at the words on the page until they blurred in his vision. He thought about what signing would mean for the future. For him.

And most of all, for Meg. A swipe of the pen and every-thing would change.

The coffeepot finished its brew cycle with a happy trio of beeps. Mike jerked to attention.

He wrote a single word across the front of the manila envelope and then slid the divorce petition back inside. Then he stowed the pen in the junk drawer before he could change his mind.

※ ※ ※ ※

By Wednesday, Margaret had heard nothing. So she did what she did best and worked as many hours as possible. Each day, she spent ten hours at the jewelry store, leaving for work before Mike got out of bed. Since it was family dinner night, Margaret planned to stop at her grandmother's house on the way home so that she wouldn't get back until after Mike was asleep. A cowardly way to avoid running into him and having another awkward, painful conversation.

There were no texts from him about what to have for dinner, no communication from Mike at all during the day. That left an odd hole in Margaret's day, but she told herself the feeling would pass and eventually, this would become the new normal.

And yet, a weird part of her missed him. Missed seeing his face as she grabbed a cup of coffee, missed those small interactions during the day. It was simply because they'd been together for so long. A decade was a really long time to spend with anyone. This was an adjustment time, nothing more.

She pulled up in front of her grandmother's house, which was still swarming with balloons. Gabby and Jake were in Jamaica on their honeymoon and undoubtedly having the time of their lives. The balloons bobbed in the breeze, like happy little punctuation marks.

Margaret shut off the car and sat in the gathering darkness, procrastinating about seeing her family and answering questions about why she was here without her husband. Again. Her family meant well, she knew, but their concern made her feel suffocated.

Margaret fished her phone out of her purse and dialed a number she dialed every few weeks. After several rings, the call went to voicemail, which it often did. Maybe he didn't want to talk to her. Or maybe he was just feeling down again. Either way, she worried and wished she could change the complicated situation that existed in those unanswered calls. "Just wanted to let you know I put a check in the mail today. I hope you're doing okay." Then she ended the call, put the phone away, and went to the toughest trial of all: the regular Wednesday-night family dinner.

When she walked inside Grandma's house, the warm scent of roast beef and mashed potatoes wafted up to greet her. She could hear laughter and conversation coming from the dining room, Luke's deep voice telling a story, Emma adding her own details, and Scout's giggles in between.

Margaret was halfway to the dining room when she remembered the basket of fresh-baked rolls she'd left back in her office. At lunch, she'd popped down to her friend Suzie's bakery for a dozen dinner rolls, her promised contribution for tonight. She was about to turn around, using the rolls as an excuse to dodge her family, when Emma saw her in the foyer.

"Margaret!" Emma scrambled to her feet and crossed to her sister, wrapping her in a hug that somehow also had the two of them moving closer to the dining room, as if Emma had read Margaret's mind and was determined to prevent her from ditching family time. "No Mike again tonight?"

"He had to work late," she lied. Margaret pivoted back to the door. "I forgot the rolls. I should go—"

"No, you shouldn't." Grandma Eleanor gestured toward an empty seat. "Forgoing a few carbs won't kill us. In fact, Harry and I were just talking this morning about trying this keto thing, so we are skipping the mashed potatoes. Janice Stalwart lost fifteen pounds when she cut out bread."

"You don't need to lose a single inch, my dear," Harry said. "You're already beautiful."

Grandma blushed. "Wait till you get that cataract surgery, Harry. You'll see the truth then."

Their flirty conversation filled the room with a warmth and happiness that Grandma had not had in decades. After Grandpa died, Grandma had sworn off dating, saying she would never find another love like her Russell. Margaret, however, had seen the truth in her grandmother's single life—she was afraid of enduring another heartbreak.

Would that be Margaret ten, twenty years down the line? Living alone, avoiding any hint of commitment?

"Where is your head, my darling granddaughter?" Grandma covered Margaret's hand with her own. Her touch was soft, comforting, and concerned. "You look troubled."

"I'm fine." Margaret tugged her hand away to settle her napkin on her lap. She tried to work a smile onto her face. "Can someone pass the mashed potatoes?"

Luke picked up the glass bowl full of fluffy, buttery mashed potatoes and dropped a big spoonful on his own plate before handing them to Margaret. "Here you go. Everyone's avoiding the carb devil, so have an extra helping and join me on the anti-keto train."

Margaret's appetite had deserted her a long time ago. The mashed potatoes were more of a misdirection than a need. She was rarely hungry lately. She nibbled on crackers when she was at the store but mostly existed on black coffee and staying busy. When she sat down long enough to eat a meal, her mind whirled with questions and doubts.

"That wedding was amazing," Grandma was saying. "Gabby was such a beautiful bride. And you two," she glanced at Emma and Margaret, "were also stunning in your pink dresses. It's such a lovely color on you both."

"And me, Grandma," Scout said. "I had on a pink dress, too!"

"Of course! Yours was the prettiest of all, Scout, but don't tell Auntie Margaret and Emma that." Grandma winked.

The family began the usual round of dinner questions and debates—how was work, how was the garden coming along, which series was better, *Ted Lasso* or *The Mandalorian*—but Margaret barely noticed. She picked at the potatoes and a little piece of roast beef, doing her best to get a few bites down her thick throat. She had to tell her family about the divorce someday. She dreaded the questions that would follow, the disappointment she would see on their faces.

Finally, the meal was finished. Margaret pushed back her chair and gathered as many dishes as she could before heading for the kitchen. "I'll do the dishes," she called over her shoulder before anyone could object—or worse, ask her a question she didn't want to answer.

She started the water in the sink and began loading the dirty plates and silverware. The rush of the water was loud enough to cover the sob that escaped her.

"Either you tell me what's going on or I'm going to tie you to the kitchen chair and bring the whole family in for an inquisition."

Margaret turned around. Emma was standing a few feet away, arms crossed over her chest, looking as stern as a mother who'd caught her child skipping school. It would have been funny if the whole situation were different.

"I don't want to talk about it," Margaret said. She turned off the water and stared at the bubbles that had started to form and then pop, disappearing into the soapy water. In the last year, her sisters had gently nudged her to open up about what was going on in her marriage, and if Margaret was honest with herself, she would admit that having their support had made her feel so much less alone. For most of her life, she'd been the one who soldiered on alone because she didn't want to burden her sisters. But they were adults now, grown women who had endured heartache and loss, and their wisdom was something Margaret knew, deep down inside, she needed right now. "But I should. Just not here, with everyone in the next room."

"Then let me help you do the dishes and then we blow this joint and go get a glass of wine at The Nightcap."

Margaret laughed, the first genuine laugh she'd had in forever. "Blow this joint? What are you, a mobster?"

"Hey, I can be tough and kinda intimidating." Emma grinned and nudged Margaret with her shoulder. "I call dibs on drying."

Harry, Luke, and Scout bustled back and forth, bringing in the dirty dishes and putting away the food. At least five times Grandma said she would do it, but Harry told her to put her feet up and let her family take care of her for once.

Margaret liked washing the dishes. It was a mindless task, one where there was an immediate result. Circle, circle, circle the plate, rinse, and woo-hoo, a clean slate, ready for the next meal. She plunged her hands into the warm, soapy water over and over again, working her way through the pile. Grandma had a perfectly good dishwasher but she said she preferred it when her dishes were handwashed. This time, Margaret agreed because the busy work helped her find her composure again so that she was no longer on the edge of crying by the time they were done.

She'd almost forgotten about promising to go out with her sister when Emma said, "I'll also drive. Which means I get to ply you with wine until you spill the beans."

Margaret rolled her eyes but followed her sister out the door in a flurry of goodbyes. She'd walk over to Grandma's tomorrow and pick up her car. "How are Luke and Scout getting home?"

"Scout is having a sleepover at Grandma's, and Luke is going over to Harry's to help him fix some plumbing something or other. Harry offered to drive him home in exchange for his help. So I'm all yours, for as long as you'll tolerate me."

They settled at a high-top inside the dim, moody bar. It was nearly deserted on this warm summer night. Bradley, the owner and main bartender, brought them two glasses of wine, exchanged some small talk, and then went back to polishing the glasses he'd just retrieved from the dishwasher.

Emma took a sip of wine and then planted her hands on the table and leaned forward. "It's just us and old McMurty over there, who's definitely asleep, even though he's sitting up." She nodded toward their neighbor, an elderly man with a fondness for plaids who had his head down and was snoring softly. "So, tell me what's going on. Is it you and Mike again?"

Margaret considered lying, those old instincts to protect her sisters roaring to life again, but all that pretending was exhausting. For months, she'd shared bits and pieces about the trouble in her marriage. In a couple of months, the divorce would be public knowledge, which meant she needed to start having the conversations she'd evaded. Some of them anyway. There was one thing she would never tell her sisters, one secret Margaret would take to her grave. "I thought things with Mike were getting better there for a while, but they didn't. We just slip right back into the same patterns over and over again. Then at the wedding, I saw how happy Gabby, Grandma, and you all are, and I just couldn't do it anymore. I told Mike it's over."

Emma gaped. "Wait. Are you getting a divorce?"

Hearing the word aloud from someone else was jarring. *Divorce.* It sounded a lot like *failure.* For the girl who had never had a bad grade, never skipped school, never bounced a check, the idea of failing at anything made her feel guilty and embarrassed. Maybe she should have tried harder to make it work with Mike. Either way, it was too late now. The ball was rolling, and stopping it would be impossible. "Neither one of us is happy. Why stay in a situation like that?"

"I remember meeting Mike when you two started dating and seeing how you were with him. I was like fourteen, but even I could recognize true love. What's changed?"

In the beginning, Margaret and Mike had been giddy and intoxicated with love. That joy eroded slowly, disappearing grain by grain like the shores of the Cape after a storm. "We became different people. After his father died, he just sort of stopped being the guy I met. I mean, he had all these responsibilities now and problems to solve. His mother was sick, and his dad had left her nearly penniless, so Mike stepped up to help her. He went to school, became a CPA, got a good job. We bought a house and…" She sighed. "I know it sounds crazy but it's the *sameness* that drives me crazy. We used to have fun and laugh all the time. Now we just talk about whether we're having chicken or fish. And we argue about everything else."

"But wasn't all that exactly what you wanted? Predictability, order, a mortgage?"

She took a long sip of wine. "At first, I thought that would be good for us. After all, you can't spend your whole life traveling the country on a motorcycle."

"Hey, I was going to do it with a backpack. Then I met Luke." She smiled the kind of smile that said she knew she'd found something incredible that day.

A fissure of envy ran through Margaret. How she missed that feeling with Mike, the us-against-the-world united front that had made her feel safe, protected, and loved. "It's supposed to be the American dream, right? The house with the fence, good jobs, a healthy nest egg. And yet…"

"And yet you're desperately unhappy."

Margaret rested her chin on her hands. "Yes."

It made no sense. Margaret was the one who had craved order and predictability all her life. The chaos of her childhood after her mother died had made her more rigid, more structured, the type of person who tried to control every element of her life so that nothing bad could ever happen again.

Then she met Mike, who was anything but, and, for once,

let go of the tight reins she held and just *was*. In those first couple years, Mike had brought out a side of Margaret she didn't even know existed. Then his father died, and everything changed.

"Do you want some unsolicited advice from your little sister?" Emma didn't wait for an answer. She just let one sentence follow another in rapid succession. "First, you stop moping about it. Nothing changes if nothing changes. Grandma says that all the time. You have to get yourself out of this... funk and do something about the situation. Stat."

"I did. I got a lawyer and a divorce petition."

"Did that make you any happier?"

"Well... no." She had expected to feel relieved or at least at peace, but instead, picking up those papers from the lawyer had left her feeling unmoored, lost. Alone.

"Then it was the wrong thing to do. Trust your gut, Meggy. It never lies to you."

"All my gut is saying is that I need some Pepto-Bismol." She pressed a hand to her stomach. "I've been sick about this whole thing for days."

Emma perked up at that. "Any chance you're pregnant?"

A weird flutter of hope went through Margaret, but anyone could do the math and see that a pregnancy was impossible. "Definitely not. Besides, Mike and I haven't... well, we haven't done anything in a long time."

"Oh. Bummer."

"Why? A baby would only complicate all of this. I just want to walk away," she brushed her hands together, "and be done with it." They had tried to have children once, and Margaret had foolishly allowed herself to hope and dream. Before they'd shared the news with anyone, they had picked out a paint color and bought a crib, so overjoyed that there would finally be a child in their lives. But then everything went wrong. The door to the small bedroom at the top of the stairs had remained closed for five years and now, always would.

"You mean you want to be done with Mike forever." Emma said it as a statement, not a question. "Really?"

"This isn't a surprise announcement, Emma. We save those for you to make."

But Emma didn't take the change-of-subject bait about her own accidental elopement with Luke in Nevada a couple months ago. "I think you're making a big mistake, but it's your life, and you're my big sister, so I support you either way." She slid off the stool and gave Margaret a long hug. "Just think about it some more, will you?"

"Coming from the one who leaps before she even looks, I'm not sure that's sound advice." Margaret grinned and hugged her sister back. Just for tonight, she'd lean on her family and let them help her carry this heavy decision.

CHAPTER 4

Mike set the suitcases by the door and sat on the steps to wait for Meg to come through the door on Thursday night. She wasn't going to like what he had to say, and it could very well backfire completely on him, but he wasn't going to land on the mat without a fight, as his dad would say.

Nathan Brentwood had died full of regrets, wishing he'd had time enough for a do-over. The years he'd spent drinking and gambling, the fights and the holes punched in walls, all of it things he wished he could take back. Mike remembered his father crying as he died, begging his only child to "make it right." It was too late to save his marriage to Mike's mother, which had become a cold stalemate of resentment. Barbara had stayed with her husband and cared for his medical needs out of obligation, not love, which had robbed her of a happy life as much as it had everyone else.

Mike had done his best when it came to his mother, but looking back, he realized he hadn't done the same with his marriage. He'd let it wither away while he was busy taking care of everyone else. Pretty much just like his father had, except without the best buddy and partner in crime, the alcohol, and the debt. He didn't want to be the man who wished he had tried harder when it was too late. He didn't want to be his father.

Meg opened the front door and stopped short. Her gaze darted to the suitcases and then back up to him. "Mike. What are you doing?"

"Waiting for you."

"Your bags are packed." Confusion knitted her brows. "You're...leaving?"

He picked up the manila envelope containing the divorce petition and turned it so she could see the single word he'd written there earlier today, the same word he said aloud. "No."

"Wait. No to leaving or no to the divorce? Because I can proceed without your signature, you know. The lawyer said—"

He pushed off the step and stood in front of her. God, she was beautiful, even when she was angry with him. Deep blue eyes and dark curly hair that she'd cut into a bob a few months ago. The cut was growing out, leaving her with curls that framed the delicate structure of her face and reminded him of the girl he'd met more than a decade ago. "I don't care what your lawyer said. She's not in this marriage."

"Actually, it's a he. My cousin George is a family law attorney." He knew that her correcting him was a reflex, a way to take charge of a conversation that was quickly going every way but the way she had predicted. Meg glanced at the suitcases again and then raised her gaze to Mike's. "If you don't want a divorce, why are you leaving?"

"One of those suitcases is yours. I'm not leaving." His shared calendar with Meg had flashed a reminder this morning that sent him down to the bulletin board in the kitchen, to unearth the marital retreat brochure that had been tucked behind an invitation to a baby shower and a notice about the town's new recycling schedule. She must have put it on their phone calendars and set up an alert for a month before the event, something very typical of his overplanning wife. He'd thought about throwing it out, had even been halfway to the trash can, but then he'd realized that maybe this was a way they could stop this runaway train from crashing. "We both are, tomorrow after work."

"That retreat isn't for another month." She waved the brochure away. "Why would we go to that thing anyway? What's the point?"

For the first time, Mike noticed that Meg had lost weight over the last few months—too much weight—and her clothes hung looser on her frame than they ever had. Meg had always been fit, with a nice hourglass figure that she maintained with running, but right now she seemed almost sickly thin. He started to say something but then stopped himself.

She doesn't need you to worry about her. That was part of the problem—Meg didn't need him for anything. She lived her own life, ran her own business, and took care of any maintenance issues that arose around the house before she even mentioned them to him. It was almost as if Mike was invisible.

But he needed her right now, or at least the Meg he had fallen in love with. He had yet to decide what to do about being laid off or to even find a way to tell Meg he'd lost his job. He felt adrift, like someone had untied his tether to shore when he wasn't looking, and all he wanted to do was to hold on to the one constant in his world. His wife.

"Six months ago, you came to me and asked me if I would go on this couples' trip with you to the Poconos. When you asked me that, we were in the same place we are now, minus the lawyer, and you thought it would be a way to rebuild what we had lost." He took her hand in his and hoped she saw that he wasn't ready to call it quits. "Six months ago, you didn't think it was too late."

"That was, like you said, six months ago."

"And what has changed since then, Meg? Nothing, except we've drifted further apart." It had all happened so gradually. One minute, they couldn't get enough of each other. The next, he started working at Cavite and she'd bought the shop, and hour by hour they began to live two different lives. "You know, the only time we have spent together this whole month has been at Gabby's wedding? Even then, we took separate cars because you had to get there early, and we only sat together long enough to argue. What kind of marriage is that?"

She threw up her hands and paced the small hallway. "Which is exactly why we should get divorced. Because we don't have any kind of marriage anymore."

He shook his head. "No. I won't believe that until we give it one more try. And I don't want to wait another month. In fact, I don't think we can wait that long, given that you're ready to file for a divorce."

"Then obviously we don't go on the retreat."

"Or..." Mike had been waiting for Meg to storm out and tell him where he could put the brochure for the retreat. She was still here, which had to be a good sign. "Today I called the woman who runs the retreat. She does private sessions at her office in Belleview. So I booked us for a session for

Friday night and a hotel room to stay up there because she has another opening Saturday morning, if you're still talking to me then."

The whole idea was a huge gamble. The receptionist he had spoken to when he made the appointment told him to be prepared to do a lot of communicating in the session, which wasn't exactly something either of them excelled at. If there were ever two people who didn't talk about their emotions, it would be Meg and Mike. That was part of what he'd loved about them in the beginning—no drama, no tears, no knock-down fights—but also a very unhealthy way to deal with other adults because it meant neither of them talked about anything that mattered.

Like their childhoods, both full of trauma and loss. Like their fears of being open and vulnerable. Like the dark day in their marriage that had changed everything.

She didn't reply, so he kept filling the space between them with words. "God knows I need a weekend away, and so do you. If this weekend turns out to be a bust and we hate each other at the end of it, I'll sign the petition and start looking for an apartment on Monday morning."

"Mike, we should just accept it's over and move on. Dragging it out will make it all more painful in the end."

"But are you sure it's over, Meg?" He shifted closer to her. A few inches separated them. He caught the scent of her floral perfume, watched the tick of her pulse along the graceful line of her neck. When Mike paused long enough to really, truly look at his wife, his body remembered all the reasons he'd fallen for her. She'd looked so damned beautiful at the wedding that he'd almost asked her to dance. Maybe he should have, and then they wouldn't be standing here right now. "Are you saying you feel nothing for me right now?"

"I..." She swallowed and cut her gaze away. "I just think we should—"

"Should what? Walk away?" Was she looking away because she hated his guts? Or because he'd latched on to a kernel of truth? "Or maybe we should kiss each other and see if it's really as dead as you think it is."

Her blue eyes locked on his. A flash of something—irritation, curiosity?—flashed in their depths. "Mike, come on, be practical. One kiss doesn't solve anything."

"I've been nothing but practical for the last ten years." He'd traded his motorcycle for a more sensible sedan, put on a dark suit and matching tie five days a week, and clocked in and out for a dependable job he'd never wanted to do, only to be let go with no notice. He'd bought the house in the suburbs, mowed the lawn on Saturdays, stayed faithful and loyal to his wife, and now he was getting divorced. Maybe all those changes he'd made to step into the predictable role of husband hadn't been the right decisions after all. "It hasn't gotten me where I want to be. I want to try impractical for a while."

"Well, if you're thinking of quitting your job and living in a monastery in Tibet, I can't stop you. We should separate our finances first so that—"

"Quit being Margaret," he said, cutting off the stern, practical voice he knew too well, the voice that was almost a different persona entirely. It was the person she projected to her family and friends, who called her Margaret, while her sisters occasionally called her Meggy, a nickname she hated, just to irritate her. Mike, however, was the one who had always referred to her as Meg. The woman he knew was there, underneath the rigid, guarded "Margaret" front. "And just for a minute, be you."

"This is me. I don't know what you're talking about."

"Maybe you forgot her. Just like I forgot myself." He cupped her neck, his fingers weaving into the softness of her dark hair. Meg was beautiful and stubborn, fiery and rigid. There was a vast, turbulent storm of emotions in her eyes, but she didn't move away. "I fell in love with *Meg*. With that girl who wanted to taste everything life had to offer. Who climbed on the back of my motorcycle and went off on an adventure without a moment's hesitation."

"That was never the real me, Mike. I just…got swept up in the moment."

"It was so much more than a moment. At least to me."

Her lips parted, as if she was about to take a breath or say a word, and that was when Mike stopped waiting for her to change her mind. He kissed his wife the way he had kissed her that first tumultuous, wild night.

Meg leaned into him for a moment. Her arms slid up his back, hands clutching his shoulder blades, drawing him into her body. The chemistry between them roared to life again, and for just a second, everything was as perfect as it had once been. The cloak of coldness dropped, and she was his Meg again.

Then she broke the connection and backed away. "We… we shouldn't do that." Her cheeks were flushed, her breath coming in short bursts. "It's a bad idea."

"You're right. We shouldn't do that now. At least not before we resolve a few things, which is what this weekend is about." He picked up her suitcase and held it out. "So, do you want to finish packing this so I can put it in the car? Or put it back in the closet?"

She worried her lower lip. Every ounce of her was as tightly wound as a spring, and he knew the slightest thing could make her retreat into the comfort of the stuffy, rule-following, by-the-book Margaret Monroe. "Why? Why should I go?"

"Because you're curious about what I said, and you would love nothing more than to prove me wrong." He picked up his own suitcase with his other hand. "So, come on, Meg. I dare you."

CHAPTER 5

When Margaret got stressed, she liked to pace. She didn't talk about her problems or call a friend or drown herself in vodka. She paced and thought and paced and thought until some kind of solution came to mind. The movement allowed her to compartmentalize her thoughts about Mike and that kiss and the weekend ahead and focus only on her business.

It was late on Friday afternoon, and the jewelry store was empty. She'd let the employees go home because there'd been no business all day, and almost none all week. They'd had a watch repair come in, and a former customer come by to sell an heirloom brooch. No sales meant no payroll, which meant Margaret was going to be in trouble pretty soon.

Ever since she took over Carats in the Cove, she'd made sure to put enough of the profits aside to carry her through the lean months between the tourist season in the summer and when things picked up again for the holidays. Then again, through the cold of the winter until spring encouraged the tourists to return to the waterfront town. That first year had been incredibly difficult, a true trial by fire in learning how to run a business. There'd been so much stress in those days while Mike was going to school and getting his CPA license and they were barely paying the rent. Margaret had done her best to balance all the bills and keep them afloat, and eventually, they had been able to get to where they were ahead more often than they were behind.

The past two years, however, had been a roller coaster of stop-and-go sales, which happened whenever there were economic fluctuations that made her customers jittery about making luxury purchases. The little shop that had done so well for so long was now teetering in the red.

Then Roger, her sole designer, broke his hand in a water-skiing accident this summer, leaving Margaret without the one-of-a-kind designs that people sought for special occasions. All of which had led her to call in a favor with another jeweler in Tiverton. Hopefully this guy could bring in the same boost in business he'd brought to the other store.

She'd come in early Friday morning to go over the books, look at the inventory, and make plans for the next two weeks. That was much easier than thinking about going to see the marriage counselor—or whatever Beverly called herself—tonight. Why had Margaret even agreed to Mike's crazy idea? Was there some part of her that was holding on to foolish hope?

Either way, going there would probably be a colossal waste of time. No one could fix a marriage in a few hours. Maybe this Beverly woman would be able to make Mike see that there was no point in keeping this charade going. Until then, there was the distraction of work.

A sleek black Mercedes rolled to a stop in front of the

shop, and a tall, dark-haired man in a well-tailored gray suit got out of the car. He rebuttoned his jacket, pushed the lock button on his key fob, and then headed toward the store.

Margaret straightened her navy dress and patted her hair. When the glass door opened, she put on a smile. "Hello," she said to the man, extending her hand. "You must be Barrett Wilson. My friend Alice at the store in Rhode Island where you did your last residency raves about your talents. I'm Margaret Brentwood, the owner of Carats in the Cove. I'm so pleased to meet you."

Instead of shaking hands with her, he lifted her hand to his mouth and kissed the air just above her skin. She could feel the warmth of his breath skate across her knuckles. "The pleasure is mine, I assure you."

A woman would have to be made out of stone not to be at least a little wowed by his dark, brooding looks and the gallantry of his greeting. He was maybe Margaret's age, maybe a little older, and was at least six feet tall, a good half foot taller than she was in flats, and still taller than she was in heels. The pictures on his website, mainly closeups of his hands at work designing jewelry, hadn't done justice to the way he looked in real life. In person, Barrett Wilson was *H-O-T*, in all caps.

"I, uh...let me show you around." She pivoted and waved at the different counters inside the small shop. She had brought him here to help save her business, not to get all flustered by his looks. "It's not a very big store, but we do have a nice volume of sales during the tourist season. We partner with the Harbor Cove Hotel and with Jake Maddox, a local photographer, to do an entire engagement weekend slash photo shoot, which has boosted engagement and wedding set sales. Normally, that's great, but unfortunately, my designer has been out sick, and I don't have anyone to create the one-of-a-kind designs that Carats in the Cove is known for."

"That is my specialty, so this should work out well." He leaned to the right and peered into the cases while he spoke.

"I saw your work on your website and was very impressed. Your designs are all unique, which should appeal to our clientele." He was also busy on social media and had an impressive six-digit following. Margaret's shop had a couple thousand followers. A mention in Barrett's social media alone could bring some internet traffic her way, and promoting his presence, especially given how handsome he was, would undoubtedly draw in a lot more female customers. Hopefully enough to offset the cost of paying Barrett to put together some exclusive designs for her. The handsome designer had not come cheap. Travel and lodging for his one-day visit, plus a hefty fee for his design work, had nearly drained her reserves. "I just wanted to thank you again for agreeing to design some exclusives for us."

"Again, the pleasure is mine." He crossed to the other side of the store and assessed the long rows of engagement and wedding rings that Roger had created out of a variety of metals. "You have a nice take on bringing vintage into the modern day. Pairing classic designs with updated metals and using modern stones in antique settings."

She blushed at the compliment. What was wrong with her? Margaret never got flustered or shy. She cleared her throat and clasped her hands in front of her, affecting a more professional posture. "Our town is known for its vintage flair. My sister Gabby owns a dress shop downtown that specializes in vintage silhouettes designed in modern fabrics. We're also located in one of the oldest states in the nation, so it only makes sense to capitalize on that historical connection."

"I'm impressed." He did a slow turn, taking in the entire shop at once. "I have to admit I expected something more..."

"Boring? Conventional?" Margaret laughed. "Well, that might be how people describe me, but hopefully not my store."

His dark eyes locked on hers. He had an intensity about him; it made her feel like he was thinking of nothing else but her. "I have only known you a few minutes, Miss Brentwood, but I would say you are neither of those things."

"Actually, it's, uh, Mrs. Brentwood." At least for now. Besides, it was a good idea to establish some workplace boundaries. She was married, she wasn't available, and he could just use those eyes on some other woman.

"Ah, my apologies. Lucky for him and unlucky for the rest of the male population." He gave her a smile and a half bow.

"Are you always this...flirtatious, Mr. Wilson?"

"Barrett, please. And only when I meet a woman who brings out the flirt in me." He held her gaze for a beat before stepping over to the main counter and asking her about a few of the necklaces she had displayed there.

The conversation finally shifted into all business, and for that, Margaret was relieved. She didn't know how to—nor want to—do this dance of flirty small talk. That had never been her strong suit. That was more Emma's kind of thing, with her unbridled confidence in virtually any setting. Margaret didn't flip her hair or make coquettish glances. She was direct and to the point. Rarely did she step outside those prescribed lines.

Well, she had when she'd met Mike, but that had been a different time and a different Margaret.

"Thank you for showing me your lovely shop," Barrett said after an hour of conversation flew by. Barrett was smart and savvy about the industry and had some great ideas for exclusive designs that would be a nice prelude to the holiday shopping season. "I'm excited to get to work. How about I sketch up some preliminary ideas this weekend and email them to you? If you approve, I will start creating on Monday."

"That sounds wonderful. If it's okay with you, I'll announce that you are here on our social media. I think the customers will be excited about having some one-of-a-kind designs from you."

"Absolutely. I'll do the same." He swiveled his gaze from the glass counters back to her. "Such a beautiful place should be valued by many, many people."

The intensity in his eyes said he was talking about much more than the little shop in downtown Harbor Cove. Margaret was going to have more to contend with than she'd expected, working with this man, especially when her own emotions were all over the place lately. "I look forward to it."

"As do I." Barrett gave her another smile, then he clicked his key fob and left the shop, leaving Margaret wondering what the hell had just happened.

❧❧❧

Mike pulled the ladder out of the garage and climbed to the top of the porch roof. The balloons from Gabby's wedding had started to droop, as if the whole house were sad that the party was over. He unfastened the strings, gathered the bunch of balloons, and tied them together with the others he'd already taken down, clamping the bunch of strings to the ladder for now. Then he climbed back down, moved the ladder a few feet, and repeated the process several times. Meg was right. Emma had used balloons to excess.

"It's too hot to be out in the sun all day doing that," Eleanor called from below him. "Come down from there and have some iced tea. I also have a fresh-baked loaf of banana bread just waiting for some butter."

"You're going to make me fat one of these days," he said as he climbed down the ladder and unfastened the big bunch of pink and white balloons he'd gathered so far. "Not that I'm complaining about banana bread, which I think you know is my favorite. What do you want me to do with these?"

"Let's put them in the house and get a few more days of joy out of them."

Mike hadn't felt joy in a long time and wasn't so sure a bunch of droopy balloons were going to do much for his mood. He kept that to himself. Meg's sunny-side-up grandmother wouldn't understand.

He pointed at the other dozen or so that were still attached to the window shutters. "You sure you don't want me to get the rest now?"

Eleanor cocked her head and gave him a knowing smile. "You sure you don't want to take a break and have some banana bread?"

"Well, when you put it like that, how can I resist?" He chuckled and followed behind her as she headed back into the house. He set the balloons in a corner of the dining room where they formed a massive bouquet of pink and white orbs.

He could hear Eleanor bustling around in the kitchen as he headed down the hall toward the scent of fresh-baked bread. The thing he loved most about Meg's grandmother was her ability to accept and love people. He'd come into Meg's life like a tornado, and although Eleanor had had many choice words for him back in the day, he had somehow always known those words came from a place of love. She was fiercely protective of her granddaughters, whom she'd mostly raised after the death of their mother, but had seen something in Mike the day he showed up on a motorcycle, and welcomed him into her home.

His own childhood had been the very definition of chaos. His mother had been gone at work more than she'd been present, and his father had drifted in and out of rehabs, casinos, and bars, usually with his best friend, DJ. His mother had worked two jobs, trying to keep the lights on, which meant Mike had been raised by his grandparents and his uncle Robert, bouncing between family members whenever his mother was gone and then back until his father slipped off the rails again.

Then he'd found the Monroe family, and it was like finally finding home. They were the kind of family that had chatty dinners around the dining room table and Christmases filled with surprises and love. He'd seen families like that on television, read about them in books, but never dared to believe they actually existed.

The more his own family fell off the cliff after his father's debts piled up and brought the Brentwoods to almost complete financial ruin, the closer Mike grew with Meg's family. When his father died nine years ago and his mother a few years later, Meg's family became the only one he had.

"Here you go," Eleanor said, sliding a slice of banana bread, glistening with butter and smelling like heaven, in front of him. She placed a frosty glass of iced tea beside it. She sat down across from him and wrapped her hands around a second glass. "It's been a while since we've seen you. I've missed my number-one son-in-law."

He grinned. "You say that because I'm the first one to marry into the family, not because I'm the favorite."

"All three of you are my favorites. You're just the first one to be my favorite." The lightness disappeared from her face a moment later. Her eyes filled with concern, and she covered his hand with her own. "Do you want to talk about it?"

He took a bite of bread and swallowed it before answering. "About what?"

"About whatever is going on—and has been—between you and my granddaughter. The two of you have barely been at family dinners. You only sat together for a blink at the wedding. Margaret has hinted at some stress but never really told any of us anything."

"There's nothing to tell, Ella." He didn't have a clear-cut answer to what had gone wrong, not even for himself. It seemed like one minute they were happy, and the next, they were, as Meg had said, merely roommates. The manila envelope still sat on the counter, waiting for Mike's signature. She'd agreed to go see Beverly tonight but had told Mike she had no hope of it changing anything. They were caught in some kind of weird twilight-zone stalemate. "We've just...drifted apart."

"You know, boats only drift apart if they loosen their moorings. You let too much slack get in the knot between you two, and that's bound to happen."

"Maybe it's a knot that wasn't meant to be tied in the first place." He picked at the bread. Most of the time, he loved Eleanor's homey wisdom, but today, it left him feeling even more dejected.

"That is a load of baloney." She waved at the air, as if she could whisk away his words. "The two of you were so deeply in love when you got married, I couldn't have pried you apart with a crowbar. That love is still there, somewhere."

"Margaret doesn't think so." He pushed the plate away, his appetite gone. "I think it might be too far gone to fix."

"Nothing's too far gone until it is," she said. "So, don't you give up on your marriage or on her. I think you're both at a crossroads. You need to decide which way you want to go, as does Margaret. Do you want to take the unpaved path or the smooth one that doesn't have any speed bumps?"

CHAPTER 6

The skies opened up the second Meg and Mike got on the freeway on Friday evening. What had been predicted to be a 40 percent chance of rain became a dark, thunderous, harsh summer storm with wind gusts strong enough to push against Mike's Audi. The wipers slapped against the windshield, barely making a dent in the torrential downpour.

"I'm glad you decided to come," he said to Meg.

"Maybe this will give us some closure," she replied.

Closure? Mike didn't want closure. He wanted a new beginning.

The storm was a blessing in disguise because all the commotion going on outside helped cut the tension in the car. It also gave him an excuse not to talk too much, in the guise of concentrating on the road.

The dry ground soaked up the first hour of rain, but as the storm kept on pounding, the earth became saturated, and the water began to rise. First an inch on the highway, then two, and then three. Mike kept his attention on the road, wondering what the hell he was doing. He knew one weekend couldn't make a dent in ten years of decay, so why was he so determined to give it one last go?

"Looks like a good weekend to be inside," Mike said.

"And a bad weekend for business. All this rain won't bring in customers, that's for sure."

As always, Meg was worried about work, not about them. He bit back the sharp retort in his head.

The exit for the hotel appeared above their heads. Mike put on his blinker and merged to the right. "Let's promise not to talk about work this weekend."

"Work impacts our lives, Mike. Ergo, it impacts our marriage." She glanced over at him. "You didn't tell me how things are going at the office. I overheard you on the phone with Larry last week saying something about there being layoffs?"

He had yet to tell her about losing his job. Maybe it was because he was ashamed or maybe it was because he didn't want to give her one more reason to walk away. The stack of topics he was avoiding was growing taller by the day.

"Work can wait until we get back home." He'd tell her about the layoff on Monday. After he'd had time to think and plan his next course of action. He needed to put in some applications and stop procrastinating on getting another CPA position.

Meg let out a frustrated huff but stayed silent as he took the exit, which dumped them into a barren, desolate area. A faded, spray-painted sign advertising fresh corn and watermelon— *buck an ear, great for BBQ*—sat to the left beside a tiny diner that looked more like a trailer. A sign on the right said the hotel was only a mile away. "Do you want to stop for an early dinner?"

Meg made a face. "That place looks like a poster child for health-code violations."

"I bet the food is great, though. Do you remember that roadside diner we stopped at in Shrewsbury? The place with those amazing Cubans?"

It had been a day much like today. Rain pelting them on the motorcycle with no sign of letting up soon. They'd both been wet and cold, but somehow being together made it less miserable and more of an adventure. They'd picked a booth in the back of the diner near a heating vent and cozied up together on the same side of the banquette. They'd spent two hours there, eating, laughing, and falling deeper in love.

"I remember," she said softly, almost wistfully. He glanced over at her, trying to read her features. "I remember more than you know, Mike."

The car behind him beeped, so Mike turned right, toward the hotel, leaving the diner in his rearview, another missed opportunity to recapture the past. It all seemed so symbolic of their history together, but maybe he was reading too damned much into a single exit off I-95.

A few minutes later, they parked under the hotel overhang and went inside to check in. Mike pulled out his credit card for the young woman at the registration desk. "Thank you, Mr. Brentwood. I have you two in a king suite on the fifth floor," the young girl said.

"Actually, can we get two double beds?" Meg said.

"I'm sorry, ma'am, but we're sold out this weekend. There's a conference in the hotel, and we don't have any other rooms."

Meg's features stiffened with displeasure. "That's fine. Just send up a cot, please."

If anything told Mike that there would be no repeat of that cozy moment in the diner, it was Meg's request for separate beds. Maybe this whole weekend had been a mistake—a foolish, optimistic mistake.

When they got to the room, they found a welcome basket full of snacks and two bottles of wine, along with a letter signed by Beverly welcoming them to the hotel. Meg glanced at it and then pulled some yoga pants and a tank top out of her bag. "I'm going down to the gym. If I'm not back in time, I'll meet you downstairs." She went into the bathroom and shut the door.

A minute later, she left the room, and Mike had to admit he felt relieved to be alone. Her questions about work meant he was eventually going to have to tell her he'd been laid off. He'd prided himself on being a provider, the one who kept them afloat when Meg's business was getting off the ground, the one his wife could depend on financially. The kind of man who would make his father proud and always be there for his family. Until now, at least.

The severance pay was going to run out in two months. He had to start looking for something new before all the nearby positions got filled by the rest of the people Cavite had laid off, which meant applying for jobs instead of wishing some job fairy would come along and grant him his wishes.

Mike opened a browser on his phone and surfed over to a few job sites. As Larry had promised, there were at least a dozen CPA jobs within thirty minutes of Harbor Cove, most of which Mike easily qualified for. The sites made it easy to apply—one click and his résumé was uploaded and sent to the employer. He'd polished his résumé a couple months ago when the rumors started circulating and loaded it onto his Google Drive. All he had to do was drag the file over to the application, and wham, he'd be one of the candidates. Yet he sat there for a long time, hesitating.

It made no sense. CPA work paid extremely well and was something that organized Mike was good at. A few of the jobs would mean a bump in salary if he got hired. There was nothing but an upside to clicking *upload*.

You're both at a crossroads, Eleanor had said. *You need to decide which way you want to go. Do you want to take the unpaved path or the smooth one that doesn't have any speed bumps?*

Where had steady-and-dependable gotten him? Stuck in a hotel room by himself while his soon-to-be ex-wife went to the gym alone and avoided the very event that was supposed to save their marriage.

The realistic side of him whispered that a divorce was expensive, and that living alone meant having a job to pay for the roof over his head. He was too old to start again, too responsible to take chances like he had in his early twenties. There was no room in his world for fly-by-night dreams, something his mother had said to his father a thousand times. *Be practical. Be responsible.* Before he could think about it, Mike hit *upload* for three different jobs. Seemed the paved road was the one he was still going to opt for, every single time.

❧ ❧ ❧

Margaret lingered outside the meeting room in the hotel, watching Beverly talk to Mike. There were three seats at the table, which seemed dwarfed by the expansive space. The counselor had offered to come to them and do the session to give them "maximum time alone" at the hotel. Margaret could have saved her the trouble and driven to the office. The last thing she needed was more time alone with Mike, with stilted conversations and awkward attempts to rekindle the spark between them.

Yes, she remembered that roadside diner and the storm that had brought them inside for the warmth and the food. If she closed her eyes, she could feel Mike's arms wrapped around her, his chin resting on her head. She could hear them giggling about something silly and doing dorky in-love things like sharing a milkshake and feeding each other fries.

When had all that stopped? When had they gone from two kids in love to two grown-ups living different lives under the same roof?

She knew that answer, deep in her heart. It had all begun to fall apart the minute she started lying to her husband.

The lie was too big now, too many years deep, to change or take back. How could she possibly explain those choices to Mike? All he'd see was betrayal. He'd never understand her need to pay that man or keep in touch with him.

Beverly glanced over and saw Margaret. Her face broke into a welcoming smile. "Hello, Margaret. Come in, come in. I've heard so much about you from Mike."

Margaret lingered a moment longer. It all seemed so intimidating. Just the two of them, talking to a stranger about the details of their lives?

Beverly Wornack was tall and thin with short, jet-black hair and smoky eyes. She had a warm laugh and was the kind of person who put a hand on a shoulder or touched a wrist to make her point, which she did a few times with Mike. Margaret could see why Suzie, who was an effusive and affectionate person, had loved Beverly, and why Margaret, who didn't get touchy-feely with anyone ever, was going to hate her.

"Join us, Margaret. Please," Beverly said. Her smile got a little more pointed, as if the *please* was a formality.

No more procrastinating. Might as well get it over with. Margaret walked into the room and shut the door behind her. The session, Mike had told her on the drive up here, was only two hours long. Surely, she could get through two hours of talking. Maybe she'd get lucky and Mike would do the majority of it, saving her from having to explain all the reasons she wanted out of her marriage.

She shook hands with Beverly and then sat down in the seat across from Mike. Beverly sat between them. It occurred to Margaret that they'd be in the same sort of position when they got divorced—across a table, with a judge or a mediator facilitating the end of a decade together. It was almost heartbreaking to think about. They'd gotten married the same way, just them and a justice of the peace, his wife across the room, playing the organ and serving as a witness.

Mike's hair was too long, she noticed, almost reaching out to straighten the one lock that always shifted out of place when he was due for a haircut. Instead, she clasped her hands together in her lap and reminded herself that her days of worrying about Mike were coming to a close.

"This is wonderful," Beverly said, reaching out each of her hands to touch Margaret's arm and Mike's hand. "I'm always so happy to see a couple who wants to do what they can to rebuild their relationship. I'm not promising miracles from one session, but if you can come into this with an open mind—and most importantly, an open heart—you can begin to make profound and lasting changes in your marriage. Are you ready to do that?"

"Yes," Mike said.

"Sort of," Margaret said.

"Well, that's as good a place to start as any," Beverly said, her voice pleasant, patient, and as calm as a windless day. "Why don't we start by you telling me how you two met, Mike?"

Good. Mike was going first. If Margaret was lucky, her normally quiet husband would suddenly become a gabber and take up the first hour with a story or two. His face softened before he started talking, as if merely calling up the memory made him happy.

"We met at a frat party. She was across the room, sitting on the kitchen countertop, drinking a Diet Pepsi while everyone else was getting plastered. I remember she had on this little pink sweater with a flower right here." He touched his left shoulder. "When I walked in, she said, 'Were you the one making all that racket with the motorcycle?' And when I told her I was, she said, 'What's that like?' It was such an unusual question that it intrigued me. Heck, *she* intrigued me because she was so different—so adult—compared to every other girl I'd ever met. We started talking that night, and it seems like we didn't stop for years."

"You remember what I was wearing?" Margaret said, forgetting her own resolution to let Mike do all the talking. "I didn't realize you paid that much attention."

"I paid attention to everything, Margaret. Every single thing."

She could feel the intensity in his eyes, hear the longing in his voice. For a moment, she was back at that party, meeting this boy who was her complete opposite in every single way. *Intrigued.* That was the perfect word for how she had felt, too. He'd been the epitome of everything she'd secretly wanted and never dared to pursue.

Beverly turned to Margaret. "What happened after you met him at the party?"

"Well, we started dating, and a few months later, we got married." No way Margaret was going to be as talkative as Mike. A single trip down memory lane wasn't going to change anything, even if the drive over here and hearing Mike tell the story of them meeting had left Margaret feeling a tiny bit wistful.

"I feel like someone just fast-forwarded through a four-hour movie." Beverly gave her a gentle smile. "Let's back up a little, Margaret. Tell me about your first date. Just that."

Margaret thought back to those dizzying first days when she'd been as hungry for him as he had been for her. For a life that wasn't focused on responsibilities and grades and worrying about everyone. She'd only been at that frat party because one of her girlfriends had begged her to come along and serve as a wingman. Then this mop-topped boy came roaring in and beelined straight for her, and it seemed like every straight line in her life had suddenly gone squiggly. "The night we met, I told him I had never been on a motorcycle before, and so he offered to take me on a ride. We road all along the coastline of Buzzards Bay and had a picnic at Fort Taber Park." Again, keeping it to the facts, as short and sweet as possible, because the truth was so much more layered.

I've never been on a motorcycle before. What's it like?

Liberating, Mike had said. *I can take you for a ride tomorrow if you like.*

She'd hemmed and hawed, suddenly shy and afraid of a machine that came with so much danger. *I probably shouldn't.*

He'd leaned close to her ear and whispered three words that had changed her life: *I dare you.*

That simple sentence had been the catalyst for a wild three months before they eloped. Grandma had been furious but eventually came around to love Mike as much as she loved her granddaughters. For a second, Margaret had considered leaving behind Harbor Cove and all the responsibilities she had shouldered, traveling the country with Mike on his Harley. But only a month into their marriage his father had gotten ill and everything she'd dared to dream came to a halt.

"That sounds like it was a lovely first date," Beverly said, drawing Margaret's attention back to the table.

"It was." *Keep it short. Keep the emotion out of it.*

"But how did it make you feel?"

Uh-oh. Beverly seemed determined to circle Margaret back around to her emotions. "It was a first date, so you know, I was nervous and excited. Worried he'd turn out to be a serial killer and leave me for dead in the park." Margaret let out a little laugh but Beverly either didn't see or didn't like the joke because her face remained impassive. Across from her, Mike cracked a half smile.

"Thanks for sharing that, but I'm more interested in how it made you feel to be on Mike's motorcycle?" Beverly asked. "When you met him, you had asked him what it was like, which intrigued him. Now I want to know what it was like for you."

The memory of that first date was still so vivid that Margaret could close her eyes and be there again. The motorcycle, wild and powerful, rumbling beneath her. Her arms around Mike's solid chest, his hand touching hers from time to time, the warmth of the leather between them. The wind roaring past her ears, sneaking under the helmet, tangling the loose ends of her hair. "It felt...free."

"Free of what?"

"Uh, free of you know, responsibility. Homework. Life." The freedom had been so much more than that, but Margaret didn't have the words to express the emotions she'd had in that moment. To sum up how one wild ride had loosened the strings that she had used to keep herself in place for so long.

"And had you felt constrained by your life up until then?"

It was such a simple question, yet the answer, Margaret wanted to say, had layers of complexity that she didn't want to uncover. Constrained? Maybe more responsible for everyone and everything. Their father fell apart after Momma died in that car accident, which left Grandma as their primary parent. Even Grandma, for all her dedication and love, had been burdened by her own grief, so Margaret had shut her own emotions off so she could step in and help with the parenting. She got up earlier than her sisters, went to bed later, made sure they got to school on time, asked about homework. At least once a day she'd get a hall pass to go to the bathroom but instead, she'd stop by each of their classrooms to peek in and make sure they were okay. *Constrained* wasn't a big enough word to describe the way she'd totally and completely consumed herself with the need to protect and shelter them. "Yes," Margaret said.

"How so?"

Wasn't it time for Mike to be asked a question? Why was Beverly's attention solely on Margaret? Maybe if she answered with more than one word, Beverly would turn her kindly, nosy spotlight on Mike instead. "My mother died when I was nine. I had two younger sisters, and I guess I just kind of felt like it was my responsibility to watch over them and protect them."

"And make sure you didn't lose them, too?"

All of a sudden, Margaret's throat was thick, and the back of her eyes burned. She'd done everything she could to make sure nothing and no one was going to take Gabby or Emma away, too. The fear that she would lose them—as irrational as it might have been—had haunted her nights for so many years, even long after Gabby and Emma had grown up and moved into houses of their own.

"You felt responsible for making sure they were all okay?" Beverly probed again.

"I felt responsible for everyone," Margaret whispered. The weight of that worry seemed like a set of bricks on her shoulders, relentless and ever present. Her father, her grandmother, her sisters. Responsible and worried all the time.

"Just like Mike felt, with his parents," Beverly said. "He and I were chatting a little before you came in the room, and he told me he grew up in a home with a father who was an alcoholic and who was in and out of rehab several times. He lost his father, in a way, and I'm sure he worried about losing his mother, too."

As Mike nodded, Margaret realized she had never thought

of it that way. When they'd met, it had been her tragedy that seemed so much worse. A loving, wonderful mother, taken from Margaret when she was in elementary school, forever gone to all three girls. But Mike's father, who had bounced back and forth between sober and drunk until finally dying of cirrhosis in his early fifties, had been taken from Mike again and again. "I guess I never saw it like that before. No wonder we clicked."

"Both of you are caretakers who put others ahead of yourselves." Beverly looked at each of them. "Which is what you're both doing right now, I suspect."

"How is Margaret filing for divorce putting others ahead of herself?" Mike asked. "It seems like the opposite."

Hurt edged his words, softening the hard shell Margaret worked so hard to maintain. Their marriage might not be working anymore, but she never wanted to hurt Mike. He was a good man, kind and compassionate, and hearing how the divorce was breaking his heart took her by surprise. She hadn't thought past getting the papers—checking off the item on her list, essentially. She had, as always, done her best to keep emotions—his and hers—out of the entire equation.

"I know you're just as unhappy as I am," Margaret said to Mike. "And I'm positive that you can find a better life with someone else."

"So, you're filing for divorce to give me a *gift* of a new life? A new wife?" He shook his head and cursed under his breath.

Beverly touched his hand. "Now, Mike, let's try not to be bitter here today. I know there are a lot of emotions flying, but let's try to come back to center. Tell me why you asked Margaret to marry you."

The frustration took a while to leave his face as he shifted gears into memories neither of them had revisited in a long time. "Actually, I didn't ask her. One day, she said to me, 'We should get married. Right now, before someone talks us out of it.' We knew that New Hampshire no longer had a waiting period, and you didn't have to be residents of that state to get married there, so we hopped on my bike and got married in Portsmouth that same day."

"You eloped?" That seemed to surprise Beverly. "How exciting. What was it about Margaret that made you want to settle down?"

"Meg was everything my life wasn't." The answer came so quickly from Mike that it was almost like he'd known Beverly would ask the question. Or maybe he'd thought about something similar over the years. "She wasn't a partier, like my dad and his friend. She was responsible and dependable, but also had a fun side of her that sometimes took a little coaxing."

"Or a lot," Margaret said. There had been times when Mike had to cajole her into skipping class or trying some new adventure. "Mike would ask me to do everything from hike a mountain to camp under the stars, all things that made me hesitate to step outside the boundaries of my life. But you know what? Every time, the moment with Mike was worth the letting go."

It was the most she'd said about her marriage in a long time. Margaret sat back in her chair, battling a wave of wistfulness.

"Why did I stop asking?" Mike said softly.

"Maybe because I stopped saying yes." The responsibilities had suddenly piled on with caring for Mike's parents and running the store. Instead of cruising around New England, they spent their weekends balancing the checkbook and talking about the lawn. There was no time—or money—for spontaneous fun. Then, just when they had something to celebrate, it was all yanked away and the two of them never seemed to get back to that space of lightness again.

"This is all great stuff," Beverly said. "I find it so interesting that Margaret popped the question instead of Mike. It's just less usual for a woman to do the asking instead of the man, particularly a decade ago. Mike, how did it feel to be the one asked, instead of the one doing the asking?"

"Good question. I've never really thought about it." Mike took a moment, doing what he always did: giving his thoughts time to process before he answered. It was a habit that both drove her crazy and made her admire him because he was rarely reactionary, even in arguments. "Like Meg said, both of us liked to experience life, maybe because we both went through difficult childhoods. If I said let's go to the beach, she said yes. If I said let's go skydiving, well..." He chuckled. "Okay, she might not say yes to that, but she would have said yes to almost any adventure I proposed. When she said we should get married, it was like she was inviting me on the ultimate forever adventure."

The ultimate forever adventure—that was exactly what Margaret had imagined when she'd proposed the idea of eloping. A lifetime of experiences and fun. Except it hadn't really turned out that way, had it?

Secrets have a way of building a wall between you, her grandmother once said. If that was true, then Margaret had built a really big wall over the years. One check, then another, and then an entirely separate bank account that Mike didn't even know about. She'd wanted to tell him a thousand times but it never seemed like the right time. It was too late to try to explain her complicated reasoning for what she had done, and how it had smothered that spontaneity in her.

Beverly shifted her attention to the other side of the table. "And why did you ask him to get married, Margaret?"

She had a short answer all ready, a simple *Because it sounded fun*. But that wasn't really the truth, was it? Like every one of Beverly's questions, the answers were tangled up in backstory. His vulnerability earlier made her want to be honest, to put everything out there, and so she ventured forward with the truth, a little at a time. "Because Mike was the only person who had ever allowed me to be me, I guess. I didn't have to be perfect; I didn't have to be responsible. With Mike, I was just…Meg, a girl he loved for who she was underneath it all. Being with him was like being on that motorcycle all the time."

"Liberating," Beverly said.

"Yes. Exactly." Nostalgia washed over Margaret, filling her heart with a lightness that had deserted her long ago. In this nondescript meeting room, she was young again, feeling that rush of giddiness when Mike said *I dare you*. Three words that loosened everything inside of Margaret, as if all she'd been waiting for was permission to stop being so stoic and controlled. "I guess I thought if I married him I could…"

The words lodged in her throat. Saying them seemed like a betrayal in a way. Even though her family wasn't here, saying aloud that she wanted to be freed of the self-imposed burden of caring about them seemed wrong somehow.

"You could let go, too, and have your own life," Mike finished softly. "We never should have stopped having those adventures."

"Then who would have paid the mortgage?" She said the words like a joke, but there was a ring of truth in the words. Mike had always known her so well, maybe too well, because right now, he was finishing every thought she had.

"We would have figured it out. Frankly, we should have figured it out long before now." Mike let out a long, deep sigh. "I miss you, Meg. I miss us."

God, she missed him, too. It had felt so lonely all these months, living separate lives, barely interacting. She ached for him to be with her, for him to tell her a silly joke or touch her with desire. She missed the man she had married, the man who had changed everything about her life for one brief moment in time.

"I miss us, too," she admitted.

"Then why?"

Margaret could hear the hurt in his voice, see it in the slump of his shoulders. The icy wall she had put between them began to crumble. "Right now, I honestly don't know," she said. It seemed like the divorce was a big mistake, a moment of rashness that she desperately wanted to undo. Maybe they could rewind and find where their paths diverged. Maybe...

Maybe there was still time. Before she could think about it, she reached across the table and took Mike's hand in hers. He looked up in surprise. And joy.

She knew she should let go, that she shouldn't send this mixed message, but right now, she needed, as Beverly had said, someone else to do the caretaking. She needed him to love her and want her and make it all stop hurting. "I miss all of it, Mike. I miss being spontaneous and fun and...so many other things."

Beverly clapped her hands together. "This is all wonderful. Great progress. I want you two to talk about when you can take your next adventure because it sounds to me like that's exactly what you both need. We did great work today. We can do even better work in our next session tomorrow."

The counselor looked at both of them, but Margaret barely noticed. All she could feel was the growing tension in that simple touch, the need to get the hell out of this room and recapture what they had lost somewhere along the way.

Mike held her hand all the way out of the room and into the elevator. The doors shut, and as he turned to her, his hand slipped from hers and slid around her waist, settling into the sensitive valley above her hip. He grinned, and the devilish glint she knew so well appeared in his eyes. "Is this what you were thinking of for our next adventure? What if—"

She put a finger over his lips. Even hearing the word *adventure* sent a little thrill of freedom through Margaret, just as it had a decade ago. "Let's not *what if* this, Mike. Let's just see where it takes us."

CHAPTER 7

Harry had become as familiar to Eleanor as her own grand-children. Her handsome neighbor, who had done his best to woo her ever since he moved in next door a year ago, had become a constant fixture in her house and in her life. They went out at least once a week and had dinner together most nights before he wandered back to his house, and Eleanor sat on her sofa and wondered how on earth she could be falling for another man.

Even though she'd been resisting their relationship nearly every step of the way, Eleanor couldn't imagine life without Harry. He'd become her friend, her confidant, and sometimes her partner in crime, like when they'd crashed the father-daughter dance to do a little meddling between Emma and Luke. Meddling that had turned out quite well in the end.

Tonight, as they drove over to Bella Vita, one of their favorite Italian restaurants and also one of the locations of Eleanor's matchmaking, she thought about Mike's hangdog face the other day and the months of trouble between him and her eldest granddaughter. Something seemed different now between them, almost as if...

No. Things weren't that bad, were they? Yet, as she recounted her conversation with Mike and her granddaughter's frequent avoidance of family dinners, the truth filled her with a sinking feeling of doom.

"Harry..." Eleanor's voice trailed off as a plan began to take shape in her head. She couldn't let them break up, absolutely couldn't.

"Hmm?" He was busy navigating the car into a parking space. He was a cautious driver, something she appreciated more the older she got. Massachusetts's roadways were difficult and dangerous enough without adding another aggressive driver into the mix. But sweet Harry had a way of making even rush-hour traffic seem sort of calm. Which, by extension, made her feel calm—and gave her mental space to devise well-meaning plots like this one.

"Harry, I have an idea."

He shifted the car into park and turned in his seat so that every ounce of his attention focused on her. She liked that. Harry was a man who didn't do anything halfway. "This sounds like trouble."

"My ideas aren't trouble...exactly."

He laughed. "Your granddaughters would disagree with you. There was a fair amount of matchmaking going on this past year."

"Yes, but look at how it ended up. Gabby is happily married, as is Emma. I have two new sons-in-law who are amazing young men."

"I hear a *but* in your sentence."

"You know me well." She laughed. "Too well, I think."

"Whatever it is, I'm in. Because I've never had as much fun as I've had with you, Ella."

Heat filled her cheeks, and the butterflies in her stomach danced with joy. This man was growing on her more and more. "You are too good to me, Harry."

"We have never had an argument, but that is an area where I completely disagree. It's you who is too good to me." He waved at the console between them, which she had populated little by little with his favorite tissues, an extra water bottle, a backup charging cable, and even a flashlight after he'd had car trouble last month. "You take care of me and worry about every little thing with me. Why, you even put one of those window-breaking gadgets in the glove compartment."

"Well, more than ten thousand people end up in the water in their car each year. You never know when you'll have to break out and swim for the surface."

He chuckled. "Ten thousand people out of eight billion is a pretty tiny percentage, so I'm not too worried. Anyway, what's this idea you wanted to talk to me about? Should we wait until after we order dinner?"

Eleanor thought of Mike's face and the resignation in his voice. For all Eleanor knew, he and Meg could already have called it quits. "The restaurant will still be there an hour from now. But Mike might not be."

Harry's eyes widened. "Are Meg and Mike in bigger trouble than we thought? Do you think they might get divorced?"

"I think they're in the process. Mike said something about things being too far gone to fix. When we talked, he was sadder than I've ever seen him. Almost...resigned to the end." She sighed and stared out the window, watching a couple walking by, arm in arm. Once upon a time, that had been her granddaughter and her husband. When they'd first gotten married, they'd been deeply in love and inseparable. "They used to be so happy when they were younger. I truly believe they can be happy again."

"Some marriages fall apart and there's nothing you can do to put them back together."

"And some marriages just need stronger glue." She refused to entertain the thought that Mike and Meg were completely over, that there was nothing she could do. "Either way, I have a plan. I'm going to ask Mike to work on a book for me."

She'd been tossing around the idea for a book of her advice columns for a few months. Leroy, her editor at the *Gazette*, had first planted the idea when they toasted her twentieth year of publication of the Dear Amelia column. She'd resisted because she hadn't wanted to unmask her anonymity, but right now, Meg and Mike's marriage was far more important than people knowing the face behind the column.

"Wait. Mike's a CPA," Harry said. "What does he know about writing books, and how does that bring them together?"

"He used to want to be a writer, and then his dad got sick, and it was a whole thing where he had to grow up quickly." Eleanor did not have time to get into the details, not when there was a relationship at stake. She had to formulate this plan and execute it before things got much worse. "Margaret will be the voice of family history, helping her husband compile the stories to link the columns together."

"So, you're going to use your advice column to matchmake

between your granddaughter and her husband, just as you used it to bring Gabby together with Jake and work some magic between Emma and Luke?"

When he put it that way, it almost sounded like she was scheming. This was merely a nudge in the right direction. "It worked before. Why can't it work a third time?"

"You have a point," Harry said. "We might be able to pull this off."

Except that Meg was headstrong and intuitive and might figure out what Eleanor and Harry were doing, especially since Eleanor had a reputation for meddling a little. "I think that all Margaret needs is more reasons to talk to Mike. Spend time with him."

"Maybe give the whole thing a little room to breathe and see if they can work it out on their own first," Harry said. "You don't know for sure that they're getting divorced, nor do you know if this is even something Mike wants to do."

Harry was missing the point. Yes, there was still a chance they'd find their own way back to each other, but a bigger chance that they wouldn't, at least not on their own. Which was exactly why God invented meddling. "I don't know for sure what he's thinking, but I've seen how he looks at Margaret when he thinks no one's watching. Mike's a man. He doesn't share much of what's going on in here." She tapped her chest.

"Hey, I might resent that remark."

"You share far too much." But she smiled as she said the words because her dear Harry always shared what was in his heart and was the sweetest person she'd ever met. "And I hope you never stop."

"I am wearing you down." He grinned. "My evil plan is working."

"It is not. Not one bit." But as Eleanor raised her chin and feigned indifference, she could see the twinkle in Harry's eyes and knew he could see right through her.

❧❧

Early Saturday morning, Meg lay in Mike's arms, her body warm against his. An empty bottle of wine sat beside a still-full second bottle and a stack of dishes from room service. In the space of a couple hours, everything had shifted between them.

As they'd left the session, Meg had slipped her hand into his and then turned into his arms in the elevator. Maybe she was feeling vulnerable after being so emotionally open; maybe she had missed him. He didn't know. He didn't ask. She'd been sentimental and vulnerable, and he'd read that familiar need in her eyes, the need that he'd thought had disappeared.

He'd kissed her in the elevator, a simple kiss that quickly turned into a tempest. The hunger and passion they'd had ten years ago returned, leaving Meg and Mike stumbling into the room, tripping over pants and jeans and shoes, and landing in bed together in a frenzied rush to be together. Afterward, he'd ordered room service and she'd cracked open the wine. They'd lain in the bed, eating junk food and watching an old movie they found on cable. Things they hadn't done in forever. And for just a moment, it was wonderful again.

Faint sunlight peeked between the curtains. He figured it was around 6:00 a.m., maybe a little after. Too soon to get up. But as he turned to curve his body around Meg's and grab a couple more hours of this heaven, she slid out of the other side of the bed. She rooted around in her bag for some clothes. "Just going to get in a quick run before we start the day."

Her voice held a distance he knew too well. Already, she was slipping back into the regimented Margaret who wore her guard like it was a wool coat. Mike flipped onto his back. "Of course you are."

The bathroom door snicked shut and he heard the sound of water running. He had just started to drift off to sleep again when he heard her voice. He jerked awake and sat up. "What did you say, Meg?"

"I said, what the hell is this?" Meg was holding his phone, forgotten last night on the bathroom counter when they'd come back from the session. Ever since the layoff on Monday, Mike had made sure to keep his phone with him because he didn't want a text from Larry or one of the other guys to broadcast the information about the layoff before he had a chance to sit Meg down and tell her. "How could you not tell me?"

And apparently what he had been dreading had happened. Even from here, he could see the white box of a text message, most likely Larry, nudging him to apply for a job. "I was going to tell you," Mike said, "but then all of this happened, and I just couldn't find the right time."

It was a lame excuse. He knew it; Meg knew it. He'd been afraid, plain and simple, that being jobless would give her one more reason to leave him.

"According to Larry's text, you guys got laid off on Monday. That's six days ago. *Six*. And yet, every morning, you've left to go to 'work.'" She made air quotes around the word. "Where have you been going if not to the office?"

He slipped out of the bed and pulled on his jeans. This wasn't a conversation to have naked. Getting dressed also bought him a couple seconds to compose his thoughts and maybe try to find a way to defuse the betrayal on her face. "I've been hanging out at your grandmother's house."

"My grandmother knows about this and didn't tell me either?"

He found his polo shirt under Meg's sweater and wrangled it back on. "No. She thinks I switched to flex hours. I've been helping her with a project."

Fury flushed in Meg's cheeks and she started to pace, her words sharp spikes in the air. "Last night, when I was baring my soul, and you were supposedly baring yours, you could have told me about this. Instead, you kept it from me, had sex with me, and pretended like everything was fine. You've lied to me, Mike, all week." Margaret tossed his phone on the bed. "I can't believe I let myself believe we could maybe... Whatever. I was wrong."

"You threw divorce papers at me the day I got laid off. Do you really think that would have been a good time to tell you?"

She turned on her heel and opened the hotel room door. "Sign the papers, Mike. We're done."

CHAPTER 8

Margaret had done a good job of avoiding Mike and her life ever since that morning in the hotel six weeks ago. She'd walked out of the room, caught an Uber home, and hadn't spoken to her husband since. She'd spent that Saturday at work, avoiding him by spending her day ostensibly working on an online ad campaign for Barrett's designs. The task had kept her there until long after the shop closed.

By the time she got home, Mike was gone. His half of the closet emptied, his space vacant in the garage, and the divorce petition signed and on the kitchen counter. Everything she wanted, in a neat and tidy package.

Yet, why had she felt so empty ever since then? It wasn't just the space in the house, it was something deeper, harder to put into words. Every day seemed ten times more draining and depressing than the one before. Maybe it was all the paperwork to do with the divorce, the categorizing of their things, and assigning a value to a decade of life together. Whatever it was, Margaret hoped the feeling would pass after the divorce was final.

She sat in her car and watched the beehive of activity on

the UMass Dartmouth campus, so like the college she remembered when she'd gone here. It was a warm mid-October day with just a hint of coolness in the air. The trees had begun to turn, blanketing the grounds with a rich tapestry of color that would only deepen in the coming weeks. Margaret sat in her car and watched the students bustle between the buildings.

The irony that life had come weirdly full circle didn't escape her. Eleven years ago, she had been the one on these concrete paths, hurrying toward the Charlton building where the majority of her business administration classes were held. She'd sat in the turquoise chairs behind curved white desks and soaked up everything she could, knowing that someday she wanted to run her own business. She hadn't expected to buy the jewelry store so soon after graduation or deal with so much financial upheaval in those first couple of years. The degree had prepared her in some ways, but her main education had come from the school of hard knocks.

A thin blond young woman with a streak of magenta in her hair came hurrying out of Willow Residence Hall with a group of her friends, the four of them chatting as they made their way down the concrete walkway and onto the path to the Visual and Performing Arts building. The young woman stopped for a second and turned her face to greet the sun. One of her friends laughed and grabbed her elbow, hauling her along with the group. "We're going to be late, Tabitha. Work on your tan later."

"I'm just appreciating the sun for being here," the blonde said. "A little thank-you for the rays."

"You are so weird," the other girl said. "But we love you anyway."

The four of them laughed and the rest of their conversation was lost to the breeze. Margaret watched until they disappeared from view. Tabitha seemed to be doing well, much better than she had been last year. That was a relief. Margaret had dropped a check off at the bursar's office this morning, more than enough to cover fall tuition and a little extra for books. Tabitha had no idea who her benefactor was, and as far as Margaret knew, the young woman had been told it was all part of some mysterious scholarship.

It had been more than two decades since Tabitha's birth in the same hospital where Margaret's mother had been declared DOA. Joy and sorrow, intertwined. Tabitha had had a late start on college, but here she was, in her mid-twenties, clearly enjoying her life and the possibilities before her.

Would Mike understand what Margaret had done if he could see this young girl enjoying a normal life, with college and friends? Would he forgive her for keeping a secret all these years?

Unlikely, Margaret knew, especially because she had stopped talking to him after finding out he'd been lying about his job. She knew the two secrets weren't at all on par with each other, and deep down inside, she had to admit she'd used his lie as an excuse. Another way to avoid coming clean about what she'd been doing for years.

She put her car in gear and pulled out of the lot. A few minutes later, UMass Dartmouth, the memories she had of that place, and the girl she had watched grow up from the sidelines were all tucked firmly in the back of her mind.

She'd go to work, even though both Tara and Duane were there and Margaret had the morning off. It was far easier to work until she could barely see straight than think about everything that was happening around her. She knew that someday she'd have to deal with all the emotions surrounding the divorce, but that day was not today.

Thankfully, the shop had been busy after featuring Barrett's designs. They'd sold out of everything he had created and gained hundreds of new followers on social media. It had been enough money for Margaret to hire a second full-time employee and run an ad campaign for the fall. Customers, particularly female customers, had been clamoring for more from Barrett, especially before Christmas.

A text message dinged on her phone and, a second later, appeared on the screen in her car. "Let's grab lunch at the diner at noon," Emma texted. "It's been forever since we caught up. Gabby and Grandma are already in, so be there or be square. Love you!"

Undoubtedly, her sisters and her grandmother wanted to check on her and maybe get an update about where things were with Mike, all in a well-meaning but nosy way that would result in some just as well-meaning advice Margaret didn't want to hear.

She needed to tell them that she'd filed for divorce. As far as she knew, Mike hadn't said anything, but it was only a matter of time before everyone realized Margaret and Mike were no longer living together.

She started to reply with a no but then stopped herself. It had been an emotional few weeks ever since Mike had left. Maybe it would be good to spend a little time with her sisters and Grandma.

"Sure. I'll see you there," she read to the AI interface before hitting send.

By the time noon rolled around, Margaret had considered

canceling a half dozen times. She had a long list of excuses—she was behind in her bookkeeping, she had a new employee who needed some more training, she wasn't hungry—but in the end, she found herself heading down to the diner. Emma, Gabby, and Grandma were already inside, sitting at a booth by the window.

"You came!" Emma grinned. "I knew you couldn't resist seeing us."

"Or maybe I just need to eat like the rest of humanity." She hugged her sisters and grandmother and then sat down beside Emma. "I only have—"

"A little bit of time," Emma cut in. "We know the Margaret rules."

"Margaret rules?"

Emma and Gabby exchanged a look before Gabby spoke. "Only one family dinner a month, stay less than an hour at any family event—"

"Except for Gabby's wedding," Grandma cut in. "You made it all the way to the end of that."

"And dodge as many personal questions as possible in between the entrée and dessert." Emma crossed her arms over her chest. "Do I have that about right?"

Margaret scowled. "If this is going to be a criticism of me, I don't need to eat that badly."

Grandma clasped Margaret's hand. "We're sorry. We don't mean it like that at all. Emma is just a little cranky because Scout had too much sugar last night at a birthday party and was up until two in the morning."

"I had no idea one kid could have that much energy," Emma said with an exhausted sigh. "I can't even imagine what it would be like to have a baby."

"Are you and Luke...?"

"No." Emma shook her head but then brightened. "But we decided to start trying. With any luck, I'll get pregnant when Gabby does."

"Jake and I are kinda trying," Gabby admitted. "But we're in no rush to have kids."

"The trying's the best part," Grandma cut in with a wink. When the girls all gasped, she waved at them. "My goodness, you'd think the three of you were created out of thin air. Sex is not a bad thing. Especially with the right man."

Emma put her fingers in her ears just like she used to when she was little and her older sisters would start squabbling. "Ew, Grandma. TMI. TMI!"

Margaret laughed at her youngest sister's clear discomfort with the idea of their grandmother being intimate with Harry. It was nice to see her grandmother so happy. "That's what happens when you're in love, right, Grandma?"

Grandma blushed. "Oh, I don't know if I'd say I'm in love with Harry."

"Yet," Margaret said, "I've seen how you two look at each other." Both of them had stars in their eyes whenever they were together. Margaret noticed they found tiny moments and excuses to touch each other, whether it was a hand on Grandma's back as they walked down the sidewalk or her hand in his as they walked into a restaurant or sat side by side at the dinner table.

It had been like that in the beginning for Mike and Margaret, too. Then somewhere along the way, it all just stopped. She prayed that never happened to her sisters or her grandmother. None of them should have to come home to an empty house like she did every night.

"Well, we're not here to talk about me and Harry," Grandma said. Her cheeks were nearly red now, but there was real happiness in her eyes, a joy that was wonderful to see. Grandma had spent far too many years alone after Grandpa died. "How are you doing, Margaret?"

"And you guys wonder where I get my conversational avoidance skills from?" Margaret pointed at her grandmother. "I'm not the only one who changes the subject when it comes to my love life. And as much as I'd rather talk about anything else..." She sighed. "I have something to tell all of you."

The other women grew quiet as if they sensed the gravity of the moment. No waitress came along to interrupt or give Margaret a chance to avoid talking about the divorce, so she plowed forward with the news. "Mike and I are getting divorced."

There was an audible gasp at the table. Gabby's jaw dropped. "Really? Why? When?"

"I filed a few weeks ago." Margaret put up a hand to cut off her family's protests. "I didn't tell you all for exactly this reason. I didn't want anyone talking me out of it or trying to change my mind."

"Which we would certainly do," Grandma said. "You two were always so happy. What went wrong?"

"If I knew that answer, Grandma, we wouldn't be here."

"Well, we're here for you, Meggy, no matter what happens." Emma wrapped an arm around Margaret and drew her close.

"You know I hate that nickname, right?"

"But we love you anyway." Emma grinned and hugged Margaret tighter. She leaned into her sister's embrace and soaked up all that love and support. Gabby and Grandma slipped out of their side of the booth and sandwiched Margaret in a giant Monroe-girl hug.

When they were done, Margaret sat back and swiped tears away from her eyes. "Thank you, guys. I needed that."

"Anytime," Gabby said. "I mean that. Anytime you need one of us, just call or text or send up a smoke signal, and we'll be there."

"Do you need anything, honey?" Grandma said. "Do you want to come stay with me?"

"I really don't need anything but a whole lot of distraction." Margaret toyed with the menu and glanced at each of her sisters. "So, can we talk about any other topic besides love lives and babies and how damned happy everyone else is? Don't get me wrong, I'm thrilled for you all, but also not in the mood for Hallmark movies, if you know what I mean."

"We know exactly what you mean." Emma thanked the waitress as she set three glasses of water on the table. "So, let's talk about my favorite subject. Food. What do you want to eat? I'm starving, so I hope you're both ready to order."

Grandma, Gabby, and Emma ordered sandwiches while Margaret opted for a small cup of soup. Her appetite had yet to return, and eating had become more of a way to stop losing so much weight than anything she really wanted to do. She saw the look of concern on her grandmother's face and added a side salad to her order just to keep from having a conversation about calories—or the lack thereof.

"I stopped by the store this morning," Grandma said. "I wanted to see some of those designs that Barrett Wilson guy did, because all the women in my book club have been raving about them since you started carrying them for Labor Day weekend. I was so pleased to see that you're sold out of them."

"He was a hit with my customers." *Hit* was an understatement, given how often her customers remarked on the poster advertising his designs. A poster that happened to also feature a photo of his handsome face. "I just talked to him this morning, and I'm going to bring him back next week for an in-person residency. I'll set him up in the front of the shop by the windows so any foot traffic we get can get a peek of him in action, so to speak."

"I saw that poster. I bet you're going to get a lot of foot traffic just to see him, never mind his designs." Grandma grinned.

"Ooh. Maybe I'll have to come by the store myself," Emma said. When Margaret shot her a look, she put up her hands. "Hey, I might be married, but I can still appreciate a handsome stranger."

"He's not that handsome." Even as Margaret said the words, she felt her cheeks flush. Barrett had those classic tall, dark, and handsome looks. He was the kind of guy that pretty much any woman would find attractive.

"So, you have noticed him." Emma plopped her chin in her hands. "And...are you going to ask him out?"

"Emma, I've only been separated for a few weeks. I have no desire to ask out or go out with anyone." The mere idea of dating again terrified Margaret. She'd barely dated before she met Mike. The whole world of dating had changed in that decade. Was she supposed to sign up for an app? Hang out at a bar? All of it sounded like a nightmare in the making. "Besides, I don't have time to date. This whole thing has been..." Margaret might as well be honest. There was no reason to lie about the difficulties she'd had in the last few weeks or the emotional roller coaster she'd been on ever since Mike had signed the petition. "Tougher than I expected. Mike moved the last of his stuff out over the weekend and the house is just so quiet."

"I bet it's hard." Gabby clasped Margaret's hand. "I'm so sorry."

"It's okay. Or it will be." The waitress dropped off their food. Margaret's stomach rebelled against even the idea of the salad now, so she dipped a spoon into the warm, thick chicken noodle soup and told herself to at least take a couple bites.

"I just think it all sounds so sad." Emma sighed. "Call me a romantic, but I think you two could still work it out."

"We are way past that, Emma." There was no calling this back, even if Margaret wanted to. As soon as Mike signed the petition, the two of them had stopped talking. There had been a few emails back and forth between cousin George and Mike's lawyer, but no contact between them. She told herself it was easier that way. No drama, no arguing over the lamps.

"It's never too late until it is," Grandma said.

Margaret chuckled. "What is that supposed to mean?"

"I just love the french fries here, don't you?" She popped one in her mouth and gave Margaret a mysterious smile.

The change of subject shifted them into small talk about the food, which led to an update on the community center that Emma had opened at the beginning of September in memory of their late mother, who had always dreamed of running a place like that. "We have a whole slate of programs coming up for the holiday break," Emma said. "The community center is growing by leaps and bounds."

"That's fantastic, Emma. I'm so glad." Margaret's youngest

sister had turned her part-time gig as an activities director into a full-time community effort when she and Luke had renovated an abandoned meeting hall and turned it into a center specifically to support kids and single parents. "You're so good with kids. I can't even imagine having that kind of patience or creativity."

"To be honest, I'm winging it most of the time." Emma laughed.

"That's what all parents do," Grandma chimed in. "It's not like you go through a certification program while you're pregnant."

"Hey, if there were such a thing, I'd sign right up." Emma ate one of the fries in the communal dish. "Either way, Luke and I have our hands full right now just getting the community center off the ground, so there's not a lot of time for baby making. That's all on Gabby right now."

"Me? Why me?"

Margaret listened to her sisters' banter about babies and marriages and envied them. It was a repeat of the moment at the wedding when it seemed she'd never been that happy, when really, the memory was so far in her past that she could barely bring it to mind.

"Well, if that's the case, you should eat more of those pomegranates," Grandma said, nodding at Gabby's salad.

"Why pomegranates?"

"I read that pomegranates are supposed to increase your fertility," Grandma said. "And I may or may not have been putting them in the smoothies I make you, Gabriella."

"Grandma!" Emma said. "You're incorrigible."

"And eternally optimistic." She grinned. Then she sobered

and put a hand over Margaret's. "It's too bad you and Mike never had kids."

The words sent a sharp pain through Margaret's chest. There'd been a time when they thought that dream would come true. A moment when their lives couldn't get any more perfect. A moment that was cruelly taken from them almost as quickly as it happened. Margaret shoved those thoughts aside and avoided looking directly at her grandmother. "I'm a workaholic with perfectionist tendencies. I'd be the worst kind of parent."

Grandma danced her fingers in the air, dismissing Margaret's words. "Children change everything about you in the very best of ways. And you, my darling Margaret, will make an amazing mother someday. I have no doubt about that."

Someday wasn't going to come for a long, long time. If ever. Instead of saying that, Margaret just nodded and directed her attention toward the soup she could barely stomach.

CHAPTER 9

Mike sat at Eleanor's kitchen table, eating leftovers from the family dinner he hadn't felt comfortable attending. Now that Meg had told her family about the divorce, he had decided to stay away from the group events. Instead, he tried to come by as often as he could during the quiet of the day, because he still craved that family connection and Eleanor's warm welcome.

"I know you love lasagna, so I saved you that corner piece," Eleanor said as she sat down across from him with a cup of tea. "There's another one if you're still hungry."

He patted his stomach. "I don't think I can eat any more."

"Then I'll box it up and you can take it with you when you go. Frozen dinners are like not eating at all, and you are probably not feeding yourself very well these days." She patted his hand. "You have to take care of yourself before you can take care of anything else."

He chuckled. Eleanor always had quirky advice for everyone she talked to. It was no wonder she'd been so successful with her advice column. He loved every one of her corny sayings, even if they didn't always make sense. "I'll remember that. Yet another Dear Amelia gem."

"That reminds me of something I wanted to talk to you about." She got to her feet and began packaging the rest of the lasagna into a plastic storage container. "I was wondering if you could...help me with something. If you have some spare time, that is."

"Sure, anything." All he had was spare time right now, but he didn't tell Eleanor that. He had yet to decide what he wanted to do about his job, and was watching those weeks of severance tick by. He'd had callbacks from two interviews but had no desire to take another full-time CPA position. Maybe, he'd been thinking, he could go into business for himself.

"I've been thinking of compiling all my best columns into a book," Eleanor said. "The older I get, the more I want to leave a legacy for my family and the people around me."

"You mean you're finally going to tell everyone who you are?" He was surprised. He'd thought Eleanor would take her secret identity to the grave. Last year, when her granddaughters discovered the truth, she'd been upset about people knowing the true face behind the weekly advice column.

"I think it's about time to come clean and wear my Dear Amelia identity with pride." She smiled. "There are a lot of people who have written in and told me that my advice helped them out. Maybe putting all those wonderful letters into a book can help more people. I don't know if I could get it published, but if not, I've heard of this thing called self-publishing. Of course I could never write a whole book, which is where you'd come in—and my granddaughters, of course, who know so much of the story already. Could you help me with that?"

"Of course. I think that's a great idea. I'd love to help you."

He pictured the project in his head, already seeing how he wanted to combine the letters with a narrative that encompassed Eleanor's life and some history about the town. He'd read enough about self-publishing to handle that end of it as well, he was sure. And it would give him an excuse to finally put his writing into the world. "In a way, you'd be helping me, too."

"How's that?"

"When I was a kid, I dreamed of being a writer. You know, one of those long-haired poets who wrote about the moon and the stars, or a mystery writer, like Agatha Christie." He chuckled, thinking of those days back when he had a motorcycle and lofty goals that had never come true. Dusting off the memories now was almost bittersweet. "Maybe putting together your book will give me some inspiration for my own."

"Oh, I think that's a lovely idea! Always follow your dreams. That's my number one piece of advice." She got to her feet, excitement all over her face. "Wait here while I go upstairs and get the copies of the columns. They're in a box in the attic."

He waved at her to sit back down. "Let me get them for you. Sit, enjoy your tea."

"You're so helpful, Mike. This is why you're my favorite son-in-law. Don't tell the others."

"I'm pretty sure I already heard you tell Jake and Luke the same thing." Mike pressed a kiss to Eleanor's cheek. "I'll be right back."

Mike drained his cup of tea and then headed up the back stairs to the second floor, which opened to a small landing before the door to the attic. Eleanor's Victorian was enormous, with a stand-up attic that had been a favorite play spot for the girls when they were little, Meg had told him. As he climbed the stairs into the dim, dusty place, he could see why. Old chairs, paintings, tables, and a multitude of boxes filled the attic and surely had created a space perfect for make-believe adventures.

A stack of dusty cardboard boxes sat beside an old hope chest. He remembered Meg telling him about the day last year when she and her sisters had come up here to find their mother's wedding dress. That was when they'd discovered Eleanor's columns and realized their grandmother was Dear Amelia. He could still hear Meg recounting the story that night at dinner, and the two of them laughing about how improbable the idea had seemed. It was, he realized, the last time they'd had a conversation over dinner. Their sole communication before she'd handed him divorce papers had been a dinner debate over text, a meal they usually ate in separate rooms. The whole thought of that made him sad. Maybe Meg was right. Maybe a divorce was the best thing to do.

Just behind the box of articles about Dear Amelia, there was a box labeled Margaret's Stuff in Meg's handwriting. Mike wiped the dust off the top of the cardboard and peeled open the flaps. Inside, he saw the glimmer of brass trophies for cross-country, a stack of awards for being on the honor roll, a yearbook from high school, and then a folder labeled simply: Richard.

An old boyfriend? A friend? Mike couldn't remember Meg ever mentioning anyone named Richard. Besides, who would keep a folder on an old boyfriend? Even highly organized Meg wasn't that kind of sentimental.

He sat back on his haunches and opened the folder. Inside, he found the complete opposite of what he had expected: a pile of articles about the accident that had killed her mother. A police report from the scene. A sheet of information about Richard Hargrave Jr., the driver—where he lived, where he worked, how old he was, how old his kids were.

The name rang a bell in Mike's head, but he figured it had to be because Meg or her family must have mentioned him at some point. When they'd first started dating, she'd shared what happened to her mother, and it was like Mike had found someone who understood his own pain.

The shared history of tragedy because of alcoholism had been part of what bonded Meg and Mike. Her mother, killed in a car accident caused by someone driving under the influence. His father, an alcoholic for two decades, who had blown his paycheck at the casinos time and time again, leaving the Brentwoods without savings or insurance when they needed it most.

Mike was surprised Meg had never mentioned the folder. Maybe she'd collected all the information when she was young, some kind of morbid curiosity to know more about what happened. And yet, something nagged at him as he put the folder back in the box. Whatever it was, Mike shrugged it off and reached for the box of Eleanor's old columns. He was already itching to get to work on the book. Whatever else was in that folder could wait.

By early evening, Mike had made a nice start on the book. He sat back in the chair, stretched his back, and then leaned forward to reread the words he had just written. It was the first writing he had done in almost a decade, and he'd been amazed at how quickly the words had flowed. There was something about Eleanor's story—or maybe his own closeness to the family—that made it easy to be creative and put together the book about Dear Amelia.

There are life lessons in every letter, Eleanor has learned. Lessons for the people who write them, lessons for the people who read them, and most of all, lessons for Eleanor herself. She has learned more about the depths of love and forgiveness in the course of writing this column than she ever imagined. That knowledge helped her move past the searing grief of losing her only child and helped her to find closure in an unjust situation. "The column has been my saving grace," she said. "It helped me, quite literally, get out of my own way and see that there were other people who were hurting in this world. It is only in sharing our hurts and opening our hearts that we can become a catalyst for change and a foundation of support."

The interview he had done with Eleanor after lunch had been full of laughter, a few tears, and an honesty that he admired. Mike had never been one for sharing his feelings, but Meg's grandmother was an open book. She'd told him it was because she wanted the book to be as close to the truth as possible. To her, the only way to live was with your true self.

Mike thought about that a lot over the next few weeks as he'd been working on the book. Maybe that was where his marriage had gone wrong, where things had begun to slowly unravel. He had kept everything bottled up inside, doing what his dad always did. "Man up. Don't be a wimp," his father had said when Mike skinned his knee or fell off the monkey bars. Tears were strictly forbidden, as was any emotion more expressive than indifference.

Maybe that wasn't such a good way to live. Either way, as the date for finalization of the divorce got closer, he knew there was no way to go back and undo what had already been done or to have conversations they should have had years ago. They had a date with a mediator, along with an appointment with a judge. By Christmas, his marriage would be over.

Mike's gaze strayed to the long green expanse of lawn outside the window, the same lawn that had hosted a wedding just two months ago. What should have been a joyous occasion for everyone turned out to be another in a short line of dominos leading to divorce. Mike tried not to think about what else he was losing in the process because it was almost too painful to consider.

This house, and this family, would no longer be his soon. He wouldn't be squeezed between Luke and Jake at the dining room table, passing the turkey and stuffing around. He wouldn't walk into Eleanor's house on Christmas afternoon and see a stocking with his name on it, hung above the fireplace alongside ones for all the other adults. Those traditions that made up the Monroe family would be over, at least for Mike. He couldn't even think about the holidays this year because the whole thing was just too damned depressing. He forced himself to shake off the heavy sadness because if he dwelled in that dark mental space too long, he feared he would never leave it again.

Mike went back to the reams of paper beside him, stacked

and organized in file folders with handwritten notes he'd made attached to each folder as a reminder of what he wanted to write in that chapter. He had done his best to arrange the letters Eleanor had kept. He'd created some semblance of order that, ironically, mirrored so much of her personal story, it was as if the letters she'd chosen to feature each week had reflected what she'd been going through in her own life. He wasn't sure the order was perfect or that the paragraphs he wrote about her personal life were conveying everything he hoped, but his gut kept telling him he was on the right track.

There was a knock on the door of the guest room that Mike had set up as a sort of temporary office in Eleanor's house. He got to his feet and turned the knob, expecting to see Eleanor on the other side with some kind of treat and a cup of tea in hand. Instead, his wife stood there—was she still his wife if they had a date with a judge?—looking as beautiful as ever in a sapphire dress that skated along her curves. "Meg. What are you doing here?"

"You didn't answer my text, and my lawyer needs an answer. My grandmother said you were here, working on some book she asked you to write? Anyway, I came over to ask you in person." Her words were short and clipped, as cold as a mid-January day in New England.

Any hope that she was here to see him, to tell him she missed him, that her life was emptier without his presence, died in his chest. She'd clearly moved on in her heart and mind. He realized he'd never seen her in this dress, or in anything this vibrant in color, and a jealous part of him wondered if the dress and heels had been chosen because she had a date. He told himself it didn't matter and that he should just answer her questions and get this over with before the moment started to hurt.

"I turned my notifications off while I was working on your grandmother's project."

"She mentioned you were putting together her columns into a book," Meg said. "I think that's a great idea."

"Thanks." Somehow, knowing Meg approved made him even more excited about the project. He opened the door wider. "Do you want to come in and we can discuss whatever it is in private?" He loved Eleanor but had no doubt she was standing at the bottom of the stairs, trying to overhear their conversation. Meg's grandmother had a terrible—but well-meaning—tendency to meddle in her granddaughters' lives, especially their love lives.

Meg hesitated. "I . . . I don't want to bother you."

"You're not a bother, Meg." *Ever*, he wanted to add, but didn't. It was just that she was so . . . breathtaking. It reminded him of the first time he met her. Today her hair was swept up into a clip that held most of her dark curls in place. A few tendrils had escaped to skate along her neck and brush her cheeks. Beneath the foundation and blush she had on, he could see shadows under her eyes and a gauntness that worried him. Was she eating? Was she sleeping?

And why did he think any of that was still his concern? He'd signed the divorce petition and moved out several weeks ago. How she went forward with her life was none of his business anymore.

"Okay," she said finally. "But I can only stay a minute. I need to get to the shop."

Of course she did. Any excuse to immerse herself in work

and avoid him. It was a pattern that both of them had fallen into over the years. Escape and avoid while their marriage withered away. "That's fine."

She entered the room, leaving the door slightly ajar, and then perched on the edge of the queen bed that dominated the space. It felt so intimate, the two of them in a small bedroom. Instead of sitting beside her, Mike opted to flip the chair he was using and sit there, using the back of the chair as a mini wall between them.

He tried to keep his face devoid of emotion, his tone as flat as hers. It disconcerted him to have to think through such simple things, like where he should sit in order to have a conversation with his wife. Would it always be this way? Would he become the kind of guy who scanned a restaurant before being seated to avoid running into his ex? Or the kind who crossed the street when he saw her with another man? Damn it. He was sliding down that dark mental road again. He cleared his throat. "What do you need to know?"

"We, uh, both have retirement plans." She crossed her hands and put them primly in her lap. "Yours is bigger than mine because your employer had a good matching program. I don't want your money, but—"

"Half of what I have is yours, Margaret. I'm not going to fight over money or couches or any of those stupid things." The minute Meg said she wanted a divorce, Mike realized that sixty-five-inch TV they had argued about buying and the armchair that he'd insisted on having, even though it clashed with the other furniture, no longer mattered to him. He'd left all of those painful reminders behind in the house that was no longer his home.

"I don't want half of yours," she replied. "You earned your retirement, and I wanted to propose that we walk away with what we have."

"Sounds fair." And all so transactional. What had he expected? That she'd come here teary-eyed and missing him? This was a divorce, a division of property and money, not one of those reality shows with a dramatic confession.

The only betrayal of her emotions was a slight tremble in her fingers. Her back was as rigid as a wall. "Well, I wanted to be sure."

"Do you really not know me?" He leaned forward in the chair enough that he caught the scent of her perfume. The fragrance detoured his mind into happier memories, of curling up against her late at night or hauling her into his arms at the end of the day. The two of them sitting on the couch, watching a documentary, and touching hands from time to time.

Those times had ended years ago. Except for that single night in the Belleview hotel, Mike couldn't remember the last time he'd held Meg, touched her, reached for her. God, he wanted to touch her now, but that would be weird and awkward and a hundred different kinds of wrong.

"What do you mean, do I not know you? Of course I know you, and I know you like to have the numbers settled fairly."

He scoffed. "Meg, I've never cared about how much money I have or you have or whether we are middle-class or upper-middle-class or anything in between. Other things are important to me."

She looked like she was about to ask, "Like what?" but instead she gave him a terse nod. "Good. Thank you."

This whole cold, dispassionate act frustrated him. He didn't know if she did it because she truly didn't care or because it was the only way she could keep her emotional distance during this process. She sat there, straight and still as an arrow, and barely looked at him.

Let it go, he told himself. *Let her go. It's over.*

Yet, there was this little voice in the back of Mike's head that said there was something else at play here. Something that Meg hadn't told him. He thought of that session with Beverly and how Meg had dropped her guard and opened up—and for a few hours, had been his girl again. *With Mike, I was just . . . Meg, a girl he loved for who she was underneath it all.*

A part of him wanted to be bitter and angry, the typical divorced man who blamed the detonation of his life on the ex. But that wasn't who Mike was. It never had been. He was a guy who let the woman with two kids cut in front of him in line even when he had two items and she had two hundred. He was the kind of guy who didn't care who voted for whom or who opposed what and still invited those friends to a barbecue. He worried about his own lawn, as Eleanor would say, and didn't stress about the neighbors'—or complain to code enforcement about the weeds. He knew that he was just as much to blame here, for taking their marriage for granted and letting it die.

He had pulled away from her instead of leaning into her when things got tough. Much like Meg, he'd become an island who pretended he didn't need anyone. Childhood defense mechanisms roaring to life, time and time again. Now that things had come to a head, his hindsight showed him where it had all gone wrong. The problem with hindsight was its crappy timing.

It might be too late to resurrect what they had, but that didn't mean they had to end on bad terms. "Let's put the divorce to the side for a minute," he said. "I want to show you what I'm working on."

As good a friend as Larry was, and as much as Mike loved Meg's family, his best friend still was—and probably always would be—his wife. She'd been his sounding board, his voice of reason, his encourager when he struggled to make it through college. She had a way of calming him and bringing him back to the center he had lost along the way. She'd read what he wrote, back when he was young and dumb and dreaming of being a writer, and given him her honest thoughts. Right now, when his only reader was Eleanor, who didn't have a critical bone in her body, he wanted Meg's unvarnished reaction.

She waved off the idea. "Oh, I shouldn't... We aren't..."

He spun back toward the desk, picked up his laptop, and held it out to her. "You know your grandmother better than I do. I'd like to get your opinion on how the book is going."

"I'm sure you're doing a great job." She perched on the edge of the bed like a bird ready to take flight. Yet, she hadn't left yet. Curiosity flickered across her features.

He wiggled the laptop. "Take it. Read a page. Two if you're feeling ambitious. Just let me know if I'm on the right track."

She shifted her weight. He could see the gears turning in her mind. Did she open a door toward détente with her soon-to-be ex and possibly change the trajectory of the divorce, by giving in to her interest about what he was writing?

Finally, Meg relented and took the laptop from him. "Well, if it'll help you..."

"Oh, it will. Enormously." He got out of the chair, and before he could realize what he was doing, he leaned over her to scroll up in the document to a section he'd written a couple days prior. They were so close together that he could feel the whisper of her breath against his arm. Feel the warmth radiating from her body. She sat very, very still, and he swore she was holding her breath, just like he was holding his. So aware, so very aware, of the woman who had come into his life like a hurricane. "Uh...yeah. Here. This is a great place to start. A lot of the letters to Dear Amelia were on this same theme and I wanted to connect it to Eleanor's own life."

She took the computer from him and settled it on her lap. He had no reason to stay next to Meg, so he sat back down in the chair. Was it his imagination, or had the desk chair gotten cold in the last few seconds?

Meg began to read from the screen, her voice rising and falling in that soft, lyrical tone she had, with just a touch of a Boston accent blurring the occasional *r* with the nearest consonant. "At least 70 percent of the letters that were sent to Dear Amelia came from a place of heartbreak. Loves lost, loves rebuffed, loves that never were. Eleanor met her own great love when she was only nineteen. Russell Whitmore swept her off her feet, married her a year later, and brought this Georgia girl up to the cold of Boston where they settled down and had a beautiful daughter. For more than twenty-three years, she and Russell lived a life that wasn't perfect and was certainly not a storybook, but was, as she put it, *real*. 'We fought like cats and dogs sometimes, but I always knew that Russell loved me. Sometimes that love would be in a word he said or a touch on my shoulder. Every time, we found our way back to each other, and the arguments we had seemed like they were someone else's memories. He was the best part of me, and his love was sweeter than any song you could ever sing.'"

Meg looked up. Her eyes glistened with unshed tears. "That's so sweet. I knew my grandmother and grandfather loved each other but never knew how much. He died two weeks after my mother found out she was pregnant with me, so I never knew him. Grandma always said that it was us girls who got her through losing Grandpa and then losing Mom."

"Your grandmother has endured so much loss, and yet she still believes in love and happily-ever-after."

Meg scoffed. "It took her years to even consider the possibility of dating. I think she believed in it for other people, not necessarily herself."

"Because Russell was her love story, and maybe she wanted to preserve that instead of muddling it with someone else." And, he wanted to add, her granddaughter had many of those same traits of guarding her heart and keeping her emotions to herself.

Meg tucked a lock of hair behind one ear, a habit that meant she was feeling a little nervous or anxious. File that under "things that Mike knew about his wife that someday would be knowledge for someone else."

"Grandma didn't put Grandpa on a pedestal, exactly," she said, "but she reserved part of her heart for him for decades. Remember how she always set a place at the table for him, until Harry came along and we had to use that seat to fit everyone around the table? Our family expanded, and as that happened, I think she gradually learned to open up her heart again."

"And find joy one more time."

"I'm glad." Everything about Meg had softened. Her expressions, her words, the way she sat on the bed. It was as if reading about her grandmother's history had opened a teeny, tiny door between them.

"Me too," he said. "She's so happy, and that makes everyone around her happy. She took a chance on love and look where it got her. Meg, I..." He paused and then opened his mouth to say something stupid, like ask her to grab lunch with him, when she suddenly got to her feet.

"I should go." She shoved the laptop at him. "Thanks for sharing that. I think it's going to be a great book."

"Thanks." He stood there for an awkward second and then said, "Well, I should get back to work." A much smarter choice than sitting here writing some impossible happily-ever-after in his head. Real life wasn't lyrical poetry and rainbows. It was heartache and loss, and somehow, someway, picking yourself up again.

CHAPTER 10

The house echoed now. Margaret swore she could hear herself breathing in the emptiness. Mike had been living in an apartment just outside of Harbor Cove for two months and had left nothing behind, except for some tools he was storing in the garage until they had to put the house up for sale. She told herself she was happier alone, but that was a lie. So, she spent a ridiculous amount of time at work and told herself this was exactly where she wanted to be.

Fall had started early this season, ushering in colder than normal temps the first week of October, which had been great for business because it brought the leaf peepers into Harbor Cove. They rented rooms in B and Bs or little cabins around the lake and spent their afternoons toting binoculars and cameras around the state parks, hoping to capture the vibrant colors of the changing trees.

That had kept Carats in the Cove busy, too. Roger's hand was still not at 100 percent, which had allowed Margaret to bring Barrett back for a one-week residency that had yet to end, three weeks later. His leaf-themed collection had sold like gangbusters this month.

She saw the handsome designer several times throughout the week when she was at the shop. He had a way of making her blush every time he talked to her with his smooth voice and combination of compliments and business. It had been a long time since anyone had flirted with Margaret, and quite frankly, she wasn't sure what to do with that.

Margaret parked her car in the rear parking lot and headed into the shop through the back door. Barrett was already there with Tara, an hour earlier than she'd expected him to arrive. He might be flirtatious, but he was a hard worker.

Tara, who had floundered when she first started as a salesperson at Carats in the Cove, had found her groove. The young woman was great at helping customers, finding just the right piece for each person. While Tara helped one customer, Barrett was up front, talking to an older woman and explaining the process of creating a pendant. He had a brilliant topaz in one hand and a filigree platinum setting in the other. "When they join together," he said, slipping the gem into the setting, "they should be like two people in love. Complementing each other in every way." He turned the design around for the customer to see.

"I'll take it," the woman said with an emphatic nod. "I just love your work, Barrett." She giggled and blushed, clearly enamored by more than just his knowledge of gemstones.

Barrett smiled and exchanged small talk with her as he finished setting the stone. He hung the pendant on a matching chain and then waved the customer in Margaret's direction. "The beautiful Mrs. Brentwood will ring you up."

Even though he had some kind of flirtatious remark or compliment for every person who came into the shop, the word *beautiful* left her scatterbrained. "Uh, sure."

Tara was still busy with another customer, so Margaret took the pendant from the customer to complete the sale. She had to enter the price into the register twice because her entire body was acutely aware of Barrett, waiting and watching a few feet away. Finally, she concluded the sale and handed the woman a cranberry-red bag containing a matching velvet box with the necklace nestled inside. "Thank you so much. Be sure to think of us if you have a special occasion, because we do a lot of custom work for birthdays and anniversaries."

"Oh, I'll be back." She glanced over at Barrett. "For sure."

The woman shot him a smile and then walked out of the store, joining her middle-aged friends waiting on the sidewalk. They left in a burst of giggles and chatter, like high school girls at homecoming walking past the quarterback.

"You are popular with the ladies, I'll give you that," Margaret said. "Which has also been very good for business."

Barrett smiled. "I'm glad. And I'm especially glad you invited me back, Mrs. Brentwood."

"Actually, it's not Mrs. Right Now, but...well, it's complicated." Flustered and off-kilter, Margaret started arranging the pile of gemstone leaflets beside the register. "I'm sorry. The *Mrs.* just makes me feel weird. Can we stick to Margaret?" Maybe if she kept defining that boundary enough, she'd be able to stick to it herself.

The queasiness she'd woken up with this morning had returned. She'd skipped her usual morning run and avoided coffee, thinking maybe those would just make her upset stomach worse. She'd nibbled on crackers on the way to work and prayed she wasn't getting the flu. Now her stomach was rolling again.

"I get it. I have had a few...complications of my own in the past," he said. "Would your complications preclude you from having lunch with me today? I eat alone so often. It would be nice to have some company for a change."

She shouldn't. The divorce was far from final, even though her cousin George filed the paperwork to make the separation official. And going on a date, if that's what this was—because Margaret hadn't been single in a long time and could easily be misreading this—was definitely a bad idea.

Yet, there was nothing wrong with another man calling her beautiful, or her feeling flustered by the intensity of a man's look. The part of Margaret that had gotten on that motorcycle all those years ago yearned for that heady rush she'd once felt for Mike. "Sure. It's a beautiful day. Do you mind if we walk?"

A few minutes later, Margaret and Barrett headed down the sidewalk to Earl's Diner on an unseasonably warm day for fall. It felt odd—wrong, almost—to be heading out for a meal with a different man. Mike had been her everything for so long that she couldn't imagine being with someone else. Did she even want to be with someone else?

That was too much to consider, especially when she wasn't feeling well. Margaret put the back of her hand to her forehead. Didn't seem like she had a fever. Maybe it wasn't the flu. Maybe it was something she ate yesterday.

When they reached the diner door, Barrett opened it with one hand and lightly touched her back with the other. The contact sent a flutter through her. "I'll, uh, get us a table," she said, just to rush forward and greet the young woman at the front counter.

The hostess led them to a booth toward the back of the diner. It was early for lunch, only 11:30 a.m., so the place was still relatively empty. In a half hour, Earl's would be bustling with customers and the sound of orders being called across the kitchen.

Just a couple weeks ago, she'd been here with her sisters and grandmother and told them about the divorce. It seemed like a lifetime ago. Her family reached out often, checking on her, but Margaret replied with short, don't-want-to-talk-about-it answers.

"You look so sad," Barrett said. "If you want to share what's troubling you, I'm told I have very big ears." He cupped his hands behind his ears and grinned.

"I'm pretty sure your ears are normal sized. And I don't really want to talk about it." Not to mention that she shouldn't bring her personal problems to someone who was working for her. No matter how many times he called her beautiful. "But thank you."

"You keep everything inside, I notice. Not good for the soul or the stomach." He pressed a hand to his abdomen. "I notice you rarely eat. Which is why I asked you to lunch. You should have the biggest sandwich they make."

Margaret shook her head. "I'm not really in the mood for anything. My stomach is a little off, that's all."

"All the more reason to have a good, hearty meal." Barrett gestured to the waitress.

The thought of a big meal made her nauseous. Ever since she'd filed for divorce, her stomach was cranky almost every day. If this was stress, it was some kind of never-ending stress. Normally, a run would help her feel better, but lately she hadn't even wanted to lace up her running shoes. She'd started skipping breakfast, opting for a package of crackers for lunch, maybe some pasta for dinner. Cooking just for one made it easy. Pop something into the microwave, and three minutes later, she had dinner. But even those she rarely finished.

Barrett was looking at her expectantly, and she realized the waitress was waiting for her order. "Oh, nothing for me, thank you."

"Eat something," Barrett said. "You must."

"Fine. I'll have a grilled cheese." Something simple and bland would probably go down easily.

But when the sandwich arrived a few minutes later, Margaret took one look at it and shook her head. "No, I can't. I just…" She put a hand on her stomach. "You have it." She pushed the sandwich across the table to Barrett.

He chuckled. "If you weren't in a 'complicated' situation, not-Mrs. Brentwood, I would ask you if you were pregnant. I'm sure it's just stress."

"Yeah, there's no way I'm…" Margaret's voice trailed off. There had been that one night in the hotel with Mike, the first time in a long time that they'd slept together.

No. It wasn't possible.

And yet…that night in the hotel had been the only time she'd had sex in months and months. Margaret had run out of birth control pills back in the spring and had been meaning to make an appointment with her ob-gyn, but there didn't seem to be an imminent need when she wasn't having sex and her marriage was dissolving.

"I need to go," she said as she slid out of the booth and grabbed her purse, fishing out her cell phone and unlocking the screen. "I, uh, have, uh, an errand to run. I'll see you back at the shop later today." She tossed some money onto the table and left her sandwich behind, uneaten.

❧ ☙

Larry wiped the sweat off his brow and plopped onto the sofa. "Remind me to pretend I don't know you next time you need help moving furniture."

Mike chuckled. The two of them had spent the better part of a very warm Sunday moving some furniture into Mike's apartment, hauling everything from end tables to a couch up three flights of stairs and around concrete pillars to get it into his tiny one-bedroom place. Next time, he was going to choose a building with an elevator. His back ached, his shoulders ached, and he hadn't been this tired in years. "I have some cold beer for you in the fridge as a thank-you."

Mike wondered if that was how it started with his dad and his best friend, DJ. Did they begin as two friends sharing a cold beer on a hot day? Maybe both of them had had addictive personalities and that friendly moment had stoked fire with fire, sending them both spiraling into decades of bad mistakes. At some point, DJ had stopped hanging around with Mike's dad. Maybe because at that point, Nathan had gotten so bad he was barely functioning.

Larry propped his feet up on the coffee table they had just set in place. "Tell me you have some bachelor food to go with the beer. Cold pizza, some wings. Maybe some chips?"

"I have fruit and some carrots I just chopped up." In the weeks since he had moved out of the Harbor Cove house,

Mike had spent too much time eating crap food and feeling bad for himself. As his apartment began to feel less like a prison cell and more like a home, he had weeded out the junk food and begun to return to his regular diet of mostly vegetables and lean protein. Not to mention the fifteen pounds he'd gained that needed to come off or he'd be buying new pants, along with the new sofa.

Larry rolled his eyes. "You are not helping me maintain my dad bod."

"I'm trying not to get a dad bod, considering I'm not a dad." Mike laughed and disappeared into the apartment's kitchen—which was really just two six-foot counters and a handful of cabinets—to retrieve a Stella for Larry and Heineken 0.0 for himself. He popped the caps off and then handed the beer to Larry. Mike took a seat on the folding chair that had formed the extent of his living room furniture until today. "Thanks for helping me move all that stuff, especially that thing." He nodded toward the sectional that had required multiple trips and a flurry of curse words to get its rectangular pieces around the corner and into the apartment.

Larry patted the cushions, and they replied with a soft thump. "It's a good couch. What'd you pay? Two hundred?"

"A little less than that." Every single thing he had in his apartment he'd bought used, most of it from an estate that was clearing out a home and had advertised pretty much every piece of furniture he'd needed. "I've been watching Marketplace for a deal. I didn't want to buy a new one in case…"

Larry shook his head. "You can't keep hoping for something that isn't going to happen. Your mediation is a week away, man. It's over."

A fact Mike stared at every morning when he passed by his refrigerator. The calendar that hung on the front had the date circled in red and the time of the mediation written in the little box for the day. The rest of the month was starkly empty, as was the next one, save for the court date to finalize everything. It was all a big, fat message that Mike refused to heed.

"You're right, and I know you're right. But every time I make some move toward the single life, like buying this couch, I hear my dad in the back of my head saying, 'It ain't over till it's over.'"

"Yogi Berra said that, right?" Larry took a long sip of beer. "Damn, that's good after a hard day's work."

"Depends on which urban legend you believe. But whether he did or he didn't, the Mets came back from the bottom and won thirteen in a row that year, ending up in the World Series." One of the happy memories Mike had with his dad was watching Mets games on television. The two of them loved baseball, and those Saturday afternoons were some of Mike's best afternoons as a kid. By the time Mike was in high school, his father's drinking had gotten so bad that there were no baseball games, nothing but arguments and the sour stench of alcohol.

Larry took a long drink and avoided looking at Mike. "You can tell me to keep my nose out of your business, so, if this is too personal, tell me."

"Shoot."

"What went wrong?" Larry asked. "Seriously, man, you and Margaret seemed to have a great marriage. I'm still honestly pretty shocked you broke up. I mean, if you guys couldn't make it, where's the hope for the rest of us?"

If Mike had those answers, he knew he wouldn't be sitting here in a crappy apartment searching for even crappier furniture. "It wasn't any one thing; that's the worst part of it. We just drifted apart a little more each day until we couldn't find a way back to the middle again." Mike knew the day their marriage had begun to sour, the moment they had stopped talking and instead retreated to their own corners, in such deep pain they could barely talk to each other.

Meg's miscarriage five years ago had been the death knell for their marriage. He could see it now, when it was far too late to go back and change their course.

Mike had been weirdly optimistic after he'd signed the divorce petition, maybe because that session with Beverly had gone so well. He kept thinking Meg would realize the whole thing was a mistake and that she didn't really want a divorce. That night in the hotel, he'd had a glimpse of the woman he'd met all those years ago, and some part of him kept expecting her to show up again. Which was, as Larry and the red circle on the calendar made abundantly clear, nearly impossible at this stage of the game. They were in the bottom of the ninth with two strikes and no runners on base. There was no way the two of them were going to resurrect this marriage. "If I ran the world, we'd have a do-over. I think maybe we'd get it right the second time."

"What would you do differently?" Larry, who had just gone through his second divorce last summer, leaned forward, as if he wanted the secret to rebuilding a marriage. Maybe both of them were romantics underneath it all.

Mike peeled off the label on his bottle as he spoke, amassing a tiny pile of shiny green strips of paper. "We were thrown into a lot of stress pretty much as soon as we got married. My dad got sick, and my mom realized their life savings had been left on a roulette table. My dad hadn't paid the insurance bill, so she was in the middle of a financial nightmare. To help her out, I started working constantly and going to night school so I could get a better job, the job my dad always wanted me to have."

"CPA, like him." Larry knew that much after years of being friends with Mike.

"It paid well, and I thought I'd have enough stability to help my mom and support my family. Meg was working at the jewelry store as many hours as she could, and we became two ships passing each other in the fog." They'd also stopped being able to talk after they lost the baby. It was as if the pain was too great to bear if they brought it out into the light. Instead of being there for each other, they'd let that distance become a massive chasm.

"Most marriages have money problems, Mike. Especially when you're young."

He let the bottle dangle from his fingers and thought about all those years of sacrifice, the endless hours he spent with numbers, sitting in the same office his father had, working the same job. "I never wanted to work in accounting. I hate the job, actually. And I think that I let a lot of those feelings build a wall between Meg and me."

Larry's eyes widened in surprise. "You hate it? Like really hate it?"

Mike had thought long and hard about this topic in the weeks since he'd been let go, as he watched the severance checks come and go and knew the weeks of indecision were coming to an end. The writing had been a gift from the heavens, to be sure, but he clearly wasn't going to be able to pay the bills from one book he did as a favor to his in-law. Still, he realized in the writing of Eleanor's book that he wanted to be sure he had enough time—and finances—to pursue writing part-time. All those years of putting his dreams on hold had gotten him to the exact opposite place he wanted to be. "Let me put it this way. I would rather chew off my own arm than go get another full-time CPA job."

Larry laughed. "But what are you going to do, man? You still have to eat."

"I have a plan for that." A plan that had created a surge of optimism in Mike, a weird kind of anticipation for what the next day would bring. If he hadn't been laid off, who knows if he ever would have had the guts to make these moves.

He chatted with Larry for a few more minutes, until his friend finished his beer and headed out the door. When Larry was gone, Mike sat down at his computer and surfed over to the business card design site he'd been looking at last night. He chose a simple design, a white card with one vivid blue angled stripe across the front. *Brentwood Accounting*, he wrote in the business name box and then filled in the details for his email address and phone number. He put in his credit card info before clicking order.

It was official. He was going out on his own. He pulled up his email and wrote two messages to the firms that had answered his job applications with interviews and, later, great job offers. *I regret to say that I won't be accepting the position*, he wrote, feeling a weird mix of excitement and terror.

He looked around the empty apartment and missed Meg

in a deeper, harder way. She should be the one he was telling about his new venture. She would, he knew, be thrilled and supportive. They'd talked more than once about him striking out on his own, but every time, Mike had felt the pressure to be a good provider and so he'd kept clocking in and out for the dependable paycheck.

And now, with a week of severance pay left, he'd taken a leap and opted for the only choice he ever truly wanted: autonomy. It felt good to do this on his own, to know that he wasn't just stepping into his father's shoes but rather forging his own path. It was weirdly empowering.

It was also an enormous risk. But he couldn't afford to sit in the middle of this life reboot and spend one more second repeating the mistakes he'd made the first time.

CHAPTER 11

On Monday, Margaret stood in the doctor's office that had suddenly become some kind of weird twilight zone. Five years ago, she'd heard these same words and had dared to dream of a bright future. She was almost afraid to breathe, to do anything that would make this moment a figment of her imagination. "Are you sure?"

Dr. Gibson, who had been Margaret's gynecologist for a decade, smiled and nodded. "I'm positive. There's no doubt you're pregnant, Margaret. I'm so happy for you."

Dr. Gibson had been there the first time, giving Mike and Margaret the news together, then holding Margaret's hand in the hospital when the ultrasound confirmed her worst fears. She'd been the shoulder Margaret had leaned on after the miscarriage, the one who had told her that, someday, they could try again. For five years, Margaret had been terrified of losing another baby and had avoided the conversation. For five years, she and Mike had danced around the subject and the closed door at the top of the stairs. And for five years, her marriage had eroded bit by bit as that loss tore them apart.

A frenzied rush of emotions ran through her. Elation.

Fear. Excitement. Panic. "But what if...?" Margaret couldn't even voice the questions in her mind, the overwhelming thought that it could happen again.

Dr. Gibson's face softened. She waved at the dozens of photos of newborns that covered the back wall of her office. "Worrying about all the wouldas, couldas, shouldas won't change the future. It will, however, rob you of the joy of this moment. Just take each day as it comes and allow yourself to celebrate this news. Just because you had one miscarriage doesn't mean you'll have another, Margaret. Enjoy this time, because your little boy or girl will be here by May."

Pregnant. About to be single. This wasn't what Margaret had envisioned for herself, but it was, as Dr. Gibson said, a moment of joy. A moment Margaret never thought she'd have again. She was going to have a *baby*. Waves of happiness washed over her. She put a hand on her abdomen and whispered a prayer of gratitude. Tears rushed to her eyes. She couldn't tell if they were tears of joy or grief or something in between. "I'm still stunned but also totally ecstatic."

"Sounds like every other new mother I've ever met." Dr. Gibson smiled as she handed a bottle to Margaret. "These are prenatal vitamins. Take one with a meal every day. And other than that, try not to worry. Get all the sleep you can because sleepless nights will be here before you know it."

Margaret thanked her and stumbled out of the office, still reeling with the news. She was pregnant again. The baby they had dreamed of and lost had been the most heart-shattering moment in her life. But now she had a second chance, another pregnancy. Another reason to hope. That one night with Mike had changed everything.

As she drove over to meet Emma, she thought about what to do next. Should she go through with the divorce? Or call it off? Should she tell Mike now or wait until she was 100 percent positive that the pregnancy was progressing? She should probably wait three months to tell people, just in case the worst happened.

No. She wasn't going to go down that mental path.

"We'll get through this together," she whispered to the life inside her belly. "Nobody has to make big decisions overnight. Right?"

The baby, of course, didn't answer. Margaret decided she would keep this amazing news to herself for a little while, just until she got used to the idea of being a mother. Then she'd tell Mike and her family. As for the divorce, she knew children didn't repair marriages. A baby was no reason to ask Mike to stay in an unhappy relationship.

Margaret parked and headed inside the community center, where Emma was in her element. Margaret watched her youngest sister bustle back and forth between the women and children who had arrived at the Penny Monroe Community Center on a beautiful fall afternoon and marveled at Emma's ability to stay cool under pressure. She had her little dog—given to her by a bridezilla she'd worked with—in her arms as she hurried from person to person. Marshmallow took it all in stride, loving both being in his adopted mom's arms and the extra attention from other people.

Emma had a kind word for every person she met and would work little tidbits into the conversations that showed she remembered details, like that woman's birthday party and this woman's new job. Emma seemed to move in a constant bubble of people as the women angled to be close to her, drawn in by her charming, thoughtful personality.

None of those were skills Margaret had. Honestly, she was continually amazed that she'd managed to be reasonably successful in a customer service industry, because she was the exact opposite of someone like Emma. Margaret was what other people called "uptight" but she liked to call "structured." She didn't have the conversational skills of Emma or the creative skills of Gabby, but she did have a business that had done a pretty good job of staying in the black for many years. Granted, there were times when that profit margin was thin, but Margaret knew that the business would move in the right direction as long as she kept the reins tight.

Yet, a part of her envied Emma's ease with others and with life in general. Emma hadn't thought twice before pouring her energies into this dilapidated building and bringing their mother's dream of a community center for women into existence. She had the spontaneity gene that Margaret lacked, the ability to just ride through whatever storms came her way; and somehow, it all worked out for Em.

As soon as Emma held the grand opening event, the workshops, events, and spaces were full. She'd charmed the community with her enthusiasm, and people couldn't wait to be a part of the positive energy Emma put out into the world.

In the background, Margaret could hear the sounds of Luke renovating the rest of the center, once a function hall for a church that had fallen into disrepair. Every once in a while, there'd be the whine of the table saw followed by a short bam from the nail gun. In another month, Emma would have dedicated class space for the single moms and struggling young women who wanted to learn new skills or brush up on the latest technology before they reentered the workforce. There was already a waiting list for the classes.

After the doctor's appointment, Margaret had headed here, more or less against her will. Last week, Emma had begged Margaret to give a short workshop on running a small business. Even though Margaret hated public speaking, being here was a great way to avoid talking to Barrett again after their lunch. When she came into work today, he'd asked her if she was feeling okay. She lied and assured him she was fine, even as her stomach reminded her she wasn't.

Emma had promised there would be "a teeny tiny group of people" in attendance. Even from here, Margaret could see at least fifteen women sitting in the break room/temporary classroom. A few women were standing in the back because the space had run out of available seats.

"Em!" Margaret whispered. "Em!"

Emma spun around, saw Margaret gesturing, and said something to the group of women she had been talking to. Three of them headed into the classroom, while two walked over to the craft table where a dozen kids were gluing together Popsicle sticks in no discernible shape that Margaret could make out.

Emma pointed at the classroom. "Looks like you have a big group, sis. Isn't that awesome? So many women are interested in starting their own businesses."

"You said it would be a few people. Not standing room only." Margaret had spoken in front of groups before, during festivals in town and at Suzie's wedding, but this was different. These women were expecting her to be the expert who had all the answers. All Margaret had felt for months was unsure.

"What a pity I was wrong about how much interest there would be." Emma grinned, and Margaret could tell she'd known full well that this event would have a lot of sign-ups. "Besides, if I told you twenty-five women signed up, you would have gone all Margaret on me."

That is so Margaret of you, Mike had said to her during their argument. Was she really that bad that everyone in her life had turned her name into a label? "What's that supposed to mean?"

"Now don't get all scowly on me, because no one likes a grumpy presenter." Emma gave Marshmallow a stroke and then lifted her hand to wave at a mom carrying a toddler on one hip while her preteen trailed behind with a grumpy face, as if God had decided to show Margaret exactly what Emma was referring to. "You know I mean that phrase with love."

"Using my name as an adjective is not loving."

Marshmallow, completely oblivious to the tension between the sisters, snuggled her little white body deeper into Emma's arms and let out a happy doggy sigh. "Your first clue to what I mean by that phrase is your use of the word *adjective*, Meggy. This group isn't a bunch of buttoned-up bankers or a convention of lawyers. These are ordinary women who are interested in doing everything from selling Mary Kay to opening a bakery. Talk to them like you'd talk to me." Emma tapped her lip as she thought about what she'd just said. "Scratch that. Talk to them like you'd talk to someone you *didn't* want to lecture."

"Emma!" Margaret's retort was instinctual because they both knew Emma was right. As the eldest, Margaret did have a tendency to tell everyone else what to do and how to do it.

Her little sister gave her a devilish grin that made it

impossible for Margaret to be annoyed. "Just be yourself, Meggy."

I don't know who that is, she thought. For months, she had felt lost, as if the person she'd turned into when she grew up had become a stranger. Was she the responsible eldest sister who peered into classroom windows and checked homework? Was she the carefree girl who had eloped in New Hampshire? Or was she the soon-to-be-divorced business owner who had spent last night adding up the value of the furniture in her house and staring at the white plastic test sitting on the bathroom counter?

Worrying about all the wouldas, couldas, shouldas won't change the future. It will, however, rob you of the joy of this moment.

Emma grabbed one of Margaret's hands, startling her out of her thoughts. All around them, a happy hubbub of conversation ebbed and flowed in the room, punctuated by the sounds of Luke building something on the other side of the wall. "You are the smartest person I know and one of the most caring people I've ever met. But you have a tendency to act like you're wrapped in barbed wire around other people. Don't worry about what anyone thinks or whether you're going to get a word wrong. Be honest with these women and let them see the real you. They don't need a bunch of charts—"

"Well, there goes my whole presentation."

Emma laughed. "As funny as that is, sadly, I think you're actually serious. Promise me that you won't whip out some PowerPoint presentation. Just be honest and real. Okay?"

The idea of that made Margaret even more nauseous. The laptop in her tote bag had felt like a security blanket until now. Was Emma really suggesting that Margaret just *wing it*? "I'll try."

Emma drew Margaret into a tight, fast, one-armed hug. Marshmallow let out a little yip of agreement. Before Margaret could return the embrace, Emma had released her. "You'll do great. Oh, look, there's Cassie."

Cassie Wallace, the groomer who owned Dogs 'n Suds, walked into the center with her nephew Drew holding tightly to her hand. When Cassie stopped beside Emma and Margaret, Drew shyly tucked himself behind Cassie's thigh, watching Emma with wary eyes. "Hey there, Drew," Emma said, bending down to his level. Marshmallow lowered his inquisitive nose in Drew's direction. "You came to my rock painting event at the hotel back in June. Remember? You painted a hamburger on your rock because your daddy loves cooking on the grill."

Drew inched his way around Cassie's leg, still clutching the denim like it was a lifeline. He watched Marshmallow, who was already wagging her tail, eager to make friends. "Uh-huh."

"And today we're going to paint leaves and make a picture for your fridge. You can use any color you like on your leaves. Does that sound fun?"

Margaret marveled at Emma's adaptability. One minute she was consoling a single mom who was worried about her upcoming custody hearing, the next she was convincing an elementary schooler that he was going to have a great time, if only he'd trust her. Given the way Drew's eyes had widened, Emma had definitely spurred his interest.

Finally, Drew released his death grip on his aunt. "Can I paint mine purple? My mommy loves purple." He closed the distance between them and started petting Marshmallow like they were old friends.

"Absolutely." Emma grinned and cupped her hand around her mouth as she leaned toward Drew's ear and feigned sharing a big secret. "Purple is my favorite color, too. You know what, though? My sister is having a bad day, and I think we should make her a picture, too. What do you think her favorite color is?"

"I dunno." Drew looked up at Margaret. "What's your favorite color, Emma's sister?"

"Yeah, Margaret, what is it?" Emma gave her a conspiratorial wink.

All three of them turned in Margaret's direction. She could feel her face heat. It shouldn't be so difficult to engage with a first grader, for goodness' sake. Maybe this was why Margaret had struggled to have kids years ago. God realized she had no skills when it came to mothering or pretending to play dolls and build forts. The idea of being a mother terrified her in a way nothing else ever had, and yet, here she was, going to be a mother. Which meant she needed to figure it out. "Uh...I'm not sure. Uh, purple sounds good."

"Perfect! Purple it is." Emma's grin widened. "Drew and I are going to make you the purpliest-purple leaf picture you've ever seen."

Margaret groaned. "Is it going to involve glitter? Because that is so hard to vacuum up and—"

Emma grabbed her arm. "Margaret, sometimes a little glitter in your life is a good thing. Trust me."

Then she handed Marshmallow off to Cassie and took Drew's hand. The two of them crossed to the craft table, inserting themselves amid the noisy, busy kids already gluing, painting, and glittering with abandon.

Margaret watched them and thought she was going to be a terrible mother. Heck, she barely had time for a goldfish, and like Emma said, she was not the warmest person on the planet. How could she ever feel that at ease with kids?

That's your fear talking. Stop letting it override what is the best moment you've had in a long, long time.

"Hey, I have to walk Marshmallow for Emma," Cassie said, interrupting Margaret's thoughts. "I'll see you around, Margaret. Good luck with your class."

Oh, yeah—that. Margaret shifted the weight of her tote bag. The laptop she'd stowed in there—complete with a PowerPoint—seemed to weigh a hundred pounds. "Nice to see you, Cassie."

With the groomer gone and Emma occupied, Margaret had no choice but to head for the class that was waiting for her. As much as she was dreading it, she was grateful for the distraction from the other thing she was trying not to think about.

Just as Emma had promised, there were more than two dozen women in the room, of all ages and walks of life. Several of them had notebooks out, ready to write down whatever they learned. She recognized a handful as customers from the jewelry store. The nerves in her stomach became a full-on riot of wild monkeys.

Margaret introduced herself and took the laptop out of the bag, setting it on the bar stool at the front of the room. A small, late-model TV hung on the wall above it, ready and waiting for a connection. "I, uh, have an HDMI cable in here somewhere, and I can hook this up to the TV so you can all see the presentation." Emma's advice be damned. Margaret had a PowerPoint, and she wasn't afraid to use it.

One woman chuckled. "Sounds like the kind of thing that will have a quiz at the end."

Margaret's cheeks flared. "No, not at all. But if you have questions, I can answer them."

A thin blonde who was in her late thirties raised her hand. "I want to know where you found the courage to open your own business. I'm so scared to do that." Several other women around her nodded in agreement.

They thought she was brave to have her own business? If only they knew how often Margaret had been on the verge of a full-on panic attack because sales were slow or inventory was delayed. How many nights she had worried about the store, about her ability to be a good leader, especially in those early days when she knew virtually nothing about being a store owner. She'd never told a soul about her fears, not even her sister Gabby, who knew exactly what it was like to be a solo-preneur. Margaret's constant stiff upper lip didn't allow her to cry on another's shoulder or ask for help. She was supposed to be the one they relied on, not the other way around.

"Courage?" Margaret scoffed as she dug deeper in her hunt for the HDMI cable. "I don't think I'm courageous at all."

"Then what was it?" the woman asked.

Margaret stopped searching and glanced up at the sea of women waiting for her answer. "I . . . I don't know. Um, are you sure you don't want to start with my checklist of things you need to start your own business?"

Because that was where Margaret felt comfortable, in a

world full of slides and lists, where there were no curveballs she couldn't predict. Frankly, if Margaret had known then what she knew now, she would have opted for a nine-to-five job with a steady paycheck.

"No offense," the blonde said, "but what good is a checklist if I'm too scared to take that first step? I'm so worried that people will think my ideas are dumb or they won't buy what I have to offer and it'll be a failure."

"Me too," said the woman behind her. Murmurs of agreement spread throughout the room.

Margaret remembered feeling that way the first day she was on her own. She had stood in the store, looking around at the inventory she had ordered for the summer tourist season and panicked that everything on the shelves was too tacky and no one would buy anything. She was so sure she'd fail that, for three months straight, she ran a profit and loss statement every day, fully expecting to see a negative balance.

"You took over that jewelry store when you were like twenty-two or twenty-three, right?" said Jackie, a woman who had been in Carats in the Cove last month to buy a watch for her dad's birthday. "That's when most people are out partying. What made you do it differently?"

None of those answers were in Margaret's PowerPoint. She stood there, mute and disconcerted without the security blanket of the slides she had spent hours preparing. *Just for a minute, be you,* Mike had said to her, just like Emma had.

Being herself would mean exposing what a mess she was. All those insecurities she had felt from day one, and still felt—pretty much in every area of her life, these days. Especially now with the knowledge that she was pregnant. The worries she had about the future, about whether she could juggle possible motherhood—a word she couldn't even think yet—and entrepreneurship, and whether she was crazy to even attempt it. She craved the crutch of the PowerPoint, but as she looked at the earnest faces in front of her, she saw that these women were like her—scared and worried, probably pacing the floors at night—and they wanted honesty.

Margaret stopped hunting for the cable, set the tote bag on her lap, and perched on the edge of the bar stool. "You want the truth?" Several women nodded. "Half the time, I have no idea what I'm doing, and the other half, I'm positive what I just did was wrong."

That earned a smattering of laughter from the group and calls of "me too," which emboldened Margaret. Maybe it wasn't such a bad idea to let other people see that she didn't have it as together as it looked on the outside.

"When the owner of the jewelry store first asked me if I wanted to buy him out, my answer was no," Margaret went on. "I had worked there for a couple of years at that point but I didn't feel like I knew enough to run a store. I was only twenty-three, and I had a business degree, but not an MBA or anything. Who was I to think I had what it took to go out on my own?"

"I feel the same way." Jackie looked around at the other women. "I've won ribbons at the county fair for my cakes and pies, but turning those into a business? That sounds so tough. What if I'm not as good as I think I am? What if people hate my desserts?"

"Heck, become a mom. Every day is a crisis of confidence." The other women laughed at Jackie's statement. But Margaret felt understanding and solidarity. These were people who had been in Margaret's shoes and knew what she was going through.

"I worry about the same thing every single season," Margaret said. "And if it's not inventory, it's employees, or pricing, or heck, what day I put up the holiday decorations. Every single day, there is something to worry about." Just saying those things out loud was like taking a hundred-pound weight off her shoulders. She had two dozen other women nodding along, getting it, and getting her. "The only thing I can tell you for sure is that you're going to make mistakes. I made so many my first year that I was shocked I made it through without going bankrupt. Even so, I was going to close the doors because I had no confidence in my abilities."

"What changed?" the blonde asked.

Margaret picked at an errant thread on the handle of her tote bag. "My, uh, husband was, is, um, an accountant." All of those words were so laden with double meanings that she stumbled over them. Was he her husband still? Was he even working in accounting anymore? She had no idea. "He sat me down and went over the numbers with me. He never told me what to do. He simply let me see the pieces, and I put them into the right order myself. Once I knew what had to be done, I had a plan, and that gave me a boost of confidence that I could do this. It wasn't so difficult anymore because I wasn't..."

"Alone?" Jackie supplied. "That would be nice. My husband doesn't do anything but complain his dinner is late because I was working on a cake."

A couple other women laughed. The blonde shrugged. "I

don't have a man, and I don't want one. Too much maintenance." That elicited even more laughter.

If there was one thing Mike wasn't, it was high maintenance. He was an easygoing guy who rolled with the punches,
and by extension, had always calmed her nerves. That night
when she'd come to Mike on the verge of tears, he had
patiently gone through her books and taught her how to read
her balance sheet and how to set up a forecasting budget for
the next year. He'd broken big concepts into simple, digestible
parts that Margaret was immediately able to understand and
implement. He hadn't tried to tell her what to do. He hadn't
criticized her decisions—and there were definitely some mistakes she'd made that had hurt the bottom line. He had simply been his normal, patient self and that had been enough for
her to stop feeling panicked and start taking action.

Then they lost the baby and that loss created a chasm
between them that became too wide to traverse. Mike had
thrown himself into work, stacking up sixty-, seventy-hour
work weeks, which left Margaret coming home to an empty
house that was too full of dark thoughts. To pull herself out
of that despair, she'd started spending even more time and
energy both at work and trying to fix someone else's life.
Because that was one place where she felt like she was making
a difference.

At first, she'd kept all of that time and money she spent
a secret from Mike because she knew he would never understand her need to fix it, to make amends for a past that wasn't
even her fault. To help someone who had been a driving force
in the hell that had been Mike's childhood. That, she knew,
was an unforgivable sin.

And quite possibly, the core secret that had eroded their marriage from the inside out.

Margaret shook off the thoughts and turned back to the group. "Let's talk about the businesses you ladies want to start and how you can make that happen."

Even when your life is falling apart, at the same time, you've just been handed a miracle.

CHAPTER 12

Mike ran through the numbers. Then he ran through them again. He got the same result every time.

Meg had been hiding money from him.

It didn't make sense. They both made good livings, or at least Mike used to when he was at the firm. Yes, Meg's income could be inconsistent because the store went through seasonal sales lulls, but the overall money coming in had been pretty good for the last few years. He'd done her taxes every year and never noticed anything amiss, not in the business returns or their personal returns.

And yet, the more he dug into their finances to prepare for the meeting with the mediator, the more he realized that there'd been a slow siphoning of funds from their accounts for years. A total just shy of twenty-five thousand dollars, taken out in monthly installments each year, every single year, for as long as they'd been married. In the early years, she'd only taken out a few hundred a year. Explainable, for sure. Maybe she'd needed cash to pay for vegetables at the farmers market or to tip the hairdresser or something. But as the years passed and their income climbed, the amount she took out also rose, until she was withdrawing thousands per year. A difference of a couple hundred bucks a month in their checking account balance could easily be overlooked or attributed to something like an extra-high grocery bill or electric bill during the winter, which made sense as to why he hadn't noticed it before. He'd trusted his wife and never done a deep dive into their accounts. The mediator had sent over a thick stack of sheets to fill out that got into the nitty-gritty of their finances, which had sent Mike delving deeper into their bank accounts.

When he looked closer and saw month after month where she had withdrawn a thousand dollars or more, he'd been stunned, unable to believe Meg could do such a thing. That discovery had sent him into the attic of their house to get the financial records for the rest of the years, hoping they would prove him wrong.

They didn't. If anything, the whole thing became more confusing. It would have been fine if she'd bought a pair of designer shoes or a handbag or something that she didn't want to mention. Maybe even setting aside cash for a new set of golf clubs for him or something like that. However, as far as Mike knew, Margaret didn't own—or care about—designer clothes, and neither of them had ever exchanged a present worth more than a couple hundred dollars.

Was she giving money to one of her sisters? Gabby, to help with her store's financial woes last year? Or Emma, to help pay for the community center? If so, why would his wife cover up something like that? And how could she think he would never find out?

And why would she do that knowing he'd watched his

mother go through the same thing with his father? Missing money, excuses piled on excuses, and trust eroding by the minute.

Mike added the stack of financial documents to the growing pile on his apartment's countertop and then gathered up the rest of what he needed for the mediation hearing tomorrow. There was such a finality that came with that date, and it had left him in a sad funk for days. In just under twenty-four hours, they would divide up everything they had built together and it would all be over, except for the judge's signature.

Over. The thought weighed on his shoulders. Eventually, he told himself, he'd get past these feelings and find a new normal. One with no secrets or lies. One where he could move on. Except he still didn't want to move on or even imagine a life without Meg.

God, he must be a masochist. What was wrong with him?

Just as he was putting everything into a folder, the doorbell of his apartment rang. Eleanor Whitmore stood on the other side with a stack of plastic containers in her hands. "I suspect my book writer has not been eating well, so I took the liberty of bringing you some meat loaf, mashed potatoes, and a batch of my homemade chocolate chip cookies."

He chuckled as he opened the door wider and invited her inside. "You spoil me, Eleanor."

"Oh goodness, I do not. This is merely some leftovers." She brushed past him and headed for the fridge. He heard her tsk-tsk when she opened it and saw the bare shelves inside. "Clearly, I came just in time."

"I appreciate it. I've been eating a lot of frozen dinners."

She closed the refrigerator and then turned to survey his

apartment. "Well, you are living like a bare-bones bachelor."
She made a little face.

"It'll become home." He glanced at the few pieces of furniture he had, the décor-free walls, the unpacked boxes stacked
beneath the windows. "Eventually."

She crossed to the pass-through window in the kitchen
and picked up one of his new business cards. "You're going
into business for yourself?"

"Yup. I've been talking to my former clients, and several
of them said they wanted to continue working with me, so
I started an LLC and hung out a shingle. It's only part-time
while I'm working on the book."

Even with the few clients he already had, he knew that he
was always going to worry about having enough next month
and the month after that. Clients had come and gone from
Cavite with each year, which had left the company continually scrambling to replace that income.

Mike now had a better appreciation for Meg's stress as a
small business owner. He had caught her pacing the floors late
at night during the slow season, and sometimes pacing when
everything was going perfectly at the store. She was always
worried about having enough sales or enough help, enough
uniqueness or enough inventory. Now that the same kind of
stress was eating him up at all hours of the day, he understood
what she went through all those years.

Was that where the money had gone? Into the business?
Had she been reluctant to tell him she was struggling? No. If
that were the case, he would have noticed big dips in sales or
seen unexplained deposits in her general ledger.

"I don't have any tea," Mike said to Eleanor, "but I can make you a cup of coffee or something if you want."

"Oh, I'm only here for a minute. I just wanted to see how the book was going."

"It's going great. We'll have to set up another interview sometime soon."

Eleanor unsnapped the lid of the plastic container, took out a cookie, and handed it to Mike. "You eat it so I can imagine I am. This whole keto thing with Harry is putting a serious dent in my dessert consumption."

"I think that's the whole point." Mike grinned and took the cookie. Like all of her desserts, the cookie was soft and dense and delicious. "Awesome, as usual."

Eleanor busied herself with refastening the lid. "About the interview..."

"Yes?" Mike snuck in and stole a second cookie before she finished snapping it shut.

"Maybe you could talk to the girls. Margaret especially. She remembers the most because she was the oldest. I think their perspective would be a great addition."

Mike's gaze went to the stack of bank statements. If he sat down with Meg without the buffer of a mediator, he was pretty sure he'd say some things he'd regret. "I don't think that's a good idea right now, Eleanor. I'm sorry. Maybe after the divorce is final and we've all moved on."

"That sounds like such a sad concept," she said. "I'd much rather we all moved sideways than on."

Mike chuckled. "Sideways?"

"When you get lost, it's best to stay where you are and

wait for the other person to find you. If you're moving on, you're leaving that place behind. How on earth can the other person ever find you again?"

Those bank statements told Mike that his marriage hadn't been what he thought at all. That he'd been caught in a deceptive circle just like his mother had been with his father.

"I don't think the other person wants to find me," Mike said. "I think she's done and moved on when I wasn't looking." If Meg had lied to him for years about the money, what else had she lied about? What else had he missed?

❧ ❧ ❧

Margaret walked down the sidewalk along Main Street in Harbor Cove on a beautifully warm and sunny fall day, a rarity at this time of year in New England. Across the street, a mother was standing in front of a window with her preschool-age daughter, pointing out a toy in the display. The little girl was on her tiptoes, peering in beside her mother. She said something that made her mother laugh and then swing her daughter into her arms, the two of them looking like they were having so much fun it almost hurt Margaret to watch.

How on earth was she going to raise a child on her own? How was she going to create that magic and happiness, as she saw other women like her sister do so easily? And juggle all that with running her own business? She'd seen firsthand how tough of a job raising kids could be when she was younger. She'd watched her grandmother, so exhausted by keeping up with three little girls, fall asleep in her armchair as soon as she finished cleaning up after dinner. Grandma had cut back to working part-time so that she could get the girls off to school in the morning and be there to greet them when they came home in the afternoons.

Margaret couldn't work part-time in a business she owned and was entirely responsible for, because her employees were depending on her to keep things running smoothly and bring in money to pay them each week. She certainly couldn't ask her grandmother to fill in the gaps and tell her how the hell to change a diaper or make a bottle.

Margaret wandered down the sidewalk and into Suzie's bakery. The scent of fresh-baked muffins and croissants normally made Margaret's stomach rumble, but today it made her feel nauseous. It had been weeks of this upset stomach, which hadn't been the flu after all. "Hey, Suze. You busy?"

Suzie poked her head out of the kitchen and grinned. "Margaret! I feel like it's been ages since we talked."

She'd met Suzie at the YMCA when Suzie unfurled her yoga mat next to Margaret's and introduced herself. The class had been ridiculously difficult, and when Suzie suggested they go get some dessert as a reward, Margaret had agreed. They'd been friends ever since. When Margaret had started thinking seriously about hiring a lawyer and filing for divorce, she'd confided in her friend, whose own marriage had gone through a rough patch. That was when Suzie told her about the marriage retreat, which Suzie had seen as the cure-all for the decade of problems between Margaret and Mike.

Margaret laughed. "We text almost every day."

"Exactly what I said. Ages." Suzie pulled the apron over

her head and hung it on a hook before coming around the corner to gather Margaret into a hug. "You're a terrible texter because you never tell me what's going on."

That was true. In the weeks since she'd filed for divorce, Margaret had avoided talking about what was going on because she knew that talking to Suzie about the divorce would result in a long conversation about how Margaret and Mike were meant to be and how they really should give it another go. Suzie was an awesome friend but also a hopeless romantic, who thought pretty much every relationship could be salvaged.

"Do you want some coffee?" Suzie asked. "One of my apple streusel muffins?"

"No, thanks. I just ate." That was a lie, but Margaret wasn't ready to share the news about the baby with Suzie, not yet. Partly because she knew that Suzie would see this as a prime reason for Margaret and Mike to get back together. And partly because she was still processing the news herself. It was like a tender, sweet secret she was holding on to just for herself, something she hadn't yet dared release into the world.

"You look tired," Suzie said as the two of them sat down at one of the small round bistro tables. Suzie had brought along a glass of water for Margaret and a cup of coffee for herself. "How are you holding up?"

"I'm okay."

"You always say that, even when you're not okay." Suzie covered Margaret's hand with her own. "How are you *really* holding up?"

Margaret bit her lip and shook her head before the tears that always seemed to be waiting in the wings could fall. All the worries about being a single mom, coupled with the overwhelming joy and hope and fear that warred within her, came to the brim. "It's been tough. Harder than I expected."

"Did you think you'd just hand him the papers and never feel regret or sadness?"

Margaret nodded.

"Hate to tell you this, but divorce is a loss like any other." Suzie sipped her coffee. Her sympathetic eyes softened when they met Margaret's. "Even the people I know who had terrible marriages and horrible divorces went through a grieving period. You are losing something, and you have to give that grief room to breathe."

Margaret could barely breathe most days. How on earth could she give these feelings space, too? "I feel like, if I do that, I'll be swamped. All these feelings I'm trying not to have are like a giant tidal wave being held back by a paper wall. If I so much as nudge that wall, it's going to come crashing down and pull me under."

"All the more reason to let those feelings out." Suzie set the coffee mug down in the saucer. "Are you seeing anyone?"

"Oh God, no. I can't even imagine dating."

"I meant a therapist. Maybe it'd be good to talk to someone about what you're going through."

Margaret toyed with the water glass. "Mike and I saw that woman Beverly you recommended for one session."

Suzie's eyebrow raised, and that optimistic romantic side of her sprung to life. "You did? Why didn't you tell me? Oh, I bet it was so good for you guys. How did that go?"

Margaret put a hand on her abdomen. *Not at all how I expected.* "We talked some things out but ultimately, we decided to go through with the divorce because neither one of us is happy."

"Really? Oh, Margaret, I hate hearing that. I truly thought Beverly could help and maybe get you guys to change course before it was too late."

They'd changed course all right. She was going to be a mother—a *mom*—and a divorcée at the same time. She could feel the excitement rising inside her but she tamped it down. These were early days and she had already learned the hard way that no pregnancy was guaranteed. She reined in her joy and roped it in place with a little reality. "We were never as solid a couple as you and David are."

Suzie scoffed. "We were far from solid when we went on that retreat. Not everything is as it seems on the outside looking in, you know."

"Oh, I know that well." Her own marriage had seemed to be solid to her family and friends. Margaret had kept most of her worries and stresses to herself. She'd told herself that she was doing it to protect her family, but in truth, she was avoiding dealing with all the confusing emotions swirling inside her or talking about all those things she'd spent years pretending didn't exist.

"I hope you know that you can talk to me about whatever's going on, Margaret." The door to the bakery opened and Suzie popped to her feet. "Sorry, it's a customer. Wait here and I'll be done in a sec. Then we can catch up some more." Suzie leaned down and lowered her voice. "And you can tell me what's got you looking like a deer caught in headlights."

Margaret watched her friend bustle around the bakery, humming a love song under her breath. As much as she wanted to confide in Suzie about the baby, she couldn't handle a conversation that ended with "You guys should get back together." Too much had happened, too many secrets had been kept, for their marriage to ever go back to what it was.

"I'll catch you later, Suzie," Margaret said as she slipped her arms into her coat and fished her keys out of the pocket. Suzie was wrong about Margaret and Mike getting back together, but she did have a point about talking to someone. Maybe it was time Margaret got some advice from an expert.

❧ ❧

The last person Eleanor Whitmore expected to see out of the blue, and in the middle of the day, was her oldest grandchild. Margaret stood on the doorstep, her eyes red and her cheeks flushed, as if she had been crying. "Oh, honey, what's wrong?" Eleanor opened her arms and pulled Margaret into a hug.

"I...I...I just need to talk to someone." She wiped the tears off her face with an angry swipe. "God, I hate crying. I just got so emotional in the car, and it just started and...Did I tell you I hate to cry?" Margaret finished in a slightly weepy laugh.

"Crying is good for getting what's in you out on the table. So, you go ahead and shed all the tears you want and come on in. I just put on some hot water for tea, and I have a few leftover chocolate chip cookies from a batch I made for..." She caught herself before she mentioned seeing Mike. Better to find out what had Meg all upset before bringing up the divorce. "Anyway, Harry and I aren't eating the cookies because we're doing that whole keto thing." Eleanor made a face. Going without carbs seemed like an offense against nature. After all, people had been making recipes from starches and grains for centuries. How bad could they really be? Or maybe she was just cranky because she hadn't had a cookie in a week.

Margaret put a hand on her abdomen. "No, no cookies. Please."

Eleanor pressed the back of her hand against Margaret's forehead. "Are you sick?"

"No. Yes. Sort of." Margaret shrugged out of her leather jacket and hung it on the hook by the door. "It's a long story."

"Well, it's a good thing I have a lot of time." Eleanor ushered Margaret into the kitchen and moved about the sunny space, fixing them each a cup of tea. She gave the Tupperware container of cookies a longing glance but then tucked them into a cabinet. Out of sight, out of mind. Mostly. "You'll have to take them home with you or I'll get too tempted and eat them all."

"Okay. I'll bring them to work and share with the staff. Barrett is still there, and we've been busier than ever."

"As much as I can tell you want to talk about work, and that man that 90 percent of the women in town are gossiping about, I'm not going to go there." Eleanor covered Margaret's hand with her own. Her eldest granddaughter was usually so stoic and controlled. For her to come in here crying meant something big was bothering her. "Tell me what's going on."

"I should probably start at the beginning," Margaret said as she swiped away another tear. "Before Mike and I filed for divorce, he booked us this one-on-one session with that woman Suzie and David went to for their marital retreat."

"Oh, yes. Suzie raved about that when I saw her in the

Save-Lots. She was positively radiating with joy." Eleanor was so glad to see Margaret's best friend and her husband work everything out. Suzie had seemed happy ever since they got back together.

Margaret nodded. "It went well for us at first, too. Mike and I worked through a couple things that night, and I felt all close to him again, and we, well, we..."

When Eleanor saw Margaret's cheeks redden, she realized what her granddaughter was avoiding saying aloud. "Nothing wrong with that at all. I've been known to do that myself with my husband. How do you think Penny came about?"

"Like Em said, TMI." But that made Margaret laugh a little bit, which lifted some of the sadness hanging on her like an oversize coat. "Anyway, the next morning I found out he'd lied to me about losing his job."

"He didn't tell you about something as big as that?"

Margaret shook her head. "I found out when his friend Larry texted him. I looked down at the phone when it buzzed and saw the notification on the screen. I was so angry and so I told Mike we were through. It's been two months, and I totally thought I was okay with it, but then..." She shrugged and smiled the biggest smile Eleanor had ever seen. "I found out I was pregnant."

"Oh, Margaret!" Eleanor exclaimed. "Really? That's so wonderful. I'm so excited for you! The first Monroe Girl baby."

Margaret's features filled with worry. "But I'm getting divorced, and it wasn't my dream to be a single mother, and I'm just so..."

"Scared and unsure? Afraid you'll mess it up?" Eleanor gathered Margaret into her arms and placed a kiss on her forehead, just like she did when the girls were little. "Oh, honey, that's exactly how your mother felt when she got pregnant with you. She was so scared that she would be a terrible mother, but she turned out to be the best mother possible."

Eleanor had had almost the exact same conversation with Penny, who had just gotten married when she found out she was pregnant. Margaret came along, then Gabby shortly thereafter, and finally, Emma. If Penny had lived, Eleanor had no doubt her daughter would have filled her home with children. Once she became a mother, it was like she had found her calling.

Margaret sat back and wiped away another tear. "She was pretty great. And so were you."

"And so will you be. Margaret, you've been a little mother from day one, even before your own mother died. You were always setting up pretend classrooms and restaurants and taking care of your sisters. You've been their guardian angel for three decades." Margaret might have doubts about her ability to parent, but Eleanor had seen that trait in her all along, just like she had in Penny.

"But how am I going to do this alone?"

"You have an entire family helping you, so you won't be entirely alone." Eleanor knew how hard the road ahead would be for Margaret. How many nights she'd stay up late, comforting a crying child or just trying to finish the dishes. The years she raised the girls were the most exhausting, rewarding years she'd ever known. "With everything else, you find a way. I had to when your mother died and your poor dad fell apart. Three little girls, all needing someone to hug them and be there for them every day. You'll get some things wrong, and you'll get some things right, and somewhere in the middle of all that, you'll make a life that's wonderful."

Margaret got to her feet, bent over, and hugged Eleanor tight. "Thank you, Grandma. I don't know what I'd do without you."

"And I don't know what I'd do without you three girls. You are the best parts of my life." She drew back and looked at her granddaughter. "Have you told Mike?"

"Not yet. I want to tell him when things are calm between us. Maybe after the mediation is over, and we're not discussing who gets the bedroom set." Margaret began slipping on her coat. "Anyway, I have to get back to work. Thank you for listening."

"Anytime. Truly. Why don't you take tomorrow off and come with Harry and me to the outlet mall? We're going to make a whole day of it. Shopping, lunch, more shopping. Harry will positively hate it, but he's a good sport for taking me."

"I can't. I have the mediation tomorrow."

Eleanor had completely forgotten about that. Maybe she should reschedule the shopping trip so she could be there for Margaret. No, she'd just make sure that Harry got them back home before the mediation ended. She'd make a special dinner for Margaret and invite the other girls, surrounding her granddaughter with family on what was bound to be a tough day. "I'm so sorry, honey. If you want me to be there, I can."

"No, you don't have to. I mean it. It's okay. Or it will be okay. Somehow." She pressed a kiss to her grandmother's cheek. "I gotta get to work. Love you."

"Love you, too," Grandma replied. "Remember to take care of yourself, not just your business."

"My business is all I can focus on right now, Grandma.

That's going to have to be good enough." Margaret slipped on her jacket and headed out the door, leaving the cookies behind.

※※※※

The next day, Harry arrived on time and with a little gift, something he had done ever since he moved in next door. There'd been homemade jam and flowers, doughnuts and muffins, all of them thoughtful little tokens that had grown on her, just as he had.

"Oh my goodness. An entire jar of Silver Needle White Tea leaves." She clasped the gift to her chest. "Wherever did you find it?"

"I ordered it a couple weeks ago when you mentioned you ran out." His smile crinkled the corners of his eyes and lit up his entire face. "They only harvest those leaves in the spring because the Chinese say that's when the Luxueya, the little green shoots, hold the most flavor and benefits."

"You are so thoughtful." She raised on her tiptoes and kissed him. "Thank you."

"No sarcastic remarks today?" Harry arched a brow. "Does that mean you're starting to fall for me?"

"Of course not. I have merely learned to tolerate you." She turned away before he could see the smile on her face and the truth that she had, indeed, begun to fall for her determined, handsome neighbor.

"Ah, Ella Bella, you will one day grow to love me. I am determined."

She glanced at him over her shoulder. "Not if you're only going to break my heart."

"Your heart, my dear, is more precious and rare than the Luxueya."

She pressed a kiss to his cheek and inhaled the woodsy scent of his cologne. This man was going to drive her crazy with his dogged insistence that they were perfect for each other. The thought of ever falling in love again and then losing the man she loved terrified her. She'd been through that pain once, and once was enough. "Let me just grab my coat and then we can get going."

A few minutes later, they were in Harry's Cadillac sedan, heading west toward the Wrentham Village outlet mall. He navigated the back roads leading out of Harbor Cove to the highway with ease, slowing for every turn and stopping at every stop sign. She always felt comfortable riding with Harry because he was a cautious and skillful driver. Her late husband had more of a lead foot and received more than a few speeding tickets over the years.

They stopped at an intersection and waited for the light to turn green. "It's such a lovely day," Harry said. "Maybe we should look for a little outdoor café to have lunch."

"That sounds like a great idea," she said as the light turned green and Harry started to accelerate through the intersection. "What kind of food are you—"

Before Eleanor could finish the sentence, there was a massive boom and the ear-splitting, horrifying sound of metal being crushed. And then everything went black for Eleanor Whitmore.

CHAPTER 13

The mediator, Caren something or other, sat at the head of the table, a thin woman in a dark gray suit with a white silk top. She had her light brown hair back in a clip and looked far more severe than she sounded when she spoke. She was friendly but professional, exactly the kind of person Margaret expected a mediator to be.

Margaret had arrived ten minutes early and took the seat on the mediator's left, across from the door to the conference room. Margaret tried not to fidget, but her nerves about this meeting made it almost impossible to concentrate. The two women made small talk about the weather that Margaret knew she would never remember. Even though this was what she wanted—what had to happen—she was more nervous than she'd ever been in her life.

She placed a hand on her abdomen. She was only a couple months along, too early to show and too early to say anything. It still seemed like she'd imagined the whole thing. The doctor had mentioned that at the next appointment, they could listen for the heartbeat.

That, she knew, would make it all real. The baby would become a person in her mind, one she had no doubt she would love fiercely long before she met him or her. And if anything happened—

No. Not this time. She'd been careful and diligent, taking her vitamins, staying hydrated, making sure she sat down and got some rest throughout the day. She had written down every instruction the doctor gave her and followed them to a T. It would all be okay, she told herself. This time was different. This time would work out.

Because it had to. She couldn't go through that, not again.

The door opened and Mike slipped into the room, followed by Margaret's cousin George, who was serving as Margaret's lawyer. Mike said hello to the mediator and told her he wasn't going to bring in his lawyer, which Margaret wasn't sure was a good sign or a bad sign. Did that mean Mike planned to agree to the terms Margaret had worked out with George?

Either way, she was grateful for the distraction of her cousin maneuvering his large body between the table and the wall because she was afraid that Mike would make eye contact and instantly discern somehow that she was pregnant. That was not a conversation Margaret wanted to have, at least not at their divorce mediation. Eventually, she'd have to tell Mike, but that day was not today. Thing number seven hundred and fifty-two that Margaret was procrastinating on dealing with, lumped in with a big pile of emotions.

George finally made his way around the table and sat down beside Margaret. He was a portly man with glasses and a receding hairline that he tried to cover with strategic combing. He'd worked in family law for most of his career and had a calming way about him that made Margaret grateful she'd asked him to be here today. "How are you?" he asked.

"Good. Nervous." The last bit she added in a whisper. Across from her, Mike had sat down and started talking to Caren. He looked good, damn him. He'd clearly been outside a lot because his normally pale skin had a slight tan. Meanwhile, Margaret was still dealing with morning sickness that clearly didn't care what time of day it was and barely sleeping. She was sure she looked like crap.

Cousin George patted her hand. "It'll be fine. I do these things all the time. You guys worked out a lot of stuff already, so this should go smoothly."

"Are we all ready?" Caren began. "I have a pretty full calendar today, so I'd like to start on time."

"Actually, there's something financial I wanted to bring up," Mike said. He pulled a sheaf of papers out of the folder he'd brought. "This is—"

Margaret's phone started ringing. Damn it. She'd forgotten to silence it. Mike shot her a look of annoyance. "Sorry, sorry. I'll turn it off." The screen showed Emma's number. Whatever emergency her sister had could wait. It was probably some question about the class Margaret had taught or some other silly thing that Emma just had to ask. Her sister must have forgotten that Margaret had told her not to call today. Just as Margaret sent the call to voicemail and reached for the volume button, another call came in from Emma. Two calls in a row? That was unusual, even for Emma. At the same time, a text appeared from Emma. *PICK UP THE PHONE!* "Let me, uh, just get this and tell her I'm busy. Okay?"

Caren's features tightened. "Fine."

Margaret scrambled out of the room, pressing the answer button at the same time. "Em, this is not a good time. I'm—"

"Grandma was in a car accident." Emma barely got the words out before she started sobbing.

The world seemed to stop turning. Margaret's heart froze. "What did you say?"

Emma drew in an audible breath. She spoke fast, in little choked bursts of words. "Grandma and Harry...they were driving...and their car, it was...T-boned."

"Oh my God. I'll be right there, Em." Margaret spun back to the conference room and dashed around the table to grab her purse, fishing in it for her keys at the same time she yanked the leather bag off the floor. "I have to go. Sorry. Just reschedule for...whenever."

"Margaret?" Mike's voice. He had gotten up and come to stand beside her, his hand hovering over her arm as if he wanted to touch her. "What's wrong? What happened?"

"It's my grandmother," Margaret said, her voice a low, terrified whisper. None of the girls would be able to bear it if something happened to Grandma. She was their everything and had been for most of their lives. Margaret closed off her mind to all the worst-case scenarios that kept popping up in her imagination like Whac-A-Mole. Once she got to the hospital, she'd have answers. There was no sense in making up an ending that might not happen. "I...I have to go."

"I'll drive." Mike was out the door before Margaret could stop him. He put a hand to her back as they hurried to the elevator and punched the button. The doors opened, and Mike ushered Margaret inside. He jabbed the button for the parking garage and then the door close button, and a second later, they were on their way down.

In that moment, Margaret didn't care if they were divorced or separated, or what was happening between them. Having tall, broad-shouldered Mike beside her made her feel a little less alone. And right now, she needed that more than anything in the world.

❧❦

Emma and Luke were in the lobby of the emergency room when Margaret and Mike rushed through the hospital's sliding glass doors. Emma's face was white, and Luke was holding her hand, stroking his thumb across hers. Emma popped to her feet and hurried over to Margaret. She wrapped her arms around her sister. "Thank God you're here."

"Where's Grandma?" Margaret asked. "Why aren't you with her?" The words came out harsh and sharp, punctuated by the fear coursing through Margaret's veins. If Grandma was in the emergency room, it couldn't be good. "How's Harry?"

"I don't know anything, really. They wouldn't let us back there." Emma glanced at the double doors. A nurse came through and all of the Monroes froze, waiting for news. But the nurse headed left, away from the lobby and the spirits in the family circle deflated. "I don't know what's going on. Gabby and Jake are out of town, at some work thing she's doing. I left her a voicemail and told her to call me right away."

Emma lowered herself onto one of the camel-colored love seats. Luke put his arm around her shoulders and drew his wife close. Margaret sat across from them in a hard visitor chair with metal arms. Alone. Mike took the chair beside Luke. Margaret told herself she wasn't envious of Luke and Emma and their closeness in a moment when everything was scary and unknown. "What happened?"

"They were driving to the outlet mall. This guy ran a red light, I think, and hit Harry's car on Grandma's side." Emma's eyes were wide. Neither one of them needed to mention how eerily similar this accident was to Momma's. Except Momma had died and the drunk driver who hit her came very close to dying. That wouldn't happen to Grandma. It couldn't. God wouldn't be that cruel.

"Oh my God." A chill ran down Margaret's spine. "Is she okay?"

Emma shook her head. "I don't know. But if they won't let us back there..."

She didn't need to finish the sentence for all of them to understand what that meant. If the hospital was keeping the family out, they didn't want them to see the shape Grandma was in yet. Maybe they were just putting bandages on her or they were too busy to come get Emma and Margaret. Or maybe it was something much worse.

A silence descended over the group. The four of them sat in the waiting room, watching the double doors. Every time they opened, everyone stood up, hoping it was the doctor coming to talk to them. But it wasn't.

Harry's son, Roger, and his grandson, Chad, came rushing in. Emma caught them up on what little she knew. The two of them slumped into the other chairs, everyone terrified to speak their worst nightmare aloud. They just sat in worried silence.

Fear rolled through Margaret in waves. She couldn't lose her grandmother. She just couldn't. Grandma was the lifeblood of this family, the one who held it all together. She was mother and grandmother and everything in between, the one constant for Gabby, Emma, and Margaret from the minute they were born. To say she loved Grandma was an understatement, because Margaret's love for her was more fierce and powerful than anything in the world.

Margaret jumped to her feet, needing to move, to stop this painful, agonizing waiting and doing nothing. A tight knot of fear and anxiety twisted in her stomach, as if someone was tugging on her intestines. She started to pace, twenty steps from the chairs to the soda machine, twenty steps back, over and over again. Instead of calming her like it normally did, the pacing only seemed to tighten that knot in her gut.

"You okay?" Mike had come up behind her, his voice soft with concern. "Maybe you should sit down."

"I can't. I'm too nervous. I have to move." She spun on her heel. Twenty steps. Coke machine. Twenty steps. Chair. Mike kept pace beside her. "You don't have to walk with me."

"I'm worried about you. I can't change what's happening behind those doors, but I can do this."

Why did he have to be so damned nice? Where was all this concern and caring in the last few years? She didn't trust herself to speak because, right now, all she wanted to do was curl into Mike's chest and cry, to lean on the man she had fallen in love with a decade ago. She placed a hand on her abdomen as she paced. "My stomach is a mess."

"You're worried. Of course it is." Mike's hand lit on her back for a second. "Maybe try some deep breaths."

"That'll never work." Twenty steps. Coke machine.

"It's worth trying, Meg."

This stress was surely no good for the baby. She could only imagine how high her blood pressure was right now, with her heart beating like a jackrabbit and her throat tight with fear. She did need to calm down, but it seemed impossible with Grandma just on the other side of those doors, possibly dying.

No. She wouldn't think that word. Grandma was going to be fine. The doctor hadn't come out because...

She couldn't come up with a reason why that didn't end horribly. A tsunami of anxiety roared through Margaret. Her breathing quickened. She felt faint. "I...I...don't feel so good."

Mike took her by the hand. "Here, sit down." He lowered her to the tiled edge of a massive planter filled with dusty plastic elephant ear leaves. "Take a deep breath."

Her throat was closing. Breathing was getting harder and harder. "I...I can't."

"You can, and you will." He leaned closer, one hand on her back, the other clasping her tightly wrapped hands. "Come on, do it with me. Breathe in..." He made a loud sound of inhaling.

Margaret cut him a sideways glance but did as he said. Her breath was shallow, only a couple seconds in and then a rushed exhale.

"Again. Breathe in, Meg." Mike inhaled, long and slow.

This time, her breath wasn't as fast. She drew in deep, feeling the oxygen rush through her veins, easing the faintness in her head. An exhale and the knot in her stomach unwound a fraction.

"Breathe," Mike said, again and again, as she sat beside him and matched his inhalations. Slowly, her anxiety eased, and her throat relaxed. "That's good. You're doing great. Just keep breathing, honey."

Honey. The endearment took her by surprise. It had been ages, maybe even years, since Mike had called her anything other than Meg or, when he was frustrated with her, Margaret. Her mind wanted to hear him say *honey* again, for him to whisper that word in her ear just before he kissed her. Her heart craved those days when every word he spoke was sweet and loving.

"My stomach is still a mess." As she pressed her hand there again, a sharp pain arced through her belly. She cursed under her breath. "God, that hurt."

"What happened?"

"I don't know. I—" Another one, sharper than the first. Like menstrual cramps, only faster and worse. Margaret forgot about breathing slow, forgot about staying calm. Because she knew these cramps and knew what they meant. It was like her worst nightmare replaying in slow motion. *God, no, please. Not now. Don't do this.*

"Not again, no, no, no." She whispered the words to herself, to God, to the baby.

"Meg? What's the matter? What's going on?"

He kept asking questions but she barely heard him above the frightened noise in her head. This wasn't happening. But then another pain ripped through her, and she knew.

"I have to go to the restroom." Margaret scrambled away

from Mike and darted into the ladies' room. She grabbed some paper towels and banged into a stall, praying with every step. *Please, please, please don't do this to me again.*

She ripped down her pants and underwear, shoved the paper towel against herself, and even though she whispered another prayer as she brought the white paper up, the dark blotch in the center was enough to tell her the truth.

She was bleeding. And she was going to lose her baby.

CHAPTER 14

Meg stayed in the bathroom for so long that Mike got nervous. Something was wrong with her, but for the life of him, he couldn't fathom what. Meg rarely got sick, and even when she did, she usually soldiered on without complaint. This time, though, her face had been white, and she'd looked...terrified.

He knocked on the door. "Meg, you okay?" She didn't answer but he swore he could hear her crying. He pushed on the swinging door and opened it a few inches. "Meg, honey? Are you all right? What's wrong?"

That was definitely the sound of his wife sobbing. To hell with it. Mike strode into the bathroom and around the corner to a wall of sinks on one side and a set of stalls on the other. Meg was crumbled on the floor against the concrete wall beneath the paper towel dispenser, holding her belly and sobbing. "Meg? What the hell is going on?"

"It's the baby." She sobbed even harder, tears streaming down her face, her hair plastered to her cheeks.

At first, the words didn't make sense. Did she say *baby*? What baby? Then Mike saw the blood on the paper towel in Meg's hand and the pieces slotted into place. Meg was pregnant?

And bleeding.

Oh God. Not again. The first miscarriage flashed in his memory. The terror they'd felt, chased by a sadness so deep he didn't think they'd ever climb out of it again. This couldn't possibly be happening to them a second time. "Stay here. I'm going to get help."

"Don't leave me." She clutched at his hand, and every inch of him broke when he saw the vulnerability in his normally stoic, controlled wife.

"I have to. Only for a minute, I swear. Just stay here. I'll be right back." He careened out of the bathroom and straight through the emergency room doors, ignoring Emma and Luke's questions, and the security guard who tried to stop him. "I need help! My wife needs help!"

A tall woman in a nurse's uniform came around the desk. "What's going on, sir?"

"My wife, she's in the bathroom. She's bleeding. I think she might be pregnant. I don't know. But you have to hurry." Mike broke into a run, heading back to Meg, not even checking if the nurse was behind him. He skidded into the bathroom and dropped down beside Meg at the same time as the nurse. "The nurse is here, honey."

The other woman—her name tag said Helen—bent down beside Meg. She placed two fingers on Meg's wrist. "Ma'am? What happened?"

Mike's heart was pounding so hard in his chest that he was sure it would explode. He wanted to scream at the nurse to move faster, to get Meg into surgery or something, whatever it took to save her. All he cared about in that instant was his wife.

"My stomach hurt, and I thought maybe it was something I ate or whatever, and I came in here and," Meg's voice caught on a sob, "I'm bleeding."

The nurse unwound the stethoscope from her neck and placed it against Meg's heart. "Is there any chance you're pregnant?"

"Yes. About ten weeks, I think," Meg said. "Is the baby going to be okay?"

Mike sat back on his heels. So, he hadn't misheard. Meg was pregnant, and if she was ten weeks along, that put the conception right around the time they'd gone to see Beverly. The night in the hotel room. The hunger they'd had for each other. He hadn't thought to ask if she was still using birth control that night because she was his wife and they hadn't had sex in so long that it didn't even occur to him. "Why didn't you tell me? Why would you keep something like this a secret from me, Meg? Why?"

"Sir, that doesn't help us right now. I need to get your wife into an exam room." The nurse got to her feet. "Can you walk, ma'am? Or do you want me to get a wheelchair?"

"I can walk."

Mike tabled the whirlwind of emotions inside himself. The priority right now was making sure Meg and the baby were okay. He put a hand under Meg's elbow and helped her to her feet. She looped her arm into the nurse's and the two of them headed out of the bathroom and across the emergency room lobby. Leaving Mike behind. He watched Meg and the nurse disappear behind the emergency room doors and didn't know what to do. Was he supposed to follow Meg? Was that his role if they were getting divorced? Did she even want him there if she hadn't told him about the baby?

Did she even want the baby?

That wasn't a thought he could have. Not now. Not ever. They had tried for so long to have a child of their own, and when Meg got pregnant five years ago, they'd been so excited and grateful. Until...

No. That wasn't happening. He refused to even entertain the thought.

"Mike. Mike!" Emma shook his arm. "What's going on? What's wrong with Margaret?"

Was it even Mike's place to tell her family she was pregnant? No. He had no idea who knew about the baby and who didn't, but it wasn't a conversation that he could or should have. If she hadn't told him then there was a chance she hadn't told her family, either. "She's got something going on with her, uh, stomach. I'm going to go see if I can see her."

Emma clearly didn't buy that. "Her stomach? What's really going on here?"

But Mike was already gone, pushing his way through those double doors and not stopping until he found the curtained area where Meg was lying on a hospital bed. She was pale, her eyes closed, tears streaming down her face. She had both her hands on her stomach as if she was trying to protect the life inside her.

He wanted to gather his frail and delicate wife into his arms and tell her it was all going to be okay. That they'd get through this together. Just as quickly as he had the thought, he remembered that they weren't together. And he had no idea if any of this would ever be okay.

"Why didn't you tell me?"

Her eyes fluttered open. She shook her head, and he could see the regret and fear in her face. "I don't know. It's all so... complicated with us now."

"I have a right to know if you're having my baby." Then he swallowed his pride and voiced the fear that had been dancing in the back of his mind ever since she'd mentioned the pregnancy. He'd done the math, but that didn't mean the math equaled him as the father. "*If* it's my baby."

"Of course it is. Who do you think I am?"

He sank into the chair beside her bed. The railing was up on this side, a mini wall between them. "Honestly? I don't think I know anymore."

The Meg he married had told him everything. They'd been best friends almost from the minute they started dating.

She turned away and stared up at the ceiling. "You don't have to be here."

"Of course I do. Who do you think I am?" he said, repeating her own words back at her. He wasn't the kind of guy who left his wife when she needed him, and he wasn't the kind of guy who wouldn't worry about his unborn baby. "For now, we are still married, and that is my child. I am not leaving."

She looked like she wanted to argue. Instead, she kept her gaze focused on the ceiling. "Fine." There was a beat, and then she said, "What was the financial thing you wanted to bring up in the mediation?"

There was no way Mike was going to ask Meg about missing money when her grandmother was injured and they were both worried about their baby. That was a topic that could wait and, in light of what was happening right now, didn't matter one whit to Mike. Meg's health and their baby's future were all he cared about. "It was nothing. Listen, let's not argue. It's not good for you or for me, and it's especially not good for the baby. You're already stressed about your grandmother, so let's just table this until later."

Before Meg could answer, the curtain was whisked back, and a doctor strode into the room, followed by a nurse with a small machine on a cart. The doctor was young and looked to Mike like he graduated med school yesterday. Hopefully not at the bottom of his class.

The doctor dropped his gaze to the chart in his hands. "Mrs. Brentwood?" he asked, then turned to Mike. "And you are Mr. Brentwood?"

"Yes," Mike answered. "Is Meg okay?" he asked at the same time Meg said, "Is the baby okay?"

The doctor smiled. He had a hipster vibe with his short hair, goatee, and purple-patterned dress shirt under his white coat. "We're going to find out both those answers right now." The doctor stepped aside to allow the nurse to wheel the machine up along the opposite side of the bed.

The nurse—a different one from the woman who had brought Meg into the emergency room—pushed down the blanket covering Meg's belly and pushed up her gown, revealing the pale expanse of her belly. If Mike hadn't known every inch of Meg's body, he wouldn't have seen the slight rise above her belly button. Somewhere inside there was his child.

His child. The words reverberated in his head. After they'd lost the first baby, there'd been an unspoken agreement that they were not going to try again. He'd seen the container of birth control pills reappear on Meg's nightstand, and instead

of saying something, he'd done his best to keep on pretending everything was back to normal. When deep down inside,
Mike was dealing with a pain he thought would never go away.

"This will be cold," the doctor said as he squeezed some
lubricant onto Meg's skin. "And now, let's check out the little
guy or girl."

The doctor's confidence made Mike relax. Surely, he
wouldn't be talking about the baby as a person if there was
something wrong. Meg didn't look so sure. Her face was a
tight mask of worry. Without a word, Mike took her hand in
both of his. She glanced over at him and something in her
seemed to soften. They were in this together, no matter what
happened down the road, because this was a moment when
they needed each other.

The doctor pushed the ultrasound wand around Meg's
abdomen. The screen was mostly blackness, no reassuring
white blob. Meg's fingers squeezed Mike's. "It's okay," he whispered to her, even though he had no idea if it was or wasn't.

The doctor swooped the wand over and up her abdomen for what felt like an hour but was really only seconds.
Then he slowed his movements and adjusted something
on the machine. Mike braced himself for the worst, for the
sound of silence instead of the steady thump of a heartbeat
and the devastating news they had heard five years before in
this same emergency room, with very likely that same exact
machine.

Nothing. Not a sound. Meg's fingers squeezed his so tight
he was sure she'd break his hand.

"Here we are, hiding back here." The doctor pressed a little more with the wand and what looked like a pale lima bean

appeared on the screen. "Let's hear how that heartbeat is, shall we?" He turned another dial, and a second later, there was a fast, steady whoosh-thump, whoosh-thump, whoosh-thump.

Joy erupted in Mike's chest, and for the first time since he'd found Meg in that bathroom, he allowed himself a real, true deep breath of relief. She was okay. Their baby was okay. There was a heartbeat.

"Is that the baby?" Meg asked.

"It most certainly is. He or she sounds hearty and strong." The doctor lifted the wand off of Meg's stomach and then handed her a stack of paper towels to wipe off the lubricant. "Everything looks fine, Mrs. Brentwood."

"But I was bleeding and cramping. Are you sure? Really sure it's all fine?"

"A little breakthrough bleeding is totally normal early in a pregnancy. You told me that your grandmother is here in the emergency room, so I'm sure that stress made you more panicked than you normally would be, which can make your body react in ways it wouldn't normally." The doctor covered her hand with his. "I promise you that your baby is just fine and growing like a weed."

"Does Meg need to stay here overnight?" Mike asked.

"Nope, you're free to go about your daily activities, but just to be safe, take it a little easier than normal. Put your feet up, let your husband do the heavy lifting, and make an appointment to see your regular OB soon. Okay?" The doctor smiled at them both. "Now, why don't I go down the hall and get a status update on your grandmother? I know it's tough to sit in the lobby and wait for news."

"Thank you." Relief washed over Meg's features as if she

had finally accepted that the doctor meant what he was saying. The baby was fine. "Thank you so much."

The doctor headed out of the room while the nurse unplugged the machine, wrapped up the cords, and wheeled it out of the room. "Congratulations," she said with a smile just before she whisked the curtain shut and Mike and Meg were alone again.

Now that the crisis was over, the silence between them felt heavy and dark. The emotions he had put on hold—the feelings of betrayal, hurt, anger—all rushed to the surface. He released Meg's hand and stepped a few inches away from the bed, about as far as he could go in this tiny curtained cubicle. "I want you to know that I'm happy to pay whatever support you need and to share custody."

The words sounded so cold and clinical. Like the baby was a sofa they were arguing over. But the reality was that soon they would be divorced, and any white-picket-fence dreams Mike had had were not going to come true. There'd be handoffs of their child in parks and debates over who got Christmas and texts about school concerts. As excited as he was to be a father, the reality edged that excitement with gloom.

Meg pushed the button on the armrest and raised herself into a sitting position. Her hand remained on her abdomen, protective, loving. "I appreciate that. I think it's too early to add a custody arrangement to the mediation, but as long as you're amenable, we can schedule a court date to firm up the plan when the baby is born."

Mediation. Custody. Court. All words he'd never imagined he would hear when he found out that he was going to be a father. "Sounds like the best way to handle what should have been," he glanced at Meg and felt his heart crack a little more, "a joyous occasion. Congratulations, Margaret."

"Mike—"

He pushed past the curtain and headed out of the emergency room. Because if he stayed there one more second, he was bound to shatter.

※ ※ ※ ※

Eleanor woke up in a room so white that, at first, she thought she'd died. The light above her head was bright and she raised an arm to shield her eyes. If this was heaven, then they needed to install a dimmer switch.

"Grandma! You're awake!" Emma's voice, a few feet away, then right next to her. Eleanor blinked in the brightness, and her youngest granddaughter came into focus. Emma's arms wrapped around her, and the soft floral fragrance of Emma's perfume danced in the air. "Oh, thank God."

Eleanor looked around the sterile space. Her side hurt. Her chest hurt. Her arm…why was her arm bandaged? "Where am I? What happened?"

Then Margaret was there, on the other side of the bed, taking one of Eleanor's hands. "You and Harry were in a car accident. But you're going to be okay."

A car accident? But they never got to the outlet mall. That was where they were planning on going today, wasn't it? Her memory had a fuzzy haze, partly because it felt like every part of her body had been beaten.

Eleanor tried to push herself up into a sitting position but had to lie down again because moving made all those parts that hurt scream in reply. She reached for the covers to throw them off her legs, but it seemed like she was swimming in molasses and the covers weighed ten tons. She needed to see Harry. Why wasn't he here? "Where is Harry? I have to see if he's okay."

Margaret exchanged a look with Emma across Eleanor's body. A look that didn't bode well. Eleanor panicked. "What? Tell me. Or I swear, I'll get out of this bed and find out myself." She could barely make the threat, never mind follow through with it, but if Harry was hurt or … worse, Eleanor wasn't going to let him be alone. She cared about him, damn it, more than she'd ever realized. More than cared, but that was a thought for another time, when she wasn't so overcome with worry.

"He's still in surgery," Margaret said. "He's been in there for a while."

"Surgery?" The panic in Eleanor's chest damn near exploded. "Why is he in surgery? What happened? Is it his heart?"

"If you promise to calm down, we'll tell you," Emma said. "Just sit back and rest. No getting out of bed, not yet."

"Fine," she mumbled, as if she didn't want to agree. Truth was, she had to agree with Emma and Margaret. Her body craved rest and something for the pain that was starting to rise as she became more awake. Her entire right side was in agony. It would be a while before she was up and about, that much was clear. Which only made the worry inside her grow ten times over. "Tell me everything. Don't spare me any details. I'm an old woman. I can handle it." But could she? If something terrible happened to Harry? She'd endured so much loss already in her life. She wasn't sure she could endure another.

Margaret drew in a deep breath. "You and Harry were heading to the outlet mall. A guy in an SUV ran a red light and T-boned Harry's Cadillac."

Oh God. Just like the accident that had killed her daughter, Penny. Except with her it had been nighttime and the pickup driven by a drunk driver was no match for her little sedan. Penny had died on impact. The driver ended up in the hospital and then was arrested for what he did so he would never, ever bring that kind of tragedy to a family again.

"The driver ran into the passenger's side where you were sitting, Grandma," Margaret went on, "but thankfully, he hit mostly the front quarter panel and only part of where you were sitting. It's a good thing Harry drives such a big Cadillac because it has a huge front end, and the police think that's what kept you from getting hurt much worse. Still, you got pretty banged up, between the airbag and the collision. You've got some cuts that need to heal, some ribs that are broken, and a lot of bruising from the impact, but it's all nothing that a little time and rest can't heal."

Eleanor waved that off. She didn't care how she was. She cared how Harry was. "What about Harry? Why did he end up in surgery if the driver hit my side?"

"His car was hit so hard that it was pushed into a light pole, driver's side first. The damage on that side was much..." Emma glanced at Margaret, who nodded as if saying, *We have to tell her the truth.* "Much worse."

Eleanor held her breath and whispered more prayers in the space of the next few seconds than she had in the last two decades. She was almost afraid to ask. "And?"

"He broke his leg and a couple ribs. One of those ribs punctured his lung. He's in surgery right now so they can try to repair his leg and his lung."

"His lung? Oh God, poor Harry." She started to sit up again, adrenaline fueling her this time, the pain in her side forgotten for a blip before it came rushing back with an angry reminder. "I have to see him. I have to—"

"You have to rest and take care of yourself." Margaret gently pushed her back down on the bed. "Roger and Chad are keeping us updated about Harry. You concentrate on you and let us worry about the rest."

That wasn't the kind of person Eleanor was. She didn't sit around waiting for things to work out. She pushed and pulled and tweaked until whatever was wrong was fixed. This was something, though, that she had no control over, no ability to fix. All she could do was lie here and worry, which was so frustrating. "But, but—"

"But nothing," Emma said. "You two are okay. Nobody died."

"Not even the driver of the SUV?" Eleanor asked.

"He's fine, too. They think his brakes failed," Emma told her.

A wave of gratitude flooded Eleanor and she took in a deep breath. Okay. Everyone was fine. Thank God. "I can only imagine how scared you two have been since this happened. I'm so sorry."

"Three," Gabby said as she strode into the room. Her hair was back in a ponytail, her face bare of makeup. A fine sheen of sweat beaded across her forehead, as if she'd run to the hospital.

"Gabriella, what are you doing here? Aren't you supposed to be putting on your first fashion show?" Eleanor's mind was clearing with each passing minute, a good sign that she didn't have a head injury. She remembered that Gabby had gone to Connecticut to be part of an event with some other clothing boutiques, a sort of fashion show for the coming holiday season. The whole thing was supposed to be a great opportunity for Gabby's store.

"I couldn't stay in Connecticut knowing you were in the hospital. Jake and I turned around as soon as we heard."

"Oh goodness, that is too much fuss. Go back to Connecticut. An opportunity like that doesn't come along every day." Gabby had worked so hard to make her vintage-inspired clothing designs a success, and this fashion show was exactly the kind of event she needed to bring those designs to a bigger stage. "I'll be fine."

"Let us take care of you for once," Margaret said. "And stop being so bossy."

Eleanor looked at each of her granddaughters in turn. She saw sternness and concern in all of their eyes. A look that reminded her very much of herself and all the times she had said much the same to these amazing young women. "How did you three grow up to be so stubborn?"

"We learned from the best." Emma pressed a kiss to Eleanor's cheek. Gabby put a hand on Eleanor's leg, and Margaret kept on holding her hand. All three of them, right here, so like their mother in their looks and their demeanors. Eleanor thanked God for blessing her with such an amazing family. Then she whispered another prayer for Harry. This wait for the surgery to be over was excruciating.

When she glanced over at Margaret's hand, resting on her own, she noticed a flash of something white. It took a second for her to realize what that plastic thing was. "Margaret, why are you wearing a hospital bracelet?"

"Oh, that." She rushed to cover the white band with her hand. "It's nothing."

"What's nothing?" Eleanor looked from Margaret to Emma and back again. "Are you all going to keep me in the dark about everything?"

"Grandma, I'm fine. I got super stressed when you were in the emergency room and panicked. Mike brought me into the emergency room but I checked out just fine. All is well."

Eleanor's gaze met Margaret's, but her granddaughter was staring at the sheets like they were the most interesting thing in the room. She wasn't telling the whole story, of that Eleanor was sure. "Are you sure?"

"Yes. Very." Margaret kept on studying those plain white sheets.

"It was probably indigestion from grumpiness," Emma muttered. Margaret shot her a glare, just like when they were little and Emma teased her for being too rigid.

"Be nice, you two," Eleanor said, just like she had back then.

"Why do I feel like I missed 60 percent of a conversation?" Gabby asked.

"Because you did. You were out of town," Margaret replied. "That's not my fault."

Gabby gave Margaret a look of annoyance but let the subject drop. Eleanor loved seeing the three of them squabble because it meant everything was back to normal. They were sisters; there were bound to be arguments and complaints. Soon, Eleanor would be home again, and they'd all be sitting around her dining room table, and the sound of their voices would fill her house and heart with joy.

And Harry...Harry would be there, too. She told herself there was no other possible outcome.

There was a knock at the door, and then Chad, Harry's grandson, poked his head into the room. He was a handsome young man, with light brown hair and dark brown eyes, and a smile for every occasion. "How are you doing, Ella?"

"I'm just fine." She pushed the power button on her bed and raised herself into a sitting position. She tried not to wince when her body complained, because then her granddaughters would just insist on her resting instead of getting answers about how Harry was doing. In that moment, that was all Eleanor cared about, which told her that her feelings for Harry were much deeper than she wanted to admit to herself. "More importantly, how is my Harry?"

"He's going to be fine," Chad said. "The break in his leg was pretty clean. He's in some pain, of course, but once the cast comes off, he can start physical therapy and get back on his feet. They repaired the tear in his lung, and he's in the recovery room now, waking up from the anesthesia. The doctor said he expects my grandpa to be back up to speed before you know it."

Eleanor's breath left her in a long whoosh. "Thank God. I was so worried. Please give him my love."

Gabby arched a brow and glanced at her sisters. The word *love* had never come out of Eleanor's mouth before in any kind of reference to Harry. "Love?" Gabby asked.

Eleanor waved her hand. "The man is recovering from surgery. The least I can do is be nice to him." Except everyone in that room knew that speaking that word was a lot more than being nice.

Chad chuckled. "Will do. Before I go, tell me how you're doing? Because I know Grandpa's first question when he wakes up is going to be about you, Ella."

That warmed Eleanor's heart. Maybe she wasn't the only one who cared more than she realized. "I'm going to be just fine. And as soon as my stubborn granddaughters let me, I'll come visit Harry."

· "Good. He'll like that." Chad thumbed toward the door. "I'm going back to wait in Grandpa's room. He should wake up soon. He's in good hands, so don't worry too much."

"Of course I won't." Eleanor raised her chin and feigned indifference, but even she knew that the tears of relief glistening in her eyes and the heat in her cheeks painted her as a liar. "Take good care of him and tell him I will make him those peanut butter cookies he loves just as soon as I get home. That keto thing is on pause until Harry is back to his normal self."

Chad crossed to give Eleanor a gentle hug, promising to return soon with the next Harry update. He ducked out of the room just as a nurse came in to take Eleanor's blood pressure and listen to her heart. She held her breath, so sure that the nurse would have something negative to report. "All looks good," the nurse said.

Eleanor watched Margaret from the corner of her eye. Her eldest granddaughter was biting her lower lip and seemed impatient to leave, which meant she had something on her mind that she didn't want to share. Whatever it was, Eleanor would bet dollars to doughnuts that it had to do with that hospital bracelet. "Emma, would you be a dear and go get me some iced tea from the cafeteria? And Gabriella, could you please go down to the gift shop and get me a card I can bring to Harry? Something…" She thought a moment. Life was short. Why not? "Something sappy."

Gabby arched a brow and grinned. "Absolutely."

The two girls left the room. Margaret circled the bed and dropped into the chair on Eleanor's right side. "You feeling okay?"

"Not exactly fit as a fiddle, but I'll be all right." She patted her granddaughter's hand. "I'm more concerned about you. Is this hospital bracelet something to do with the baby?"

Tears filled Margaret's eyes. She nodded several times. "I had some breakthrough bleeding and cramps, and I just panicked. I didn't say anything because I haven't told Emma and Gabby yet. There's just so much going on."

"Is the baby okay?"

"The doctor said everything looks great. They did an ultrasound and we heard the heartbeat." A look of wonder and joy that Eleanor recognized filled Margaret's face. "Anyway, I have to follow up with my doctor next week. It was nothing, really, Grandma."

It didn't sound like nothing, but if the ultrasound showed the baby was okay, then surely it all would be fine. Now that she was awake and the pain medicine they had given her was wearing off—which made sitting in this firm bed uncomfortable—Eleanor could concentrate on the details. "You said Mike brought you to the emergency room. Wasn't today your mediation hearing?"

"Yes. But we didn't get to do any of that. The call about your car accident came in right when Mike and I arrived. It was just...instinct, I guess, to rush over here together. Then when my stomach hurt, I went into the bathroom, and he got worried and found me and practically dragged me into the ER." A little smile crossed Margaret's lips. "I was so scared, and he was so calm."

Well, none of that sounded like a marriage that was completely dead. Mike's instinct to stand by his wife's side during a family crisis and Margaret's ability to rely on him spoke to a relationship that still had at least a few embers burning. Maybe it wasn't too late after all... if Eleanor did a little of the same kind of behind-the-scenes machinations that her granddaughters had done for her last year. Machinations that had brought Harry into Eleanor's life, a change she was eternally grateful for. As soon as she was out of this hospital bed, Eleanor was going to do her best to ensure one more happily-ever-after for her darling Monroe girls.

CHAPTER 15

Margaret pulled up to the small, quaint coffee shop located a few miles away from Harbor Cove and rolled her windows down to let some of the crisp fall air into the stuffy car. Years ago, there was a convenience store on this corner. The coffee shop was just as busy as the little store had been, with a constant stream of people coming in and out of the door on their way to or from work. Now, the men and women hurrying through the door released the scent of coffee mingled with vanilla and chocolate, making the air almost as delicious as the coffee itself.

Margaret went inside and ordered a decaf latte with a sprinkling of cinnamon from the barista who looked barely old enough to drive. When had everyone become so young? Maybe it was just being here, surrounded by people who were in their late teens and early twenties, that made Margaret feel ancient.

The coffee smelled amazing, almost Christmassy, reminding her that before she knew it, the holidays would be here. Her divorce would be final, and she would be alone. The thought didn't fill her with relief so much as it did a sadness that seemed to grow heavier every day.

She watched the barista sprinkle the cinnamon on top of the foamy skim milk. Margaret had started adding it to as many things as she could after she read somewhere that a little cinnamon could reduce her blood sugar levels. The last thing she wanted was gestational diabetes, or any of a hundred other things that could go wrong during her pregnancy. That moment in the hospital had terrified Margaret, and she'd been ten times more cautious in the days since that happened, even though both the ER doctor and her own doctor had assured her everything was fine. She made sure to rest frequently throughout the day and had cut back her hours at the store so that she could be home more often with her feet up. She'd also slowed her runs to easy jogs and reduced her mileage, even though the doctor assured her that continuing to exercise was fine.

Mike reached out a couple times a day, asking simply, "How are you and the baby feeling?" She'd type back a short answer, usually "Fine," and that would be it. Yet, every time he texted her and she replied, she stared at her screen, waiting for the three dots that would mean he was typing back. Those three dots never appeared.

Was it simply habit that made her anticipate his next text? Or was there some other meaning hidden in that disappointment about the three dots? A truth that she refused to acknowledge?

She put a hand over her stomach and thought about the miracle that was growing inside her. She was not even through the first trimester, far too early to feel the baby move. The nausea had finally abated, and Margaret had started filling her fridge with organic fruits and vegetables and grass-fed, hormone-free chicken. She cooked because she had to for the baby, not because she wanted to. The joy of making a meal had disappeared, now that she was eating alone at the kitchen island every single night. She'd talk to the baby as she cooked and ate, but it wasn't the same as having Mike across the table.

Was this sentimentality a normal feeling for someone getting divorced? She had no idea and didn't know who to even ask. Suzie, Gabby, Emma, and Grandma had all been happily married. They wouldn't understand, so she kept this tumbleweed of emotions to herself. Maybe it was just pregnancy hormones.

The door to the coffee shop opened and a tall man wearing jeans and a windbreaker walked inside, his steps uneven, leaning to one side. He scanned the busy space until he saw Margaret. He gave her a little wave and then navigated his way through the tables and customers to take the seat across from her. No cane today, which meant it must be a good day for him, one free of the pain that had been such a big part of the last two decades. "Margaret. How are you?"

"Good. And you?" It was the same exchange they'd had dozens of times, ever since she'd first met Richard Hargrave almost fifteen years ago. In the beginning, she'd fully intended to confront him and demand answers. But that first meeting had been more emotional than Margaret had anticipated, and all of her plans disappeared.

Back then, Richard had still been in a wheelchair, not yet fitted into artificial legs, and the message sent by the thin blanket that hung from his knees was that the accident had claimed more than just her mother. All of the anger and recrimination she'd been carrying in her heart for years had dissipated. They'd had an awkward, painful conversation, but it had been a massive first step in healing. For both of them.

So, every year in early November, around the time Momma had died, Margaret and Richard sat across from each other and slowly built something that wasn't quite a friendship, but was a relationship that she knew she needed as much as he did. "You're looking well," he said.

"You too. I saw Tabitha on campus a couple weeks ago," Margaret said. "She looks...happy."

A smile spread across his face. "She is. It took her a while to figure out where she wanted to go with her life, but I'm glad she opted for college. She's staying in a dorm, so she gets that taste of being on her own, yet she's close enough to come home on the weekends to do her laundry or have some of her mom's lasagna." Richard chuckled. "She'll tell you she doesn't miss us, but I think she does. When I told her I'd be in the area, she asked me to come by and visit for a little bit. She's so smart and sweet. She's turned into an amazing young woman."

"I agree." Tabitha was the safe space where Margaret could tread, the one topic that didn't veer too close to a history that both of them danced around. Richard's daughter was the light of his life, the thing that kept him on track day after day, month after month, and year after year. He'd still been in jail when she was born, and as soon as he was released, he headed straight to a halfway house with a strong therapy program for recovering alcoholics, determined to turn his life around. He'd been sober now for two decades, and every time Margaret saw him, she marveled at his strength and growth.

"I wanted to give you another check," Margaret said as she

reached into her bag and pulled out a piece of paper. "I know how expensive college can be and—"

Richard put his hand over hers, refusing the money. "You've done more than enough for our family. More than anyone else ever could or should."

"Your family was just as destroyed as ours," Margaret said. "You lost so much."

"Not as much as you girls." Richard released her hand and sat back in his chair. At the same time, he extended one of his legs under the table, revealing a glint of metal when the denim shifted.

"Loss is loss, Richard. You spent months, heck, years in a wheelchair before you got these legs and learned to walk again." He'd barely touched on it, but she knew that being in jail and recovering from losing his legs had been a hellish time in Richard's life. He'd once told her that, before the accident, he'd gone back and forth between on and off the wagon, spending too much time in bars with a good friend who was going down the same rabbit hole as Richard. When he found his reason to stay sober, he left that life—and his friend— behind for good and never looked back.

"I also spent a lot of time drunk as a skunk, hating myself," Richard said. "And rightly so."

When Margaret had met him, it was several years after he'd stopped drinking. She wasn't sure the meeting would have gone the way it did if Richard hadn't gotten sober and been so committed to changing his life. She'd seen earnestness in his face and a desperate need to forgive himself for what had happened. When he became a father, he'd told her, he realized how devastating it had been for the Monroe girls to lose their mother when they were young. That had been the wake-up call he needed to never, ever let something like that be his fault again. "Yeah, but you're the one who did all that work to turn your life around and make a difference for other people."

"Because of you." He leaned across the table. He had vibrant green eyes and dark hair that was just beginning to show streaks of gray. So many years had passed, so much water had gone under the bridge, and so much had changed since that first meeting in a coffee shop similar to this one. "When you asked to meet me all those years ago, I was terrified. I had spent a lot of years beating myself up for what happened, and I just knew you were going to do the same thing. You had every right to hate me, to scream at me. Instead, you…" His voice caught. "You forgave me."

It hadn't been Margaret's first instinct that day. The minute she got her driver's license, she had reached out to Richard with a message on social media, which was still so new at the time that she was surprised to see he had a profile page. Mostly inactive, with only a smattering of posts, which meant he wasn't on there much. It took two weeks for him to respond to her message about meeting with a tentative *Okay*.

"I wanted to yell at you, believe me," she said. "I had spent years thinking about what I would say to you when I saw you. I had so much anger in me, so much grief I'd never dealt with. I wanted you to know what losing my mother had done to my sisters and me, never mind the rest of my family. I wanted you to feel the pain that we had felt." She was ashamed of the hatred that had consumed her in those days, the way it had eaten her up inside and, she was sure, been a big part of why Margaret was an expert at stuffing her feelings deep inside rather than speaking them aloud.

"I don't blame you. I would have screamed at me, too. Yet, you didn't."

"You were still in a wheelchair then, and when you rolled into the coffee shop, I realized..." She could still see him, a broken man who was depressed and penitent, unable to ever go back to work as a roofer. She had never thought about what happened to the driver of the pickup truck, because in her mind, he had been this demon who stole her mother from her. "I realized you were a human being who was suffering, too."

She remembered being stunned by his appearance. The monster in her mind was in reality a frail, broken man.

"It was a hard few years, for sure, because I struggled for so long to find work to support my daughter."

Which was why Margaret had started sending him money. Just a little at first, cash in an envelope with no return address. A few years after those envelopes started showing up in his mailbox, Richard made the connection and asked Margaret straight out if she'd been sending him money.

"I was at the bottom of my barrel that day you met me. I was a single dad who couldn't get a job because of my record. My bank account was almost empty, and I was just..."

She covered his hand with her own. "I know." They never talked about what a dark place Richard had been in back in those days. It scared her to think that such a smart, kind man would feel so deeply depressed that he would think of ending everything. That confession had come years later, once Richard and Margaret had become sort of friends.

"I'm still so glad you contacted me," he said. "I think I needed that meeting more than you did."

"We both needed it." The money had been a way for her

to help Richard out and, she supposed, do what her mother would have done. Penny Monroe was as generous with her talents as she was with her time and she would have been the first person to forgive and raise a helping hand. It was also something that Mike never would have understood. A secret she'd had to keep because telling it would have destroyed her marriage in a blink.

So, Margaret had kept sending the money, and Richard had kept protesting, even though she could clearly see he needed it. For her, it was a way to honor her mother. For Richard, it was more complicated. He felt ashamed and guilty. It was Margaret who'd said that she wanted to do it for Tabitha, to help her have a good life despite the rocky start her father's problems had given her. That had seemed to sit better with Richard, and he'd gradually allowed Margaret to help. She'd helped cover the gaps between his debts and his bills as he found a career that gave him purpose.

She sipped at her latte. A couple with matching coffees slid past the table, holding hands, him leading and her following behind, laughing at something he'd said. They looked so achingly happy that, for a second, Margaret couldn't think.

"You okay?" Richard asked.

"Yes, yes, of course." She squared the coffee mug on the saucer because putting things into order was one of the few things that calmed the rush of anxiety in her chest. "Meeting you allowed me to see that there was another side to the story."

"There's always another side to the story. Even if you don't want to see it."

She nodded. "Very true."

Three girls wearing Harbor Cove cross-country team sweatshirts poured into the coffee shop. They could have been doubles for Margaret and her sisters. The girls' cheeks were red from the chilly fall air. They talked over each other in that way close friends had, stumbling over the words as they ordered their coffees and scones.

"Can I ask you something?" Margaret said.

"Sure. Anything. You know that."

Even if they were in some undefined space between strangers and friends, the divide created by the accident had closed, allowing them to have several difficult conversations in these annual meetings and over text or the phone the rest of the year. There were still days when Richard turtled himself at home, when the waves of depression became too much to put on a happy face, but thankfully, those days were fewer and fewer as Richard's life bloomed into something joyful. He had lost everything but eventually found happiness again. "How did you do it? Start over?"

He scoffed. "I had no choice. It was literally either that or die."

Margaret fiddled with the handle on the ceramic mug. The foam on top of the latte floated across the dark coffee like spring clouds. "I am sort of at a crossroads myself right now, and I'm a little terrified about starting over."

It was easier, somehow, to tell this person who wasn't part of her family the truth. To open up about the things that she normally kept hidden inside, the fears she didn't show her sisters or grandmother or even her best friend. Richard's face betrayed no judgment, nothing but concern. "I get that."

"Mike and I are getting a divorce." Richard had always

been a listening ear whenever she was frustrated with how things were going with Mike, something she never would have imagined would happen after that first meeting. "Got the paperwork, hired the mediator, put all the pieces in place to end this marriage that is anything but a strong, loving relationship." She thought of the baby growing inside her, that night in the hotel room. With a child, there would always be a tether between her and Mike. "Sort of."

"I'm sorry to hear that. Mike's a great guy; always has been. I knew you were unhappy but not that unhappy," Richard said.

"No one did, because I'm very, very good at hiding my feelings." She ran a finger along the rim of the mug, skating over the bits of foam that remained. "I'm the kind of person who withdraws when things bother me. I've always been the one who was there to keep others on track, and I think that kept me from talking about what scared me or worried me. Mike is an avoider, too, who hates arguing. You put two people like that in a house together for years and there's bound to be a lot of things that never get talked about."

Richard's gaze went to somewhere far in the past. "I did the same thing, but with alcohol. I had a rough childhood, the kind that they'd have on an episode of Oprah's show. I don't like to talk about it because then I think about it, and thinking about it makes it real again."

"I'm so sorry, Richard." She thought of how lucky she and her sisters had been, with Grandma and Dad in their lives. All this time she'd spent on the outside looking in at Richard's life, she'd begun to understand Mike's father, and her own, in a way she never had before. She'd begun to see the complicated layers that steered some people in the wrong direction. Hopefully, from now on, Richard's life would stay on an even keel.

"Don't be. It's not your fault. Not mine, either, it turns out." He tapped his head and grinned. "Therapy works wonders."

She laughed. "I've heard that. My grandmother tried to get me to go to therapy after my mother died, but I thought I could handle it on my own."

"Sounds like that's what you've done all your life."

Her smile wavered on her face. "That's the truth."

"Hey, I get it. I'm the same way. Instead of talking about it, I drank until it didn't hurt anymore. Guess what? There's not enough alcohol in the world to get to that point."

"I understand." She thought of all the miles she had logged on her runs and the hours she had put in at the store. She'd done the same thing as Richard, but without drugs or alcohol. Even the short session with Beverly had been enough to show Margaret that maybe therapy would be a good idea. She'd gone all these years refusing to ask for help. Maybe it was time to start.

"Even after Tabitha was born, there were a lot of moments that were hard as hell. Therapy brings everything you buried right up to the surface, forcing you to face those regrets. It was hard, not gonna lie. Especially without that crutch of alcohol to fall back on. But I was determined to stay sober, not just because of my daughter, but also because..." He dropped his gaze to his hands. When he spoke again, his voice was soft but pained. "Because I didn't want to let you girls down again.

"When I hit your mother's car," he went on, "I tore your life apart. I was, and still am, so damned sorry for that." He put up a hand to stop her protests. "I know I've said I'm sorry a million times, but I feel like I can't say it enough. When I saw the sympathy in your face the day we met, I realized what I had become. What I had let the pain do to me. A sad man who offered nothing. All I did was take from people. Cause them pain. I was tempted—really tempted—to go back to drinking, but I didn't want to be that guy. The one who killed your mother and then essentially killed himself with a bottle. You had already lost so much, and here you were, trying to make me, the man who did that horrible thing, feel better. How could I just keep going further into the pit after getting the gift of your forgiveness?"

"I had no idea that you were going through all that when we met," Margaret said.

"Sometimes, Margaret, you change people's lives simply by being there." Richard fiddled with his cup. "For me, there are still a lot of people I want to apologize to. To make amends. But I don't want to do that at the expense of their peace of mind. That would be selfish."

Margaret thought of how these meetings had changed her, had helped heal the massive wound created by her mother's death. Over the years, all of the Monroe girls had struggled with losing Momma. Maybe it was time to change more lives than just her own and Richard's. "I'd like to propose an idea to you."

"I'm ready," he said.

Hopefully, so was her family.

CHAPTER 16

From a mile away, Margaret could see the two of them marching down the sidewalk, clearly two women on a mission. Margaret stepped away from the window and braced herself for the Monroe-girl invasion. It had been two days since Grandma's accident and Margaret's ER trip, which she knew had piqued her sisters' curiosity. Neither one of them seemed to buy the "stomach issues" excuse, and they looked like they were ready to perform a sisterly inquisition.

She'd just gotten back from the coffee meeting with Richard, which had left her feeling oddly optimistic. On the way to the store, she'd called a local therapist and set up an appointment. The idea of going to therapy made her nervous—talking about all these things she'd avoided sounded like the fifth circle of hell—but also relieved. As if she were putting all these weights on her shoulders into someone else's hands.

"What's wrong?" Barrett asked. Sales had been so brisk since he came on board that he had stayed on at the shop for a few more weeks, which, admittedly, made going to work a little more enjoyable.

Margaret was surprised when he'd offered to stay on.

Surely, he was in demand at jewelry stores all over the place. Why he'd want to stay in this tiny store in Harbor Cove befuddled her, but she wasn't about to turn down the uptick in business, especially now.

"My sisters are on their way in, and when my sisters show up, it usually means they have a lecture for me." That's what happened when little sisters grew up to be adult women; they flipped the tables on who was in charge. "I'm supposed to be the one who lectures. I'm the oldest."

Barrett came out from behind the design table to stand beside Margaret and glance out the window. "It must be wonderful to be so loved," he said softly.

She flicked a glance at him. He seemed lost in thought. The spicy, warm notes of his cologne drifted between them. She didn't know what brand it was, only that he smelled better than a new car and Christmas rolled into one. "It is. I'm blessed to have a great family."

"And yet..." He shrugged but didn't finish the sentence.

"And yet what?"

He turned away from the window and leaned one hip against the counter. He was wearing a dark brown suit today, and when he shifted to one side like that, he reminded her of Don Draper's character on *Mad Men*. Smooth, sophisticated, confident. Irresistible to the women around him. "You have been quite unhappy these past couple of weeks. It troubles me to see you like this."

He'd noticed her? In a way other than as his boss? Her cheeks burned, and she struggled to maintain eye contact with Barrett's dark, brooding gaze. "I'm...going through a lot."

"Ah, yes. The divorce." He put up one hand. "You do not

say anything but I hear, I see. I notice." He nodded toward her bare left hand with its visible tan line from where her wedding ring used to sit.

"Well, thank you." She wasn't sure what else to say. How was she supposed to respond to someone she'd hired talking about her personal life? She glanced out the window again, willing Tara to come in early for her shift. Margaret's sisters were less than a block away. Not the people she wanted to see today, especially when it was probably clear to the crew on the International Space Station that she was flustered by this man.

"You deserve someone who cares about you." Barrett pushed off from the counter and came to stand in front of her. Very, very close. "You deserve someone who sees your beauty and appreciates every inch of you."

Margaret gulped. A rush of something that she refused to name charged through her veins, igniting parts of herself that had been dead for a long time. "Thank you," she said again.

Such a lame answer. It screamed, *I haven't been flirted with in a long time and have no dating skills.*

Instead of laughing, Barrett just smiled. "How long has it been," he said, his hand lighting on her chin, fingers dancing across her skin, "since someone loved you?"

The door opened and her sisters stumbled in, giggling and talking as they did. They saw Barrett with his hand on Margaret, and they both came to a sudden halt. "Uh...we can come back later," Emma said.

"Much later," Gabby added.

Margaret shook her head, pulling herself out of whatever crazy trance she'd been in with the handsome designer, and stepped back. "Gabby, Emma. I'd like you to meet Barrett Wilson, my designer." Nothing said *don't want to talk about it* like ignoring what just happened. "Barrett, meet my sisters. This is Emma, and this is Gabby."

"I've heard *all* about you," Emma said with a big, knowing grin. "The women at the center are constantly talking about the handsome guy working in my sister's shop." She glanced around the room. "Alone."

Oh my God. Margaret was going to kill Emma.

"The pleasure is mine," Barrett said. He took Emma's hand and raised it for an air kiss and then Gabby's. He'd done the same thing when he met Margaret. Clearly, this wasn't anything special, and she was reading way too much into his words a moment ago. Why on earth would Barrett be interested in a soon-to-be-divorced, boring woman who hadn't been on a date since *How I Met Your Mother* first aired?

"So, what are you two doing here?" Margaret asked, changing the subject in the room and in her head. "It's barely even five o'clock."

Gabby scowled. "Nice to see you, too, Margaret. How've you been?"

Emma nudged her and gave her a look that Margaret knew well. It was the convince-Margaret-to-do-something-she-doesn't-want-to-do look. "We thought you've been working so hard lately that it might be nice to do an early sisters-only dinner. We can go to Bella Vita, have some lasagna and an extra order of yummy garlic bread…" Emma licked her lips. "And I throw that in there because I know how much you love their garlic bread. And the crème brûlée for dessert."

"Are you trying to bribe me?"

"Is it working?"

Margaret shook her head but a smile lingered behind her feigned annoyance. "You two are a royal pain in my butt."

"That, my dear older sister, is the whole point of family." Gabby crooked her arm into Margaret's while Emma did the same on the other side. "Let's go eat. I'm starving."

Tara walked in just then for her shift, eliminating Margaret's only excuse. Truth be told, she was happy to leave with her sisters and put some distance between herself and whatever was brewing with Barrett. There was tension between them, and not the kind that set off arguments. "I'll see you tomorrow, Barrett," she said.

"I cannot wait." He blew a kiss in her direction as she sailed out the door with her sisters.

"Oh. My. God. What. Was. That?" Emma asked the second the door shut behind them.

Margaret dragged the two of them down the sidewalk until they were out of view of the shop windows, because she was not having this conversation in range of Barrett's eyesight or hearing. "Honestly, I have no idea. Do you think he was flirting? Or am I just being an idiot?"

"If you don't know when a man is flirting with you, I think you need to go back to high school." Gabby laughed. "That guy could barely keep his eyes off of you."

"Never mind his hands," Emma quipped.

Margaret scowled. "Nothing is happening between Barrett and me. He flirts with everyone."

"Uh-huh," Gabby and Emma said together.

The sun was already beginning to set, a sign that the warm, breezy days of summer were far in the rearview mirror.

The cornelian cherry and Washington hawthorn trees lining the sidewalks were turning shades of auburn and ocher that matched the sunset washing over Harbor Cove. "I love fall," Margaret said, once again shifting subject gears before her sisters read too much into her comments about Barrett. "It makes me feel like I'm a teenager again, with brand-new notebooks and pens in my backpack, cutting across campus for a class in economics or sociology."

"Are you sure our sister's not a sociopath?" Gabby said to Emma. "Because Margaret just said she loves economics and notebooks."

"I think it's code for, *I wish I were back in college, meeting hot guys at frat parties.*"

"What is wrong with the two of you? Not everything I do or say is about men or dating."

"Why not?" Emma said. "After all, you're going to be single and ready to mingle soon."

Margaret and Gabby both groaned at the rhymey joke. Margaret ticked off all the reasons Emma was wrong about that: "For one, I'm not single yet, and for another, I am far from ready to mingle. Third, I have work and—"

"If you mention work again, we're going to have to gag you." Gabby wagged a finger at her. "Tonight is girls' night, which means all we talk about is wine, men, and chocolate."

They had reached the door of Bella Vita, the cozy Italian restaurant in downtown Harbor Cove. Last year, Gabby had orchestrated a meeting between Frank Rossi, the owner, and a friend of Grandma's, Sandra, which had turned into a relationship, much to Grandma's delight. For the most part, the meddling the three girls had done in Grandma's life had turned out okay and had revived Grandma's enthusiasm for her advice column. So much so that she was now writing that book with Mike, which had given Grandma something to do other than worry about Harry.

The thought of Mike caused a little pang in Margaret's chest. Her mind flashed back to him sitting at the desk in the guest bedroom, head bent over the laptop, typing away with a fervor she hadn't seen in him in a long, long time. Margaret shook it off. Thinking of Mike was unproductive and foolish. Like Emma had said, soon Margaret would be single, and that meant no longer allowing her mind to revolve around the man who used to be her husband.

A man who would forever be in her life, she realized, once the baby was born. If it was so tough to simply think about him, how hard would it be to see Mike every other weekend, especially after he had moved on with someone else?

Frank welcomed the girls warmly and led them to a quiet booth at the back of the room. He insisted on bringing them a fresh loaf of garlic bread, as well as glasses of wine on the house. "Uh, none for me," Margaret said. "I'll just have some iced tea, if that's okay."

"Whatever any of you want. You can have a lifetime of garlic bread because you brought Sandra into my life and made me so happy." He handed out menus and exchanged a little small talk before heading into the kitchen.

"No wine?" Gabby said when Frank was gone. "Since when do you turn down a glass of Chardonnay? A free one at that."

Margaret buried her face in the oversize menu, studying a list of entrées she already knew by heart. "I'm just not in the mood for wine tonight. Besides, I might go back to—" She glanced up and saw her sisters' pointed looks. "I might have something I have to do after we eat. Something to do with numbers on the computer that sits in the place that brings in income for me."

Emma rolled her eyes. "Even when we tell her not to talk about the *w* word, she manages to bring it up."

"We'll just have to eat her garlic bread as punishment," Gabby said, just as a waitress laid a basket full of warm bread in front of them.

The girls snacked and talked, slipping into the rhythm of sisters. It was a pattern of love and squabbles, teasing and advice. Every time the three of them got together, they seemed to become little girls again, cuddled up in one of their beds with after-curfew cookies, waiting out a storm or giggling about the mysteries of boys.

"So," Emma said after the garlic bread was gone and they had placed their dinner orders, "we have something super serious to talk about."

For a second, Margaret was convinced that her sisters knew the real reason she'd gone to the emergency room and why she had been nauseous for weeks. "I—"

"Grandma," Gabby put in.

Grandma. Of course. "What about Grandma?"

"She's being released from the hospital tomorrow, but Em and I are worried that she'll try to do too much as soon as she gets home."

"She's talking about hiring someone to build a ramp for Harry's wheelchair, both at her house and at his," Emma said. "And you know Grandma. She's so impatient, she's liable to do it herself if she doesn't get it built in the next five minutes."

"So, the three guys offered to build the ramps," Gabby continued, "but that still leaves Grandma alone. Emma is finishing up those classrooms with Luke this week, and I'm heading to Connecticut for a redo of that fashion show I had to skip. They already rescheduled me once so I can't tell them no again."

Margaret glanced between both her sisters. "You two want me to stay with her."

"Could you?" Gabby asked. "If you can't, I'll cancel the show again."

That wouldn't be fair to Gabby, who had left her first fashion show to be with Grandma. Margaret knew how busy Emma and Luke had been renovating the building and getting the community center running. They also had a four-year-old to raise, which had to be exhausting at the end of the day.

Margaret had employees and a store that could run itself. She was the one who chose to be in the shop almost every minute it was open because working was a hell of a lot easier than dealing with her own life. She had flexibility where her sisters didn't. Which meant she didn't have an excuse to turn them down.

Besides, she had never had a moment when Grandma wasn't there to support her or just give her a hug. There was no way she could say no when Grandma was in need.

"Of course I will," Margaret said, before she remembered one very important fact she had overlooked…

Her soon-to-be ex-husband was at Grandma's house nearly every day, working on the book. Avoiding him—and everything that seeing him stirred up inside her—would be impossible.

❧❧❧

Mike stacked the freshly printed pages into a pile and then sat down in the armchair he'd dragged upstairs. He had a red pen and, hopefully, a critical eye for his own work. He'd been so immersed in trying to get the beginning of the book down that he'd barely had time for editing. It was time, though, to start looking at these pages and see if he had holes in the story, if he'd flubbed the transitions, or had shorted the reader on the emotional connection. With Eleanor downstairs recovering from her accident, he felt even more compelled to get this book done. And do it right.

Mike spent three days a week here at Eleanor's and the other four in his apartment, working on the accounting for his new clients. His part-time business had been going well with barely time to breathe—a good thing for a man who didn't want to think about the fact that he was living in an apartment alone instead of with his pregnant wife in the house they had bought together. They'd had a painful meeting with a realtor and then he'd seen the FOR SALE sign go up on the house. He hoped like hell it never sold. It would be too hard to drive by that Cape-style house and see someone else's family in the yard.

Mike could hear Harry's voice from time to time, followed by Eleanor's notes of concern, and then the sounds of Meg moving around the kitchen, fixing drinks or making sandwiches. Eleanor had come home from the hospital three days ago and, as predicted, immediately asked her sons-in-law to install two wheelchair ramps. That night, Luke, Jake, and Mike worked together, cutting the lumber and laying out the ramp. That team effort, coupled with Luke's renovation experience, had both ramps finished in a few hours. Mike loved his brothers-in-law and had loved the opportunity to work with his hands, but every time he turned around, he was reminded that this amazing family would no longer be his after the divorce.

The wheelchair ramps were for Harry, who had been released this morning. As soon as the transport van pulled up with a haggard-looking Harry, one leg in a cast, Eleanor had insisted on having him come over to her house so that she could take care of him, even though she was still banged up and in a fair amount of pain herself.

It had taken an intervention from all three girls, as well as Harry's son and grandson, to convince Eleanor she was in no shape to be a nursemaid, not while she was supposed to be healing herself. She'd compromised on a sort of shared custody arrangement where Harry came to her house during the day and went next door to his own house in the evenings, where Chad and Roger were staying to help him maneuver with the wheelchair and casted leg.

Shared custody. Just the idea of it saddened Mike. The baby that Meg was carrying wouldn't be a child they raised together. It would be a calendar entry, with the days shuffled between them like playing cards. When Meg got pregnant years ago, the two of them had dreamed of the adventures they would take as a family, the lazy summer afternoons on the beach, the milestones they'd celebrate. Together. None of that was going to happen with this baby.

This wasn't where he was supposed to be, wasn't the life he had planned when he married Meg. Wasn't, in any way, shape, or form, what he wanted.

He heard footsteps in the hall and then a tentative knock on the guest room door. "Come in."

Meg stepped inside, as if she'd been conjured up just by thinking about her, and he forgot to breathe for a second. She was so stunningly beautiful. Her dark hair only emphasized the blue of her eyes, the graceful curve of her jaw, and the delicate swoop of her nose. She was dressed in jeans and an untucked T-shirt, a total 180 from her normal business suits and dresses. The casual clothes gave her an air of comfort, as if Mike could wrap himself around her and fall asleep in her arms.

"Uh, my grandmother wants to know if you're staying for dinner. It's Wednesday."

Family dinner night. Something Mike hadn't attended in so long that he was sure he was off Eleanor's list of family members. "She's cooking?"

"Uh, no. She's been forbidden from cooking by my sisters and Harry. And you can imagine how that discussion went." Meg rolled her eyes.

"Probably about the same as when you tell me I have to stop eating dessert."

Meg laughed. "I do remember wrestling a Ho Ho out of your hands once. Too much sugar is a bad thing."

"You only say that because *you* ate that Ho Ho." When she grinned even wider, for a second, it was like old times; so, Mike kept talking because he couldn't bear to let go of the moment. "I think it was all an ongoing plot to steal my desserts. I'm not the one who somehow always got the last piece of cake."

"I would never. Well, almost never."

Another laugh from Meg. Mike felt like a comic who had

just hit his stride with the audience. He glanced down and saw pink sparkly polish on her toes. "You're wearing glitter?"

She followed his gaze and blushed. "My sisters talked me into dinner and then a pedicure the other night. They insisted on the sparkly color."

"It looks fun," Mike said. Like the Meg he had met, but he didn't add that. "I like it."

"It won't last." And he wondered if she was talking about the nail polish or the light and easy moment between them. "Anyway, I'm making beef Stroganoff."

His stomach rumbled at the mere mention of that dish. "I haven't had your beef Stroganoff in..." He thought for a second. When was the last time he and Meg sat down for a meal together at home? Many, many months. "A really long time. It's always been my favorite dinner." He wondered if she'd remembered that and chosen beef Stroganoff entirely for him.

"Turns out it's Grandma's, too."

There went that theory. He needed to stop looking for rainbows at night. There was no romance left between Meg and him, no overtures on her part to bring them back together. It was all some silly, sentimental part of him that was living in a Lifetime movie.

"Do you want to come down for dinner?"

"I don't want to make it awkward," Mike said. "I can eat at my place." Which would mean stopping at the Save-Lots to pick up yet another frozen dinner. Mike's cooking skills didn't extend much past grilling. The apartment didn't have a balcony, so a grill was out of the question, which meant the folks at Lean Cuisine and Healthy Choice were getting rich off his divorce.

"I know you love that dinner," Meg said, "so, if you want to stay, it's fine with me. We have to learn how to be civil with each other someday."

"When have we ever been uncivil?" As soon as the words were out of his mouth, he realized how his tone came across. "Strike that. I'm not trying to start an argument. Truly. So, in the spirit of not arguing, Meg, I would love to stay for dinner." Partly because of what she was serving but mostly because there was a part of Mike that needed to bask in the familial warmth around that dinner table one more time. Maybe for the last time—a thought he could hardly bear.

"I also wanted to talk to you about one other thing." She glanced behind her and then stepped all the way into the room, shutting the door as she did. "I had an ultrasound today."

He tried to mask his disappointment that she hadn't asked him to come with her to the appointment. He wasn't her husband anymore, and he couldn't expect her to include him in everything, even if it involved their baby. She was telling him about it, though, which had to be a good sign. "How did it go?"

"I have a picture. If you want to see it."

"I'd love to." The first pregnancy had only lasted ten and a half weeks. Meg had been scheduled for a twelve-week ultrasound, but she had miscarried before they'd ever seen their baby. Somehow, that had made the loss so much harder to bear and accept because they'd had nothing tangible, nothing to point to and say, *That was our baby.* All that remained of that first time was an empty room and a crib in a box. "It's the first time we've had an ultrasound picture."

"I know. It makes it so much more real when you see the baby." She reached into her back pocket and pulled out a four-by-six black-and-white image. "I, uh, had them print two, so you could have one to keep." She held it out and pointed at the little white blob in the middle. "There she is."

"She?"

"Or he. They don't know the sex yet, but I want to think it's a she." Meg's hand drifted to her abdomen as if she was thinking of their maybe-daughter right that moment. Pregnancy agreed with her, giving Meg's body more curves. "The doctor said everything looks normal. The baby is about three inches long right now; the doctor said she's the size of a plum. Isn't that wild? That I've got a plum-size human being growing inside me?"

"It is." He studied the grainy image. He could see tiny legs and arms, the side profile of the baby's face. Would he or she look like Mike? Have the blue eyes of Meg? The anticipation inside him was almost overwhelming. "How are you feeling?"

She rolled her eyes. "You ask me that every day."

"Because I worry about you every day." Crap. He hadn't meant to say that out loud. "I worry about the baby, I mean."

"Of course," she said, but he could tell she didn't believe him.

Damn it. He didn't want to make this awkward. Why couldn't he seem to stay, as she said, civil, instead of getting so damned personal?

"I . . . I have to go check on dinner." She stepped away from him, shutting down, shutting Mike out. Again. "We should be eating around six, if that works for you."

"Any time is a good time for your beef Stroganoff." That

joke coaxed a flicker of a smile from her but it wasn't enough, because she was like a wild kitten, skittish and ready to run at any second. "I'll, uh, see you at six. And Meg?"

She had already turned out of the doorway. "Yes?"

"Thank you for including me with your family. It means more than you know."

CHAPTER 17

Margaret pushed Harry up to the table carefully so he wouldn't bump his cast. Luke and Emma were running late, still working at the community center, but they had dropped off Scout earlier so she could spend time with the rest of the family. Scout was using her toy doctor kit to pretend to take Harry and Grandma's blood pressure and listen to their hearts. Her little face got so serious when she did it that Margaret nearly burst out laughing.

If her baby was a girl, would she do the same thing? Would she be quiet and shy or exuberant and chatty like Scout? As nervous as Margaret was about how on earth she was going to juggle it all, a bubble of anticipation was slowly building inside her. Each day that passed, each week that stacked up, gave her hope that in a few months, she would be holding a newborn.

The table was relatively empty for family dinner night— Grandma on the corner beside Harry, Scout and Mike on the opposite side. Gabby and Jake had decided to stay an extra couple days in Connecticut so that Jake could meet with a magazine that was interested in hiring him for some freelance photography work.

Margaret went back and forth between the kitchen and dining room, bringing in silverware and plates and a Dutch oven full of beef Stroganoff. Every time Grandma offered to help, Margaret raised a brow and said she had it covered. She could see Grandma feeling antsy, out of her element with someone else doing all the chores.

"Uncle Mike! I gots to listen to your heart, too." Scout unwound the stethoscope from her neck and placed it on the right side of Mike's chest. She jabbed the ends into her ears and pretended to listen.

"I think my heart's over here, kiddo." He slid the head of the stethoscope across his T-shirt and onto the left side of his chest. "See? Thump-thump, thump-thump."

Scout's eyes widened and then she pulled away. "You're making that sound, Uncle Mike."

"That's my heart. It's so full of love that it beats extra loud." He tapped her on the nose, and Scout giggled.

"You're silly," she said. "Now I need to give you a shot."

"Uh-oh. What kind of shot?"

Scout dug in the black plastic bag and found a clear toy syringe. "A cooties shot!"

"Cooties?" Mike jumped back and squealed. "No one wants cooties! Better get me the shot right now!" He thrust out his arm, and Scout stabbed him with the end of the syringe. "Phew. Crisis narrowly averted."

That sent Scout into another round of giggles. Margaret watched them from the kitchen doorway, a little bit of envy rising inside her at how easily Mike engaged with the little girl.

He had dropped right into Scout's imaginary doctor's office with all the gusto of an Oscar nominee. Margaret always felt so stiff and awkward around kids. She couldn't imagine faking an aversion to cooties or having an oversize heart.

He'd make a good father, that was obvious. She'd known that almost from the beginning. Whenever Mike had interacted with children, no matter how old they were or how they were related to him, he became a different person. The goofy, fun, adventurous guy she'd met came to life, almost as if being with a child gave him permission to be his old self.

How she envied that and, at the same time, missed it. She'd never been goofy or particularly adventurous, but with him, she had the freedom to be—as he said a hundred times—Meg, not Margaret.

"Margaret, come sit down and eat with us," Grandma said. "The food's getting cold."

She couldn't procrastinate any longer. When she'd asked Mike if he wanted to stay for dinner, she'd fully expected him to say no. But when he did, she'd found herself convincing him to stay. Maybe it was because she'd known in the back of her mind that it was Mike's favorite dinner.

There was no ulterior motive. She was simply being nice. That was all.

She took a seat across from him, watching him out of the corner of her eye as she placed a napkin in her lap. Scout was snuggled up against him while she ate. Mike ate with his opposite hand and let Scout continue monopolizing his right side, undisturbed by the child's interruption to his meal.

"This is amazing, Margaret," he said. "Even better than I remember."

Her eyes locked with his, and it seemed like dozens of memories unfurled in that space. The first time she'd made him this dinner. The time they had a picnic at the beach. The night they stood outside to watch a meteor shower together.

"Uh...I think I forgot the rolls." Margaret shoved back from the table and hurried into the kitchen. She plucked the still-warm rolls from the sheet pan and dropped them into a basket, waiting until conversation around the table had shifted to Grandma's plans for her spring garden—something neutral, something that didn't make Margaret weirdly melancholy—and then she returned to the table.

Margaret remained quiet the rest of dinner, allowing the conversation to circle around a dozen different topics, from plants to parties. She concentrated on eating, keeping her gaze on everything except Mike. Inviting him had been a bad idea, especially after that moment up in the bedroom.

She'd been so excited to show him the ultrasound, to share the incredible picture with the one person she knew would be as thrilled as she was. Then something had shifted between them, and all the emotional distance she had so carefully cultivated in the few months since Mike moved out seemed to dissolve.

The only way to rebuild that wall was to stay away from him. No more moments alone. No more family dinners. She had six months to build some armor around her heart, six months during which, except for the mediation, she had no reason really to talk to Mike. Six months would be enough time.

Wouldn't it?

Dinner went by quickly, and every last bite of the Stroganoff was eaten and proclaimed amazing by everyone at the table, even Scout. Grandma started to get to her feet and gather up her plate and Harry's.

"Sit down, Eleanor," Mike said as he took the plates from her hands before she could protest. "Margaret and I will do the dishes. That way you two can talk while Scout gives out more cootie vaccinations."

Scout shot out of the chair, the plastic syringe already in her hand. "Grandma! I forgot to give you your cootie shot, too!"

Grandma and Harry played along, clearly delighted to have a preschooler around the house. Margaret realized she had no excuse to get out of doing the dishes with Mike, which meant her plan for zero contact had already failed.

"Hope it's okay I volunteered us," Mike said as he reached across the table and stacked her empty plate on top of the others. "If you want, I can do the dishes alone."

"That is far too much to ask," Grandma cut in. "You have been working all day on that book, Mike, and I am sure you are tired. Margaret has put all this work into a wonderful dinner, so she shouldn't be stuck with all the dishes, either. I think the two of you doing them together is a wonderful idea."

Grandma's enthusiasm made it impossible for Margaret to say no. She forced an agreeable smile on her face, picked up the empty Dutch oven, and followed Mike into the kitchen. He offered to finish clearing the table, so she started the water and squirted some dish soap into the sink.

Too quickly, Mike was done with the table. He grabbed a clean dish towel from the drawer and stood a few feet away from Margaret, waiting for the next dish. "Just like old times, right?" he said. "Back when we had our first apartment with that teeny, tiny kitchen."

"And no dishwasher. Or washing machine. We had to go down three flights and across the street to the laundromat."

He chuckled. "I forgot about that part. It seemed so much simpler then, didn't it?"

"Uh, no. It seemed like a lot of work. That's how I remember it." She finished a plate and put it in the dish rack for Mike to dry.

It occurred to Margaret that merely a few months ago, she'd been in this exact same position with her sister Emma. Her washing, Emma drying, while the secret truth about her marriage slowly leaked out and became a conversation over wine an hour later. That night seemed like it was years ago in one way, and a blip from yesterday in another. How quickly everything had changed.

Before Mike could take them down another memory lane, she changed the subject. "Did you get the appointment for the rescheduled mediation?"

"Yes, a couple hours ago." He took the plate she washed and circled it with the towel. "It doesn't seem real."

"It will be soon. Real and final." She set every dish she washed in the rack instead of handing them to him, inserting a millisecond of distance between them. "Assuming we can work out all the details at the mediation—"

"We will. We don't have anything to fight over." He took the next plate and dried it before turning away to slide it into the cabinet.

"At least it's gone smoothly, at least so far," she said, because she didn't know what else to say. *Great? Congrats? Finally?* Or simply, *This is sad but I don't see another way.*

Meeting with the realtor last week and putting the house up for sale had been the hardest part. She remembered buying the house with Mike, how scared they were about making the mortgage payments, the dozens of conversations they'd had about someday raising a family there. Then everything changed, and the house that had seemed so filled with promise became an empty reminder of what never was. Maybe it was better to sell the house. A clean break, a new start. Even if it didn't feel that way quite yet.

She glanced over at him and thought how weird it was to be doing dishes with the man she was going to divorce in less than a month. How many women were in the same zip code, never mind the same kitchen, as their soon-to-be ex? Margaret told herself it was all evidence of how civil and adult they could be. She and Mike were above the petty arguments, the ridiculous fights over lamps and duvets.

"I appreciate how easygoing you have been," she said.

"Ditto."

There was nothing to say to that, so Margaret washed the next plate and the one after that. They worked in silence as the bowls stacked up, then the silverware, the glasses, and finally, the pots and pans. It was awkward and comfortable at the same time, maybe because she and Mike had spent a lot of the last few years existing in the same space but not interacting.

She rinsed the last pot and pulled the drain plug. Mike dried it and then hung the damp dish towel on the oven door handle. Margaret tensed, fully expecting Mike to walk away without a word. Bracing herself for it while also feeling relieved that she wouldn't have to make small talk with this man who would soon be someone she used to know.

※⋚ ⋚※

Mike had never been a quitter. Even when he was dead-last in the high school cross-country meets, he kept plugging along toward the finish line. He'd learned pretty quickly that he wasn't much of a runner, but he was what his coach had called "ridiculously persistent." Maybe that was a good thing when he was trying to run six miles. Or maybe not, because, after all, he had to run six miles, and that was never fun.

He'd seen something earlier tonight when Meg had come to him with the ultrasound picture. A glimmer—no, more of a sliver—of the old Meg and the relationship they used to have. He suspected she wasn't as cool and calm about this divorce as she kept saying she was, because every time he brought it up, she couldn't look him in the eye.

Maybe they had a lot more than six miles between them, and maybe there was too much ground already covered to ever make this right. But when the email had come into his inbox for the rescheduled mediation hearing, Mike had realized he had one more shot—because it wasn't, as they say in the movies, quite over yet. And he'd be damned if he missed taking this last opportunity.

Because even though he had questions about the money, he still loved his wife. He missed what they used to have and knew that if there was even a minuscule chance of getting that back, ridiculously persistent Mike was willing to try.

The last of the soapy water went down the drain with a

gurgle. He could hear Scout and Eleanor laughing in the dining room. Emma and Luke weren't back yet, and Harry wasn't going anywhere in that wheelchair. That meant Mike had a few more minutes alone with his wife. And his baby.

Meg glanced over at him and found his dark eyes watching her. "What?"

Mike took a tentative step closer to her, his hand extended between them. The ultrasound image had made the baby so much more real and exciting. He was going to be a father and he could barely wait for that day. "Can I...?"

"Uh...okay. But you won't feel anything. Not until I'm further along." She shifted toward him, an invitation to share the miracle between them.

He put a hand on her belly, right above the highest point of her where she would soon have a baby bump. Somewhere in there, their son or daughter was growing, becoming a human. A plum, like she'd said, turning into a person. A person they had created together, a life that had formed because of the love Meg and Mike had once had and had recaptured for that night in the hotel. Maybe this was all a sign that it wasn't as over as they both thought. "We should go out and...I don't know, celebrate."

Meg tucked that stubborn lock of hair behind her ear, a clear sign his question had caught her off guard. "Go out? Wait...are you asking me on a date?"

"To be honest, I don't know." He was close enough to see shadows under her eyes that her makeup hadn't quite covered up, which meant Meg still wasn't sleeping well. Was she tossing and turning in that big bed alone, just as he was every night in the apartment? "Roxy's sent out an email this morning. Friday night, Chef Tyler has a special fall prix fixe dinner featuring his braised short ribs. A one-night-only special."

He waited for her to call him crazy and storm out of the kitchen. They had a date with the mediator and a judge after all. There was no real reason to do anything other than sign the papers.

She bit her lip and considered him. "We haven't eaten there in years."

Okay, so she hadn't said no, not yet. That was a good sign, right? Depended, he supposed, on why he was asking her to dinner. Was it a date? Or one more attempt to hold on to something he knew he was losing? "Five years, to be exact."

The math added up in her head, and her eyes filled with bittersweet tears. "Because we went there the last time."

The last time. Right after Meg's visit with her obstetrician where they'd heard the heartbeat of their first baby for the first—and only—time. They'd decided to keep the pregnancy a secret a little longer, something special that was just between the two of them. They'd sat in their favorite booth at Roxy's, toasting an exciting future they'd dreamed about for years, Mike with champagne, Meg with soda water and lime. "We were so excited. Ecstatic, really. We talked about names and what color you wanted to paint the nursery."

Neither one of them needed to add *and then we lost the baby* because that heartbreaking truth had never left the space between them. "Why would we go back there and dredge up that memory, Mike?"

"Because I don't want that memory to be a horrible one anymore. Yes, we lost that baby, and God, that was a horrible moment. It was, hands down, the worst day of my life, and for so long, I've let it be this dark day that I can barely think about."

"I can't, Mike. I just can't."

"You're terrified it will happen again. I can see it written all over your face." He cupped her jaw out of instinct, out of some emotion he couldn't name. "What happened wasn't your fault, Meg."

"We don't know that. My body—"

"You are the most protective person I know. You would never do anything to intentionally hurt anyone you care about. Sometimes, these things just happen."

"But why did it have to happen to us?"

The heartbreak in her voice nearly killed him. He was right back there with her all over again, standing in a hospital room watching the doctor slowly shake his head and realizing the baby was gone.

"I don't know why, honey. I don't know." Before he could think better of it, he was pulling her against his chest, the baby cradled between them. For a moment, she leaned into him, into all of it. He held her for a long time, until her tears stopped falling.

She stepped back and wiped away the tears on her cheeks. "I'm sorry. I didn't mean to get so emotional."

"Meg, it still makes me emotional. I know it was five years ago, but God, it hurts so much when I think about what happened. But here's the thing. I don't want to let that memory haunt me anymore. There was something your grandmother said in one of her advice columns about how important mindset can be in rewriting history." He'd gleaned thousands of useful tidbits from Eleanor's columns. He had no doubt that the compilation book would be helpful to everyone who read it, because it had been helpful to this clueless man who needed advice more than he realized. Eleanor had a way of giving advice that was so clear that you felt like slapping your forehead and saying, *Of course that's what I should do.*

"What does my mindset have to do with that..." She closed her eyes and shook her head. "That awful night?"

"You and I have been stuck in this deep, dark hole of grief, and that's keeping both of us from being truly excited about this baby."

"Because I'm terrified, Mike. I have a thousand what-ifs in my head. That's why I still haven't told my sisters or Suzie. What if I do and then..." She didn't voice the words.

"I know. Me too." He could see the fear in her face, the same fear that knotted in his gut almost every day. He hadn't told Larry about the baby either, or anyone else. It was almost as if keeping it secret was a way of protecting against the worst happening, as irrational as that was. "Neither one of us can predict if that will happen again, Meg. Do you really want to spend nine months worrying about something that might or might not happen? Or do you want to celebrate this amazing thing that happened to us?" He put a hand on her belly and swore he could feel the warmth of another life beneath his palm. "For a little while, we had a precious, beautiful baby in our lives, and then, for whatever reason, we didn't anymore. Now, we have a second chance, Meg, another precious, beautiful baby. I don't want to dwell on what we lost for another second. I want to focus on what we have."

For now, they had each other, and they had the baby on

the way. Two weeks from now, that would change, but he wasn't going to think about what was coming down the road. "We have spent five years not talking about it, Meg, not dealing with it. We've avoided that restaurant and avoided the conversation."

"We're living in separate houses. There's no reason to pick out a color for the nursery or talk about what kind of crib we want to get." She shook her head. "I'm sorry, but it's too late to have that conversation now."

CHAPTER 18

Harry was a terrible patient. Absolutely the worst. He drove Eleanor nuts with his insistence that he didn't need help when he so clearly did. He was a stubborn man, but she was a far more stubborn woman.

She yanked at the throw pillow they'd been tussling over and tried to wedge it beneath his cast. "Will you just let me put this pillow under—"

"Ella Bella, if you don't sit down, I will have to call your granddaughters."

That made her stop. Her granddaughters had made it their mission to keep Eleanor from moving at all. Margaret did everything around the house, cooked all the meals, and did all the shopping. Emma lectured from the sidelines and helped out whenever she was free. "You would do no such thing."

"I can." He took his cell phone out of his shirt pocket and held it up. "And I will. You are supposed to rest, and I have seen you do the exact opposite ever since Margaret went to the grocery store."

Eleanor had been home from the hospital for six days

now, and still her family hovered over her like she was the one with the broken leg. It didn't help that Harry took every opportunity to remind people that the doctor had prescribed rest for Eleanor's not-so-bad injuries.

Yes, she had a couple broken ribs, and yes, she had a lot of very ugly bruises and a ridiculously large hematoma on her right hip. And yes, her chest was still sore from the force of the airbag, but that didn't mean that she couldn't take care of Harry and herself. She wasn't an invalid, for Pete's sake. "I am fine."

Harry arched a brow. "Prove it. Take a really deep breath. A four-count."

She inhaled, trying to do it slowly, but when she expanded her lungs, a sharp pain ran through her rib cage. She let her breath out again in a whoosh. "I'm fine. Sort of," she added in a mumble.

"Case closed, your honor. Now go sit down. I am perfectly capable of putting a pillow under my own leg." He snatched the pillow out of her hand with a grin and then lifted his cast with the other hand before centering his leg on the cushion. "By the way, you're even more beautiful when you are frustrated with me."

"You are the most infuriating man in the world, Harry Erlich." Eleanor took a seat in the recliner beside Harry's. She'd had Mike and Luke carry the extra recliner downstairs from the bedroom she'd converted to a sewing room years ago and set it up beside the one that had sat in her living room for ages. Years ago, this recliner had been Russell's favorite chair. After he died, she'd had it moved upstairs because she couldn't bear looking at it every day and seeing it empty. Whenever the grief got to be too much, she'd go up to that bedroom and sit in the chair and talk to him. When the girls moved in, the recliner had served as a bedtime story spot, giving it a new life and purpose.

And now the chair had become something else. A way to sit beside the man who had captured her heart in a way she thought no one ever would again. It seemed apropos, and almost like Russell was smiling down on her, for her and Harry's clasped hands to sit on the armrest. A new beginning, in a way, something she had no doubt her late husband would have wanted her to have a long, long time ago.

"Margaret isn't back yet, and it's going on noon," Eleanor said. "Maybe I should make us some—"

Harry gripped her hand tighter as she tried to stand up. "No one is going to die of starvation in the next hour. So, that means you can keep me company while we get caught up on *Ted Lasso.*"

"I do like that show," Eleanor said. "That Ted is just a sweetie."

"Almost as sweet as you." Harry leaned over and kissed her cheek. "Though not even a tenth as pretty as you."

Eleanor felt her cheeks heat. It had been this way for a year now, ever since Harry moved in next door and had—for whatever reason that she couldn't fathom—decided that she was the woman for him. He had courted her and complimented her, making her face turn ten shades of red at least once a day. "Are you sure that accident didn't damage your eyesight?"

He chuckled. "Actually, I think it damaged yours because you are still sitting here and trying to take care of this old fool."

Harry was anything but an old fool. He was tall and trim with what her mother would have called "a distinguished air" about him. He had wonderful blue eyes and a nearly full head of gray hair that was edging more toward white every day. He had stopped shaving because his broken leg made it too difficult to get close enough to the mirror, and the scruff of beard on his face gave him a rugged look that Eleanor found she liked. Very much.

"You may be old, but you are not a fool," she said. "Because you're dating me."

He chuckled. "Very true, my dear." He held up the remote, and when she nodded, he flicked on the television and surfed over to the Apple TV+ streaming app. He clicked the first episode of season three of the comedy with Jason Sudeikis. The familiar opening for *Ted Lasso* began to play, but Eleanor wasn't watching it.

She was looking at the man beside her, this man who had changed her life and given her heart a second chance at love. A wave of gratitude washed over her and she gave his hand a squeeze.

He glanced back at her and, in an instant, read everything in her features. He paused the show and took her hand in both of his. "I feel exactly the same way about you."

"I didn't say anything about feeling anything for you," she joked, but really, it was a defense mechanism, a way to avoid speaking that *l*-word to another man. As much as she knew that Russell would want her to be happy again, it still felt wrong to say she loved someone else.

"You don't have to say the words for me to know how you feel." Harry kissed her hand. "Now, let's get back to watching the show before one of us says something mushy."

"Too late," she mumbled, but secretly, she was glad that Harry seemed to intuit how difficult this was for her. His wife had died a few years ago, and while he had struggled early on to open up his emotions, he had seemed to have an easier time with the whole idea of loving again. Maybe Eleanor had become too set in her ways. After all, Russell had been gone for more than two decades, and she'd lived all that time as if he were still going to walk in the door and sit down at the dining room table.

Being stuck in the mud was how people missed the opportunities right within their grasp, she thought. Her eldest granddaughter, for instance, was stubbornly sticking with the divorce, even though it was plain as the nose on Eleanor's face that the two of them still loved each other. Maybe it was time to take her meddling plan to another level.

"Harry? I think we need to work harder to bring Meg and Mike back together. Thus far, she has not taken any of my numerous hints and nudges seriously."

He chuckled. "Maybe because she knows you're a hopeless romantic and matchmaker."

"I am neither of those things." She reconsidered. "Well, maybe a little. Either way, when Margaret comes in, I want to push her in Mike's direction a little more by . . . well, fibbing just a bit."

"A fib? You? Never." He feigned outrage.

"You are incorrigible."

Harry shifted in his seat to face her, his face growing more serious. "You really want to try to stop their divorce? Eleanor, it's only a couple weeks away."

"Which is plenty of time, if we work quickly. There's too much at stake to let their marriage fall apart."

His gaze narrowed. "What aren't you telling me?"

She shrugged, but the smile she could barely hold back filled her face. She was so excited about the baby to come that she wanted to shout it from the rooftops. Margaret was far more cautious, refusing to tell anyone else until she got through the first trimester. "The secret isn't mine to tell, but let's just say that there's more than Margaret and Mike who will be affected by whatever happens."

It took him a minute, but then realization lit in his eyes. He leaned closer and lowered his voice, even though it was just the two of them in the house right then. "Is Margaret pregnant?"

Eleanor had promised her granddaughter that she wouldn't tell anyone, so instead she made a zipping gesture across her lips. At the same time, she heard the back door open. "That's Margaret. Play along no matter what I say, okay?"

"Your wish is my command, my dear." He winked.

There was the sound of rustling paper bags in the kitchen. "Margaret, is that you?" Eleanor called.

"Sorry!" Margaret called back. "The market was packed. I picked up some Chick-fil-A for lunch. I'll bring it right out."

"No rush, dear. But when you come...ooh...could you bring one of my pain pills?"

Margaret darted into the living room. "What's wrong? Are you okay?"

"Just a little sore." Eleanor shifted her weight and made a face that she didn't really have to fake. This car accident had left her more banged up than she'd expected. "I wanted to help Mike with the book today but I'm afraid I'm simply not up to it."

"The book can wait, Grandma. Let me go get your lunch so you can take your pill." Margaret spun back into the kitchen and a minute later returned with two plates, some silverware, and a prescription bottle. "Do you need a refill on your water?"

Eleanor touched Margaret's wrist. Even with the pregnancy, Margaret was still too thin, and Eleanor worried about her and the baby. "You do too much for me."

"It's never enough for what you did for us girls," Margaret replied, her voice soft and tender. Then she shifted back into her efficient, organized self, a role she had slipped into the day her mother died. She dished up the salads she'd brought home onto the stoneware plates, set them on the TV trays, and positioned the lunches before Harry and then Eleanor. "Here's some silverware and napkins. Do you have enough dressing? If not, I can go get some out of the fridge."

"We're fine," Harry said. "Thank you, Margaret, for lunch. This is one of my favorite salads ever."

"Great." Margaret smiled. "Let me know if you need anything else."

She had taken two steps when Eleanor said, "Actually..." as if the thought had just occurred to her and wasn't a plan in her head for the last hour. "There is one thing."

Margaret paused and turned back. "Sure. What is it?"

Eleanor moved a couple inches and feigned great pain with a little moan. "Oh goodness, this accident did leave me in quite a state. I think it'll be a while before I'm up and at 'em again."

Worry flashed across Margaret's face. "Oh, Grandma, just rest. Don't worry about anything."

"Well, I am worried about the Dear Amelia book. I should go help Mike. He needs my input to finish it."

"My dear, you know you can't be doing that," Harry said. He laid a hand on her arm, playing along like a pro. Harry should have been a movie star. "It's far too taxing."

"Harry, this book needs to be done," she said in the sternest voice she could manage. "That publisher is anxious to see it."

"You have a publisher?" Margaret asked.

Eleanor made a grimacing nod, like she was excited and in pain. The excited part was true. When she'd received the call from the editor on Friday, she'd been shocked and ecstatic. "Leroy, the editor of the *Harbor Cove Gazette*, is friends with a publisher at a small press in Boston. They called me on Friday and said they would love to put out the Dear Amelia book for Valentine's Day, but that would mean finishing it up before the end of the month, and I don't think I'm up to it." Eleanor let out a long, heavy sigh. "My book may never get out there."

Margaret waved that off, clearly not sensing the urgency Eleanor tried to put in her voice. "I'm sure they can wait. You'll ask for an extension, and the book will come out next year."

"You know the reading public, Margaret," Harry added. "Today they're interested in advice columns, tomorrow it's some tok-bok thing."

Margaret laughed. "I think you mean TikTok."

"See? You know what it is. How long before the rest of the world decides to go on that instead of reading advice that they could surely use?" Eleanor added. She gave Harry's hand a grateful squeeze.

"Doesn't Mike have the book under control?"

"Yeah, but see, I was helping him with it by filling in my life story to link the letters together. I think it would be lovely if we included some parts about your mother and you three girls." Eleanor squeezed Margaret's hand. "It would be such a wonderful way to remember Penny, don't you think?"

Okay, so that probably wasn't fair, Eleanor acknowledged to herself, pulling on Margaret's heartstrings by mentioning her mother. But Margaret and Mike's divorce date was only a couple weeks away, and if something drastic didn't happen, nothing would change.

"I don't know. I'm really busy with the store and helping you."

"It would be such a gift, not just to me but to all those people who need a little Dear Amelia advice in their lives. I'd hate for them to go one more year without a little guidance. Look at how many people have said that their lives changed because they read something in my column that helped them."

Margaret worried her bottom lip. "Maybe Emma and Gabby—"

"Oh no, not them. You know both of them are swamped right now. Gabby has lots of orders after that fashion show, and Emma's opening the learning center on Monday. I don't want to add another thing to her plate. Besides, the doctor told you to rest, and there's nothing more restful than sitting in a chair and just talking about your family."

Margaret chuckled. "I see what you're doing here."

Eleanor shifted again and winced even more this time. "Oh goodness, can you check and make sure you gave me the full dose of that pain stuff? This hurts so much."

Margaret's mistrust flipped to concern. "Maybe we should get you back to the doctor."

"Oh, I don't think it's that serious," Harry said. "Just Eleanor overdoing it again."

"Harry, you know me too well."

Margaret didn't say anything for a long moment. Eleanor worried she had laid it on too thick or maybe had been too obvious. She tried not to fidget in her seat or let any of those worries show on her face.

"I know how much this book means to you, my dear." Harry's face positively radiated sympathy and concern. "But Margaret is right. You need to rest. Maybe the publisher can release it in a couple years."

Eleanor hung her head. "You're right, Harry. My health should come first. If only there was someone in the family who knew me and my story really well and could help, just a little."

"I suppose I could help," Margaret put up a hand, "a little. Do you want me to write some notes for Mike?"

"I don't think that's the same as doing it face-to-face. Mike can ask questions then and really get what he needs." Grandma took Margaret's hand in hers. "I would be so grateful if you would do it, my dear Margaret. You're the only one I trust with such an important... mission."

When Margaret promised to help, Eleanor knew she'd successfully executed another meddling plan. Now to sit back and watch it bring Margaret and Mike together again. Hopefully before it was too late.

CHAPTER 19

By the time Margaret finished climbing the stairs to the second story, she realized she had been had. Grandma had brought Gabby and Jake together by convincing them to double date with a friend of hers. She'd done some smooth talking with Luke to convince him not to annul his elopement with Emma. And now she had just hoodwinked her oldest granddaughter into working with her soon-to-be ex-husband. Yes, Grandma was still busy recovering from her injuries, but the bit about being too worn out to talk to Mike about her past was pure baloney.

Margaret was about to go downstairs and tell her grandmother that she wasn't going to get sucked into another of her happily-ever-after schemes when the door to the guest bedroom opened and Mike emerged.

His dark hair was mussed, causing a little poof at the cowlick on his crown. His shirt was wrinkled and untucked, the sleeves rolled up. He looked comfortable and messy and so much like the young man she had met years ago that, for a second, her breath was caught in her throat. "Meg." He blinked. "What are you doing here?"

Might as well tell him the truth rather than let him get sucked into the scheme, too. "My grandmother and Harry conspired to get me to help you with the book."

"Conspired?" He chuckled. "You're the least conspirable person I know."

"I don't think that's a word, Mr. Writer."

He grinned. "Take it up with Webster's. How are you supposed to help me with the book?"

Leave it to Mike to alleviate some of the tension between them with a little joke. He made it easy to talk to him, even in the midst of everything that was going on. "Grandma says there's a possible publishing deal, if you can get the book done before the holidays?"

"I got off the phone with the editor a few minutes ago." Mike ran a hand through his hair, making it even messier. "It means pedal to the metal for me all this month, because it took me three months to get halfway through the story."

So, Grandma had been telling the truth about the publisher. A rushed schedule like that would surely require hours of Grandma sitting and talking with Mike, something that she really shouldn't be doing, not while she was still recuperating and worrying about Harry. "She wants me to do the interviews with you so that she can concentrate on getting better."

"You? I mean, that could work, to a certain extent, and take some of the pressure off of Eleanor..." His face took on a pained look. "But why you, exactly?"

"I was thinking the same thing." She glanced down the staircase to make sure there were no grandparent ears listening. Then she moved closer to Mike and lowered her voice.

"Hence my conspiracy theory. I think she's trying to get us to stay together by forcing us to work together."

Mike grinned. "I'm not surprised. If there is one thing I've learned about Eleanor in the course of writing this book, it's that she will do almost anything to help people find happiness. Her whole life has been about helping others."

"That's true."

"That said, if you really want to help, I'd love to get your opinion on some sections. Maybe you know the background of some of the stories she's told me, too." He thumbed toward the bedroom. "If you have a minute, I'd like to share something with you."

"But you were just leaving. I shouldn't keep you."

"You aren't, Meg."

"Uh, okay." Margaret followed him into the bedroom. Even though they left the door open, it seemed like they were home together in their own bedroom again. The two of them alone and the air between them a little bit charged, a little bit tense. Why had Margaret agreed to do this, knowing full well what Grandma was hoping would happen?

"Here, let me pull up something on the computer." He picked up the small laptop and sat down on the bed. Margaret debated and then sat down next to him. She could have sat in the desk chair, but it was pushed against the desk. Moving into the center of the room would be an obvious attempt at distance. Yeah, that's exactly why she chose to sit beside Mike.

Mike wasn't wearing any cologne, but she could smell soap and a different brand of laundry detergent. Was someone else doing his laundry? Someone who preferred Gain over Tide?

And why did she care?

"Meg, did you hear me?"

"Oh, sorry. No. What did you say?" Damn it. How on earth could this man—the man she was leaving—still distract her?

"Your grandmother told me a story about a woman she met at the grocery store named Lissa, a cashier who was always so chatty and friendly. When your grandmother was feeling overwhelmed with you three girls, Lissa became a sounding board of sorts because she was a single mom of two herself. They became friends and would grab a glass of wine every once in a while to commiserate about raising kids."

"I think I remember her coming to our house on the weekends for barbecues or birthday parties or whatever. She had a boy and a girl, a little older than us." Margaret's memory was fuzzy, but she could see a short woman with red hair and two children whose hair was as red as their mom's. The kids were shy at first, but by the second or third time they came over, Margaret remembered the daughter playing Barbies with Emma and the son watching movies with Gabby. "But it was only for a year or two. Not that long."

Mike nodded. "Lissa often told your grandmother that all she wanted was someone who would love her kids as much as he loved her. She was divorced, and her first marriage had ended very badly, so she was gun-shy about dating again. Then there was this." Mike turned the laptop in Margaret's direction and pointed at a Dear Amelia letter that had been centered on the page.

Dear Amelia,

I'm a busy single mom who doesn't have time to date. I don't go to bars or hang out in the gym because I'm almost always with my kids. After the kids go to bed, though, I realize how much I wish I had someone to spend my life with. A man who was funny and smart and who loved my kids like I do. Where can a mom meet a guy like that?

—Single but Hopeful Mom

"Grandma got so many letters like that," Margaret said. "I swear, 90 percent of the columns were about love."

"Close—82 percent." He shrugged, and a flush of pink showed in his cheeks. "You can take the accountant out of the office…"

Margaret laughed so hard that she put a hand on her chest to catch her breath again. "I forgot how funny you are."

"I'm not funny. You just laugh at everything I say."

"Ha. You've met me. My sisters would tell you I don't laugh at anything." Her gaze connected with his, and a tether of connection knit itself into that moment. Margaret jerked her attention back to the laptop. "So, was this letter written by Lissa?"

"As far as we know. Eleanor said that Lissa confessed to writing in to an advice column for help. She had no idea that Eleanor was Dear Amelia."

"None of us knew, not until last year. Grandma was very good at keeping that secret."

"Some people are experts in that area," Mike said under his breath.

Margaret's attention perked up. What had he meant by that? Surely Mike didn't know…

No. There was no way. He would have said something. "So, uh, what did Dear Amelia say in return?"

"In the column, your grandmother encouraged Lissa to be open to new experiences and hobbies. She told her that focusing some of her energy on herself, instead of just her kids, would open new doors that might lead to new relationships."

"That's pretty good advice."

"At the same time, Eleanor the friend invited Lissa to a Scrabble group that had started at the library. Lissa met a guy there, fell in love, got married, and moved to Cincinnati with him when he got a job offer he couldn't refuse."

"I can see where my sisters learned their matchmaking skills." Margaret laughed. "That is so typical of Grandma. Trying to nudge things along because she thinks she always knows what's best." Like she was probably doing right now.

"Maybe she does. She sent you up here for a reason. Maybe she sees something we don't."

"Or maybe she refuses to see the writing on the wall." Margaret got to her feet and crossed her arms over her chest. At least her body language spelled distance, even if some part of her yearned for closeness. "We're only a couple weeks away from the divorce being final."

"I know. I'm sure your grandmother knows that, too. But…" Mike got to his feet and crossed to stand in front of Margaret. She caught the scent of the man she had slept beside for hundreds of nights, the man she knew so well she could practically predict his next snore. "Maybe we should go along with her scheming."

For a second, her mind was muddled. Because she missed sleeping beside him, that was all. And maybe she was feeling a little lonely and nostalgic after hearing Lissa's letter. "You mean work on the book together?"

"I mean go to dinner at Roxy's tonight. Eleanor will be thrilled, thinking her plan worked out, and then we can tell her that it's over-over, and maybe she'll give up."

Margaret laughed. "Have you met my grandmother? She doesn't give up easily."

"Neither do I, Meg." There was something in his eyes, something that echoed the thoughts she had just been having. She yearned to lean into that, to lean into him.

"Give me one good reason why we should go to Roxy's tonight," she said.

He reached over and touched her. "Because this," his hand skated across her belly and the little plum-human there, "this is the last thing that is only ours, no one else's. And before everything between us is over, I want one night to enjoy this baby with you."

CHAPTER 20

Roxy's was tucked between a coffee shop and a pizzeria at the end of Main Street. The restaurant was barely wide enough for a set of booths against one wall and a long oak bar against the other. The owner had hung mirrors to give it the appearance of being bigger, but part of what Mike loved most about Roxy's was its size. Only a couple dozen people could fit inside at one time, which made the restaurant, with its walnut floors and dark brown booths, feel as cozy as his own living room.

Mike had picked Meg up from the house—he still couldn't call it her house, even in his mind—a little before six. She'd insisted that he not come to the door. "This isn't a date," she'd said. "Let's not treat it like one."

But she'd dressed up, wearing the cranberry dress he loved on her. The dark maroon fabric was the perfect complement to her fair skin and her brown hair and made her eyes seem even bluer. She'd opted for low heels and a sparkly necklace that he'd bought for her birthday several years ago. He could almost convince himself that it was back to normal between them until he glanced at her left hand and saw her bare ring finger.

She closed the door and settled her seat belt across her chest. "I could have met you there."

"You could have," he said. *But you didn't.* When he texted her about it after they'd talked at Eleanor's house, she'd agreed to ride with him, something he'd been sure she would argue against.

Meg turned to him in the dim light. The sun had already set, and the streetlights were coming to life, one after another. "Why are you still trying, Mike?"

It was a complicated answer. He knew she wanted the marriage to be over. Hell, she was the one that filed for the divorce. But every once in a while, he got a peek of the Meg he used to know, and when that side of her appeared, he saw that she was scared and that maybe, just maybe, she didn't want this as much as she said she did. That maybe it was fixable and that there was a way to make sure neither of them reached the end of their lives with a heart full of regrets and what-ifs.

"I guess it felt so normal to be with you in the kitchen the other night. Doing something you and I have done a thousand times together. I miss that, Meg. I'm not going to lie. And I know we're getting divorced and we're probably never going to do the dishes together again. Or go out to dinner, for that matter."

"We can be civil."

God, he hated that word. She'd used it at least a dozen times in the last few months. "What we're doing tonight isn't civil. I don't know what it is, but it's a lot more than that."

She had her purse on her lap, her hands curled around the handles. "I'm sad about it, too, Mike."

He kept the surprise off his face. All along, he'd thought

Meg was relieved to be getting divorced. That she was happier without him. That she'd maybe moved on already. To hear that she was struggling emotionally, too, oddly soothed him. "It's not an easy thing, is it?"

"No, it's not." She turned to him, her profile outlined by the passing lights outside the car. "I didn't make this decision overnight and I'm not going to get over it that quickly either. This is hard for me, too."

Then why do it? he wanted to ask. It was a question he already knew the answer to. Because whatever they had had before died somewhere along the way and neither one of them had cared enough to resurrect it. This dinner was his last-ditch, ridiculously persistent attempt at shoring up a marriage that had already eroded. There were so many things they needed to discuss, topics he had avoided and danced around because he was afraid of driving her even further away. "I'm glad. I know that's weird for me to say, but it makes me feel better that this wasn't easy for you, either."

The restaurant was only a few blocks from the house, which meant the drive was short. Mike parked the car and shut it off. She tapped the dash. "You traded in the Audi?"

"I'm working for myself and figured the income might be sporadic, and I didn't want to be worrying about a car payment. So, I sold the Audi and got a dependable Toyota. It's a few years old, but it's great on gas and it runs well."

"Working for yourself? I want to hear more about that when we get inside."

He got out of the car and came around to open her door, but she had already gotten out of the car, overriding his attempts to be a gentleman. She strode up the walkway to the door, but he was faster and managed to open it for her. "At least let me still get a few Brownie points."

That made her laugh a little. "Are we actually competing for who's the nicest during our divorce?"

"You beat me at gin rummy enough times while we were married that I feel compelled to win something. If only to keep my man card." He winked and she laughed again. He followed her into the restaurant, thinking how much he liked this. The easy conversation. The way they seemed to still have the same inside jokes.

"Mr. and Mrs. Brentwood!" Chef Tyler called from the open pass window of the kitchen. "I haven't seen you in forever!"

Neither of them bothered to correct Tyler on their marital status. Meg waved, and Mike said hello. "Sorry, man. We've been busy," he added.

"Always great to see you two. Sit anywhere you like. I'll send over one of my crab cakes in just a second."

"I think the baby just jumped for joy," Meg whispered in Mike's ear. "I remember those crab cakes."

Her breath was warm on his skin. Familiar. Sweet. "Pretty sure I just jumped for joy, too."

Meg laughed. "You are a dork, Mike Brentwood. But a funny one." She skipped the first booth and the second, before sliding into the third. The one where they always sat, the one that was almost always open when they came to this restaurant, like Roxy's was saving it just for them. A second later, a waitress brought them each a glass of water.

"Can I get a glass of sparkling water?" Mike asked the waitress. "And one for my . . . for Meg."

The waitress nodded and headed to the bar.

"No alcohol?" Meg said.

"I quit drinking the day you told me that you filed for divorce." He squared his place mat against the table. "I saw my life heading down the same path as my father's, and I knew I needed to change direction."

"What do you think would have happened if your father had done that, too?"

"You mean quit drinking?" Mike scoffed. It was a question he had considered dozens of times over the years, especially toward the end. His father had insisted on drinking nearly until the day he died, which had sadly robbed his father of the relationships he had wanted desperately to repair. "It would have changed everything."

"And maybe given everyone time to forgive. Rebuild."

Where was she going with this? There was no point in discussing his father or a past that couldn't change. "Maybe. I'd much rather concentrate on right now, Meg. Not ancient history. Because it's not too long until we're parents ourselves." Even saying the word *parent* aloud sounded odd to his ears.

"That is such a weird thought," she said, as if she'd read his mind. "I . . . I gave up on thinking of myself as a mom."

The day they closed the door on the nursery, he had stopped thinking about the possibility of ever becoming a father. "Me too. It was like it was easier not to—"

"Get our hopes up," she finished. Meg thanked the waitress as she set their drinks on the table. She picked up the glass of soda water. "So . . . what are we toasting to?"

Mike raised his glass and tipped it toward hers. "To a future we never saw coming." They clinked and each took a sip.

It was a little awkward and a little comfortable at the same time, the two of them caught in this weird space between a relationship and their divorce. There was the sweet familiarity of being with someone he'd known for more than a decade, tempered by the unspoken tension of what was to come in a couple weeks.

Meg crossed her hands on the table and leaned forward. "Tell me about working for yourself. When did you decide to do that?"

"I applied for a couple of CPA jobs, went to some interviews, and even got some offers, but I turned them all down. I couldn't imagine spending the rest of my life in someone else's office, clocking in and clocking out like my dad used to."

"You hated it that much?" She shook her head. "I never knew."

"Because I never told you. I always felt like it was my responsibility to provide for my family and not whine about it." To step up to the plate in ways his father hadn't, putting his mother, and his wife, ahead of the desire to work for himself. He'd done that for years because it was the responsible thing to do, the adult thing to do. "The layoff was like opening a gate and showing me a playing field I'd never seen before. And, frankly, without the added pressure of having to pay a mortgage, I thought I could take a chance on going into business for myself."

"I get that. It's freeing and terrifying at the same time." She laughed. "I wish I'd known. Maybe we could have found a way for you to do that sooner."

"You live and you learn, right?" Regrets were a waste of time; he'd learned that in the last few weeks. They did nothing but *keep a person bogged down in the past*, as Eleanor had said a few times in her column. "I have four clients already. And two more that are thinking of working with me. That's a good number to start."

"This may sound weird, but I'm proud of you." She tipped her soda water in his direction. "To new beginnings."

He clinked again. "New beginnings apart, you mean."

Her face sobered and he regretted the words. "Let's not go down that path."

Why couldn't he stop himself from bringing it up? Why did he have to keep talking about the fact that they were over? It was as if a part of him couldn't let her go. "Agreed."

The crab cakes arrived, a welcome interruption for the tension that had begun to build at the table. The conversation was like navigating a minefield. There were a hundred subjects that both of them danced around and refused to touch and a dozen others that they brushed up against, opening wounds that were barely scabbed over. Maybe this dinner had been a mistake. Because every time he looked at Meg, he wondered what made him so stupid to let his marriage with this intelligent, beautiful, stubborn woman fail.

"I was thinking, if it was okay with you," Meg said, drawing his attention back, "of naming the baby Penny, if it's a girl."

"I like that. I think your grandmother would, too. It's a nice way to keep your mother's memory in the family."

"I'm glad you agree." She fiddled with her fork. "When I was...when this happened before, you talked about Greg as a boy's name, but we never really settled on anything."

"That was when I was younger and didn't know any

better." Mike chuckled. "If you are still attached to Greg, we can put it on the list. But I was thinking it might be nice to name our son Robert."

"After your uncle? That's a great idea."

"He was the closest thing I had to stability when I was a kid. And he never got married or had kids of his own, so his name and the Brentwood name would live on, if we have a son." Then Mike caught himself, stumbling over another one of those land mines. "I mean, unless you wanted to go with Monroe, if you're going back to your maiden name..."

Meg touched his hand. "I haven't even thought about that, Mike. I like Robert Brentwood. I think it's a good name for a boy."

He laced his fingers through hers, ignoring the questions that kind of touch opened up and ignoring the way his heart skipped a beat. Every time they talked about the baby, he wanted to touch her, to share this joy. "Either way, I hope the baby is as beautiful as you."

She dipped her head and blushed. "Are you sure that's sparkling water and not champagne?"

"A hundred percent." He smiled at her. "You're even more beautiful than when we met, Meg. Back then, you were less sure of yourself. As you've gotten older, you've become more confident and stronger, and that makes you more intriguing to..." He almost said *me*, but quickly replaced it with "other people."

"Thank you." She gently tugged her hand out of his and picked up her fork. "I've always loved these crab cakes. I think it's the remoulade that Tyler makes."

The change of subject was probably a good idea. As she

had reminded him over and over again, they were over, and he was only setting himself up for heartache by drawing out the inevitable conclusion.

"I think it's the crab." Mike dug in at the same time she did. Their forks collided. "Sorry. You go."

"No, you go ahead and take the first bite."

"How about we let the baby take the first bite?" He nudged the plate in Meg's direction.

She grinned. "That sounds like a good idea to the baby's mom." She dipped a piece in the pale orange remoulade sauce and swallowed. "Oh, it's so good."

"It is," he said softly, thinking more about how good it was to sit here with Meg and enjoy each other instead of arguing, or worse, not saying anything at all. "This is nice."

Her gaze softened. "It is. Almost like old times."

Almost. And in an hour or less, this date would be over, and Mike would be left with a sweet memory and an empty bed. At some point, Meg was going to start dating again. Mike couldn't even imagine being with anyone other than this beautiful woman he'd fallen in love with years ago.

"You're staring at me," she said.

"You're the kind of woman men stare at," he said. "I mean, not in a creepy way, of course. In a *wow* way. That dress looks amazing on you, Meg."

She shook her head and laughed a little. "You are on a roll. Where were all these compliments when we were together?"

"I was an idiot. I didn't appreciate what I had until it was too late." It was true. He had taken her for granted, taken *them* for granted, figuring they would repair the divide between them someday down the road. If only he had tried harder years ago or fought harder against the divorce, maybe they wouldn't be here right now.

"Me too," she said softly.

He was about to ask her what she meant by that when the door to the restaurant opened, ushering in a gust of cold air. At the same time, a man about their age walked inside. He was wearing a dark gray wool coat with a crimson scarf. He unwound the scarf as he headed for the bar. Then he paused and stopped beside their table. "Margaret. How lovely to see you here."

"What a surprise," Meg said, her face lighting up in a way it hadn't in a long time.

Who the hell was this guy? He was the kind of guy that made other men want to hit the gym. "I don't think I've met you," Mike said as he put out his hand. "I'm Mike Brentwood."

Okay, so that was a little territorial, and Mike had no right to be that way in the middle of a divorce, but there was something about this guy that had rubbed Mike the wrong way. Maybe it was the fact that he was clearly looking at Margaret with interest.

"Mr. Brentwood." The man shook hands with him, but his attention remained mainly on Meg. "Margaret's ex-husband."

"Not ex. Not yet."

"Mike," Meg whispered, "stop it." She brightened and gave the other man a smile. "It's so nice to see you, Barrett."

"The pleasure is, as always, mine." Barrett made a point of ignoring Mike and lasering his focus on Meg. "I've never eaten here before. What do you recommend?"

That you get the hell out of here. But Mike didn't say that. He had no right to, of course. He could feel the tension hovering in the air between Meg and Barrett. There was something there, something Mike didn't want to see.

If anything told Mike that it wasn't over in his heart, it was the flare of jealousy that ignited in his chest the minute the other man gave Meg a smile that seemed meant only for her.

CHAPTER 21

For most of her life, Margaret had been the one her sisters relied on for advice, support, and a little bossing around. She was used to being the solitary soldier who didn't need anyone else. Maybe it was the hormonal swings of her pregnancy or maybe it was everything that had happened in the last few weeks, especially Grandma's accident and then that confusing dinner with Mike, but right then, she had a deep-seated need to be surrounded by her sisters.

She'd been avoiding the shop ever since the encounter at Roxy's with Barrett, claiming she needed to stay at home and work on the books. The empty house seemed to mock her decades of defiant independence, and by the time the end of the day rolled around, Margaret found herself picking up her phone and texting Emma and Gabby.

In desperate need of some girl time. Are you two free?

Who is this? Emma texted back and then added a laughing emoji and a *Just kidding. Have never heard you say that, Meg.*

She scowled at the phone. She started to type *Never mind* so she could revert to what she always did—wall herself off behind a mask of irritation. But that desire for connection, for family, roared inside her even louder, and she found herself typing, *Could really use you guys tonight* and hitting send before she thought about it too long.

Three dots appeared beside Gabby's name and Emma's. The dots disappeared. They appeared again, doing that flickering dance that filled Margaret with both anticipation and dread. Just when she thought her sisters were going to say no or worse, tease her again, Gabby texted, *Come to the shop, I have coffee cake* and Emma texted, *As long as you bring the wine, Meggy.*

You're on, Margaret replied. They settled on a time after Gabby's store would be closed for the day. Margaret flipped her phone over and set it on the desk. Even after doing that, she couldn't concentrate on work, couldn't concentrate on anything. Whatever restlessness had spurred her to reach out to her sisters hadn't quelled.

Margaret meandered through her house, fluffing a pillow here, straightening a vase there, whisking off a piece of dust there. She circled the downstairs and then began climbing toward the second floor. At the landing, instead of turning right toward the master bedroom, she found herself reaching for the knob on the door on her left. A door that had remained closed for five years.

She turned the brass knob halfway and then released it again. On the other side of that door was a room full of hope and grief. An unopened box for a crib and a single painted wall, the other three still the same dull shade of contractor white that came with the house. She closed her eyes and pressed her forehead to the oak-paneled door.

Even the whisper of going through that kind of loss again

terrified her. The toast with Mike had been tentative on her side, and almost as soon as she did it, she wanted to cancel it. She was so terrified of jinxing this miracle and losing what she had already begun to love.

She heard the ringtone that meant one of the employees at the store was calling her, so she hurried back downstairs and immersed herself in work. Avoiding the thoughts she almost couldn't bear until seven o'clock rolled around and it was time to meet her sisters.

Mike didn't text her. Ever since the dinner at Roxy's, he'd stopped even the daily checks on her and the baby. Grandma had appeared to have given up on her scheme to get them back together. It all filled Margaret with a finality that was hard to swallow. This was exactly what she wanted. Why was she struggling with it so much?

Margaret picked up a bottle of wine at the liquor store on the way over to Gabby's store and parked in front, right after Emma walked inside. From the car, Margaret could see Emma and Gabby embrace and then laugh at something Emma said, their connection light and easy. Margaret always felt like she was trying too hard to fit in, worrying too much about saying the right thing and never quite feeling like one of the girls. Maybe it was because she'd been the bossy older sister for so long.

She'd started therapy today, and it seemed like the hour with the counselor flew by. She'd had so much to talk about, so much to work out. So many thoughts that had been tucked inside herself for so long. Richard had been right. Therapy could work wonders.

Margaret grabbed the canvas tote with the bottles and

headed into the store. "Hey, guys. I've got wine." She hoisted the bag. "Gabby, do you still have those glasses from last time?"

A year ago, the three of them had been in this same place, an impromptu sisterly get-together to console Gabby after she and Jake hit a rough patch. That night had been the first time Margaret had truly opened up about the state of her marriage. A year ago, she'd had hope that they could fix it.

A year ago, everything had been so different.

"I've got real wineglasses," Gabby said. "A gift from one of my customers." She ducked behind the counter and came up with a box of stemless wineglasses, nestled inside tissue paper. The logo for Ella Penny Boutique, Gabby's shop, had been etched on the front of each one. "I designed some bridesmaids' dresses for her wedding, and she was so pleased with them, she got these made for me. Aren't they gorgeous?"

"Amazing," Emma said. "But they'll be even more amazing with some wine in them."

"I agree. It's been a heck of a day." Gabby gave each of them a glass as the three of them took a seat on the chairs that were situated by the dressing rooms in the shop. Gabby had added a small glass table to the area as a place for friends to hang out and shop together. "I have so much to tell you guys about how that fashion show went."

Margaret handed Emma one of the bottles of Chardonnay she'd brought and took a second, different bottle out of the bag. She set it on her lap and let out a big breath. "First, I have something I have to tell you both."

Gabby stared at the bottle in Margaret's hand. "Sparkling grape juice? Are you training early for dry January or something?"

"No. I'm not drinking because..." Margaret bit her lip. She had told the therapist today that she wanted to stop being afraid of what could go wrong and start celebrating what was going right, as Mike had suggested. That started with finally telling the people around her about the baby. "I'm pregnant."

Her sisters exploded with questions and congratulations. There was a flurry of words and hugs, a human tornado of joy. For the first time since she'd seen the results of the pregnancy test, Margaret allowed a little of that excitement to build in herself, too. Then the cautionary side of her tamped those feelings down and replaced them with the very real fact that she could lose this baby, too. It seemed she wasn't going to change overnight after all. "It's early," she warned her sisters. "And anything can happen."

"Meggy, it'll all be fine," Gabby said. "You're super healthy, and you look great. I'm sure everything's going along exactly as it should."

"That's what we thought last time, but—"

"What do you mean last time?" Emma asked. "You were pregnant before?"

Margaret blamed the pregnancy hormones for the inadvertent slip of the tongue. She and Mike had never told anyone in the family about the first pregnancy. In the weeks that they kept that sweet secret to themselves, every step they'd taken to prepare for the baby had felt like something sacred to only them. Back then, she and Mike had been so close and still as romantic as newlyweds, living on a planet of just the two of them. "It was years ago."

"But why didn't you tell us?"

"Mike and I were going to. We started planning a little

party and everything. That morning, I went to order a cake from Suzie and…" A twinge of a cramp had turned into a twisting pain, and before she could turn the car around, she'd known deep inside what had happened. She'd called Mike, and the two of them had rushed to the hospital, but it was too late. The same emergency room, the same machine, but a much different result. The silence of that machine had haunted Margaret for years. "We lost the baby before we could tell anyone."

Gabby and Emma wrapped Margaret in a tight hug. She held stiff for a moment but then relented because her need for her sisters' love and support overrode everything else. "I'm so sorry," Gabby said as she swiped away a tear. "And to go through that without the rest of your family there…"

"It's too much for anyone." Emma squeezed Margaret's hand. "Promise us you won't do that again. That's what sisters are for, you know, to help you get through the hard times."

"It still feels wrong for me to rely on you two." Margaret lowered herself into the chair and took a sip of the grape juice. "When Momma died, it was like something broke in me, and I could never go back to playing hopscotch and hide-and-go-seek."

"You were nine, Meg," Emma said. "That's far too young to grow up."

"I agree now, but back then, I didn't see that. I just felt so damned responsible for you two."

"I know. You told us what to do all the time." Gabby grinned, and Margaret fake punched her in the arm.

"Sometimes you needed someone to tell you what to do." Margaret laughed and then sobered. "Mike was the one who

made me feel like a kid again. He was so different from everything I knew. He had that motorcycle, and the second I got
on it, it was like stepping into a different world."

Emma sliced the coffee cake into thin pieces and handed
them out to her sisters. "And what happened that made it
change?"

Margaret set her coffee cake on the table. "I don't know.
We bought a car, a house, and the next thing we knew we
stopped riding through the hills of New Hampshire because
we had to buy a sedan. We stopped eating at the diners we
found along the road every weekend because the lawn needed
to be mowed and the laundry needed to be washed."

"You could have still done that," Gabby said. "The lawn
doesn't need to be mowed every weekend. Let the HOA complain and have fun with your husband."

"True." They had used those excuses to settle into a life
of predictability. Everything, right down to their sex life, had
become routine. Dinner out on Friday night, followed by a
glass of wine at home, and sex before they fell asleep. Then
they lost the baby, and even that routine slipped away.

Emma ate a big bite of her coffee cake. "So, what are you
going to do now? You're still getting divorced, right?"

Margaret nodded. "I don't see how we can put it back
together again. Too much has happened."

Gabby sighed. "It all seems so sad and unfortunate."

"It is." Tears sprang to her eyes. Margaret put her head in
her hands and let them fall. She'd held back her tears for far
too long, been strong when she should have allowed herself a
moment of weakness. "Honestly, it sucks and I hate it and I
wish it wasn't happening."

"Us too. The whole family is sick about it." Gabby rubbed Margaret's back. "Even Grandma called me to talk about it."

"Me too," Emma said.

Margaret rolled her eyes. "That is part of her meddling scheme." She told her sisters about the book and how Grandma had convinced her to work with Mike. "But it won't work. Mike stopped talking to me after we went out to dinner the other night."

She caught her sisters up on the night at Roxy's and the run-in with Barrett and a hundred other details of her life that she hadn't shared. That tidal wave she'd been holding back in her mind slowly ebbed with each sentence she shared with Gabby and Emma, and all those emotions she'd been so afraid to have became manageable. "Thanks, guys. You have no idea how much I needed this."

"Oh, we knew." Emma topped off her wineglass and cut another piece of coffee cake. "You're always so buttoned up, Meggy. If you ask me, keeping all your feelings locked away means you don't just miss the hard emotions, but you miss out on the great ones, too. Like joy." Emma's hand lighted on Margaret's abdomen. "You're going to be a mom. That's the most exciting thing I've ever heard. It's not even my baby, and I want to dance on the rooftops with happiness."

Gabby grinned as she hoisted her wineglass in the air. With her free hand, she nudged Margaret's arm up to do the same. "To the next Monroe girl."

Margaret laughed. "I don't know if it's a boy or a girl yet."

Gabby clinked her glass with Emma's and then with Margaret's. "Doesn't matter. We're going to spoil the hell out of that baby either way."

❦❧

Mike had been in the guest room for more than an hour and had yet to write a single word. Instead, his mind kept replaying that moment in Roxy's, the way that Barrett guy had looked at Meg and the surge of something—jealousy, anger, sadness—that had risen inside him. In a couple weeks, Meg would no longer be his wife. Why did he care if some other man found her interesting and beautiful?

"Mike? Can you come down here for a minute?" Eleanor's reedy voice carried up the stairs. "I need some help with Harry."

"Be right down." Mike shut the laptop. There was no point in leaving the computer running if nothing was happening on the screen. He took the front set of stairs down to the foyer and then headed into the living room. Eleanor and Harry were sitting in their twin recliners, looking for all the world like a couple who had been together for decades. They were holding hands in the space between the chairs and talking softly as a show played on television that no one was watching.

For a second, Mike envied their closeness. When he and Meg had said *I do*, Meg in a white dress she'd worn for her senior formal and repurposed for their wedding and Mike in a suit jacket that was his dad's and far too big for Mike's skinnier frame, he'd pictured them spending decades together. That dream, it was clear, was not going to come true.

"Uh, Eleanor? You needed me for something?"

She turned and smiled at him. "Yes, thank you. Harry wanted to make his special grilled cheese sandwiches for us for lunch, and Margaret's not here yet, so I was hoping you could help him in the kitchen."

Mike didn't reply right away. For one, Mike rarely cooked anything more complicated than a frozen dinner. And for another, the kitchen was Eleanor's domain. She was really going to let two men loose in there?

"Harry insisted that he do it for me, not with me," she said, as if she'd read his mind. "And I've been feeling awful tired today, so if you could be a dear…"

Harry had already moved himself out of his recliner and into his wheelchair, stubbornly not waiting for help. It was little wonder he and Eleanor butted heads often. They were both fiercely independent. "It should only take a few minutes," Harry said. "Hopefully you weren't in the middle of writing anything."

"Actually, it's good timing. I was stuck." Mike tapped his head. "Little bit of writer's block, maybe."

"Well, the best thing for that is to do something else," Eleanor said. "Gets your mind thinking in new directions."

"Exactly what I was thinking, my dear." Harry blew her an air kiss and began wheeling his chair toward Mike. His casted leg stuck out in front of him, making maneuvering past the furniture a complicated procedure.

"Let me help you." Mike took the handles of the wheelchair and pivoted Harry past the end tables and down the hall to the kitchen. He parked the chair at an empty space in front of the kitchen table. "Tell me what you need and I'll get it so you don't keep getting out of that chair. I'm pretty sure the doctor said not to do that unassisted quite yet."

Harry's face had that innocent who-me look. "If you don't tell my doctor, I won't."

Mike chuckled. "Just don't hurt yourself, okay? You're as stubborn as Margaret's grandmother."

"Which is why we make the perfect couple." Harry nodded toward the bread box. "Grab me the loaf of bread, please. And the tub of butter in the fridge?"

Mike retrieved the honey-wheat bread and set it on the table in front of Harry. "What kind of cheese do you want me to get?"

"Cheddar and American. And Swiss, if Eleanor has it. I call this my triple-decker delight."

Sounded more like a triple-calorie delight to Mike. He brought back all of the items Harry asked for, along with a butter knife and a plate. "Do you want me to plug in her electric griddle right here?"

"That's a wonderful idea. Then I can tell my Ella Bella that I actually cooked these myself." Harry began unwrapping the slices of American cheese while Mike found and set up the griddle. "You're a great help. Thanks."

"No problem." Mike took the seat across from Harry. The older man seemed like he had it under control but that didn't mean he wouldn't need help later. He watched Harry layer three kinds of cheese between two slices bread and then add another layer of cheese and a third slice of bread. He buttered the outsides and carefully set the sandwiches on the hot griddle. The butter sizzled and in seconds, the scent of melting cheese and toasting bread filled the room. "Those are the biggest grilled cheese sandwiches I've ever seen."

Harry slid a spatula under one of them and peeked at the color of the bread. Still too light, apparently, because he let it cook some more. "I used to make these for my son on the weekends when my wife was at work. My wife was a nurse and she'd give me a lecture about cholesterol and carbs, but my argument was always the same: What's life without a little fun?"

Mike grinned. "You're a very wise man."

"I think I'm more of a very lucky man. I was blessed to have an amazing wife who died too young, and then I just happened to move next door to another amazing woman and her incredible family. I'm so grateful for Ella and her grand-daughters. They've made this lonely man's world vibrant again."

It seemed Mike wasn't the only one who saw how amazing the Monroe family was. Eventually, the book would be done, and Mike's excuse for spending time here would be gone, as would his connection with all of them. "This family is incredible. I'm going to miss seeing them all the time after the divorce."

Harry frowned. "I can't even imagine how hard that will be for you."

"They're the only normalcy I've ever had in my life." Mike watched Harry flip the sandwiches and heard the butter on the other side begin to sizzle and skitter across the griddle's surface. "I didn't get off on the right foot with Eleanor when I first met her, but eventually, she came around. She's been like another mother and the grandmother I never had, all in one."

"She has that way about her, doesn't she? Ella may come off all tough and cranky, but she's a total softie underneath."

"The same with her granddaughter. Margaret acts like she's a fortress, but she's the total opposite inside."

Harry lifted the edge of one sandwich and then the next. "Too bad you guys couldn't work it out."

"It happens." The words came out casually, is if this were no bigger deal than spraining his ankle. But inside, his heart felt like someone was squeezing it until it burst.

"I'm sure you guys gave it all you've got."

"I'd like to think we did."

Harry shifted the sandwiches around on the griddle, moving the outer ones to the center and the nearly done ones to the cooler space on the side. "You know, my first wife and I came awfully close to divorce."

"Really? I never knew that."

"We had the papers and the date with the judge. I'd moved in with a friend of mine and was sleeping on his couch. I swear, it took a year for the bruises on my back to heal from that crappy couch. I was miserable without her but I was too damned proud to tell her."

"The whole man-up thing, huh?" In the other room, Mike could hear the television switch to a cooking competition, complete with literal bells and whistles.

"Partly. My father was the kind of man who thought crying was for sissies, so when I was younger, I tried my best to never show an emotion. I got pretty good at it. So good, my wife thought I stopped caring about her. She packed my bags and told me to leave. Next thing I know, we're dividing up the silverware." Harry slid the sandwiches off of the griddle and stacked them on the plate. He nodded toward the cabinets. "Can you get me a couple more plates, please?"

Mike retrieved two more stoneware plates and set them in front of Harry, who divvied up the sandwiches and cut them on the diagonal. Cheesy goodness oozed out of the hot centers. Mike's stomach rumbled. Thank goodness Harry made three. "So, what happened?"

"I stopped by the house one day when she wasn't home to pick up my half of the stuff. I looked around that house and thought how empty it looked without her in it. I saw the boxes of silverware and plates and couldn't bear to take them with me. They belonged in that house, with her, because that was a home. Or it had been, until I went and screwed it all up. I didn't want to live in a house by myself, I wanted to live in that home with her. So, I sat down at the kitchen table and I waited for her to come home. What I didn't expect was that she'd come home from a date."

Mike thought of Barrett's dark eyes and that intense way he looked at Meg. How she blushed when he'd flirted. If there wasn't something between them now, Mike had no doubt there would be in the future. The very idea of someone else kissing Meg, holding Meg, lying beside Meg at night, nearly debilitated him. "That had to be awful."

"It was. At first, I was angry, and I had plenty I was going to say to her. Then I thought about something my grandma had said to me when I was a kid and had gotten in trouble for fighting with Bobby Greenholt at school. I was all set to fight him again the next day and show him what's what. Then my grandmother said, 'How did it work out when you acted that way the first time? What makes you think it'll end up any differently this time?'" Harry put two plates in his lap and handed one to Mike. "Can you wheel this thing one-handed?"

"Sure." He stepped behind the chair and grabbed one of the handles to start pushing Harry toward the living room. "I take it you decided not to argue with your wife about the date she'd been on?"

"Exactly. I didn't fight Bobby a second time, and I didn't lose my temper with my wife for moving on when I was the one who bungled the whole relationship to begin with. I just nodded, polite as I could, and pretended I cared about meeting this man who had taken my wife to dinner. We were only a couple days from getting divorced, and I knew I had no right to say anything to her. But when the guy left…"

Mike maneuvered the chair around the corner and down the hallway, moving slowly so he didn't bump into the walls or the long, narrow table full of family pictures. "When the guy left, what happened?"

"I told my wife the truth. That I was miserable without her and I had been a terrible husband. I opened my heart, laid it bare on the table, and waited for her to stomp on it. But she didn't. She started to cry, and then I felt even worse." Harry put a hand on Mike's, to stop him from pushing the chair the rest of the way into the living room where Eleanor waited for her lunch. "She told me she'd been so scared that I didn't care anymore and that I was going to leave her that she left me first. All because I had been convinced that a stiff upper lip was the only kind of lip to have. From that day forward, I vowed to be more open and not be such a stuffed shirt. Of course, no one transforms overnight, so there were a few more bumps in the road, but eventually, she and I found a happiness with each other that was even sweeter than what we had when we first got married."

"That's great, Harry. It's always nice to hear about someone having a happily-ever-after." Way to make Mike feel even worse, he thought. Happy endings all around, except for Mike and Meg.

"I think a lot more of us would have those if we stopped being so damned stubborn. Poor Ella's got the evolved version of me. I tell her how I feel all the time. I'm not above shedding a few tears, either. It makes our relationship honest, and that, to me, is the most important thing you can have between two people. Honesty."

"Takes two to do that, Harry." Mike pushed the chair into the living room and got Eleanor and Harry set up with their lunches. Harry insisted Mike take the third plate with him when he left to go back to work on the book, but when Mike sat down upstairs at the desk, his appetite was gone.

CHAPTER 22

Grandma and Harry were all smiles when Margaret arrived later that day. She picked up the empty plates in the living room and spent some time cleaning the kitchen while her grandmother sat at the kitchen table and chatted about her day. Margaret only half listened. Her mind was distracted by the thought that Mike was one floor away. They hadn't talked in the week since the disastrous end to their dinner out, and Margaret was dreading seeing Mike again. It was bound to be an awkward conversation.

What's going on between you and Barrett? she could imagine him asking.

What was going on between her and Barrett? She had no idea. He flirted like he was interested but had yet to ask her on a date or anything like that. Yet, after working off and on at the store for the last month, he had learned the way she took her coffee and showed up nearly every morning with her favorite decaf cinnamon-sprinkled latte in hand. A man didn't do that if he didn't have at least some interest.

The more important question was whether Margaret was interested in Barrett in that way. She'd have to say no. All his attention had been flattering and, at first, exciting, but that feeling had quickly waned. Right now, Margaret couldn't imagine dating anyone, much less someone who worked for her. It all seemed so...exhausting. As the weeks passed and her pregnancy advanced, the energy that usually made Margaret soar through her day was lessening. Her runs had gotten shorter, and her craving for naps had gotten much stronger.

Plus, there was a part of her that still missed Mike, as weird as that was. She'd check her phone off and on throughout the day, as if he'd magically ask what was for dinner or if she was busy tonight. There'd been nothing, no contact, no flickering three dots. Just a blank screen.

"Thank you for all that you do," Grandma said as she walked slowly around the kitchen. Grandma was doing much better but wasn't as spry as she had been before the accident. Margaret could see a caution in her steps, as if she was afraid of cracking another rib or breaking a leg like Harry. "Which is far too much, I might add. You've done all the shopping, nearly all the cooking, and cleaned this house from top to bottom."

"Because you should be resting." Even though the doctor had given Grandma the all-clear yesterday, the girls still worried, and Margaret kept insisting on doing all the chores.

"As should you, my darling granddaughter." Grandma put a hand on Margaret's belly. "That little bean inside you needs plenty of energy to grow, but he or she can't do that if Mom is constantly tired."

"It's good for pregnant women to remain active, Grandma." Plus, it kept her mind off things. Like her silent phone.

"As long as you're not *too* active. Put your feet up and rest,

because you won't get a moment's rest after this baby comes."
Grandma patted Margaret's cheek and gave her a soft smile.
"I'm sorry I asked so much of you over the last weeks."

"Shopping and cooking is nothing. I have to do it for
myself. It wasn't much to add on a couple more meals." Margaret filled the teakettle and set it on the stove. She turned
on the cooktop and prayed the tea took forever to brew so she
could procrastinate about going upstairs.

"I meant working with Mike. I'm afraid I added to your
stress, Margaret."

That was an understatement. She knew her grandmother
meant well, but it was never going to work. There was too
much between them now to go back to the way they were.
Even if they could fix things, Margaret didn't want that roommate life again. She wanted a partnership with someone who
opened up to her and who didn't leave her to go through the
hard parts alone. Someone who wasn't afraid to have the
tough conversations. Someone who didn't retreat when she
withdrew or clammed up. Someone who took her in his arms
and gave her the space to let her emotions fly.

She knew she was just as much to blame as Mike was,
with her own tendency to shut people out and shoulder all
the responsibility alone. She had been a wall when Mike
needed an opening, a block of ice when Mike needed warmth.
The only thing she could do was try to do it better the next
time.

Ugh. Even thinking of a next time with anyone else made
her want to take a nap.

"So, uh, how much more does Mike need to write?" Margaret prayed her grandmother said the book was done because she wasn't so sure she could get along with Mike for another twenty minutes, never mind twenty chapters.

"Not much," Grandma said. "In fact, he said he might not need your help at all anymore."

Thank goodness. Maybe he was avoiding her as much as she was avoiding him. Yet, the knowledge made Margaret feel a little sad. Hurt, even.

"He did ask if I could bring him some tea, though," Grandma said. "Do you mind, dear?"

"Of course not." She could drop off a hot beverage, exchange a bit of small talk, and then maybe that longing for a text from him would finally disappear.

As Margaret moved around the kitchen, setting up teacups and tea bags, she thought of how this simple drink laced so many of her memories together. How many times had she sat at this maple table, talking to Grandma about a boy or school or whatever was bothering her, while the two of them sipped a hot, fruity tea?

The kettle whistled. Margaret retrieved the water and poured some into each of the cups. A part of her wanted to ask her grandmother to have one of those tea talks, but how could she when she'd been insisting to everyone for weeks that she was fine? Grandma had enough to worry about with Harry's recovery. Margaret didn't need to pile on to that.

"Well, if any of this stuff with the book or the divorce gets too difficult, please come talk to me," Grandma said, as if she'd heard Margaret's thoughts. "Your happiness is the most important thing."

Margaret sighed. "I don't know where my happiness is anymore, Grandma."

Grandma feigned catching a fistful of air. "It's right there, just waiting for you to breathe life into it again. Sweetheart, you look so down. Do you want to talk about it?"

Here was the opening she'd just been wishing for, the opportunity to dump it all in someone else's hands, someone who would give her advice and a hug. The divorce, the store, the unanswered questions in her life, and all the worry about the baby seemed like a massively heavy blanket. As much as she wanted to talk to her grandmother, she knew there was no advice to make it better. No hug that would take away the feelings of loss and grief. Instead, Margaret said *I'll be fine* again.

She grabbed one of the teacups and headed up the narrow back stairs. When she was little, she and her sisters had played hide-and-seek a thousand times, using these stairs as a way to sneak into one of the bedrooms. When Emma was a teenager, she'd used these stairs to creep out the back door and go to some party or meet some boy. When Margaret and Mike came back from eloping, he'd hauled her into this staircase and whispered that he loved her, giving her the courage to face her family and tell them about the spontaneous thing they had done. Margaret knew every riser, every tread, every dent in the wall. Some of her best memories—and a few of her worst—were contained within this house.

The hot tea gave off the aroma of blueberry and pomegranate, mingled with the sweet scent of the honey she'd stirred into the cup. A full teaspoon for Mike, who had more of a sweet tooth than she did. Who would make him a cup of tea next month? Next year? Who would remember that he was always leaving his keys on the workbench in the garage instead of the little table inside the door? Who would know that he hated cauliflower but loved broccoli? Who would leave a light burning in the hallway so he never had to come home to a dark house?

The idea of another woman doing those things for him was oddly unsettling. Margaret shouldn't care who folded Mike's T-shirts or picked up his favorite cookies at the bakery. But for some weird reason, she did.

Hormones, she told herself, just as she had a dozen other times over the last couple of weeks.

She tapped on the open door to the bedroom. Mike was hunched over his laptop, typing away, and didn't hear her. "Uh, Mike? I'm here."

He turned and looked at her. She waited a beat for the familiar smile to appear on his face. It didn't. "Oh. I didn't know you were coming."

He sounded almost disappointed. Margaret felt the hot rush of tears behind her eyes. They were getting divorced. These were irrational feelings. *Stop it,* she told herself. *Be a grown-up.* "Grandma said you wanted a cup of tea." She walked into the room. "I added extra honey—"

"For your honey," he replied, in the habitual exchange they'd had so many times in the years they'd been married. He scowled. "Sorry. It was habit. I didn't mean to say that."

She nodded because, for some reason, her throat was thick and she couldn't find her voice for a second. "No problem."

"It's just..."

"Awkward." The whole conversation could be described that way. Fits and starts, pauses and hesitations. "I just wanted to check and see if you needed help with the book before I left to go back to work."

His forehead wrinkled in that way it did when he was annoyed. She could almost read his mind. *Of course you're going back to work. When are you not working?*

"We're having a big sale this weekend, and Tara is feeling a little under the weather, so I wanted to be there to help Duane out." Why did she feel the need to justify her job?

"Can't Barrett do that?"

Was it her imagination or did she hear a hint of jealousy in his voice when he asked that question? "Barrett doesn't do sales. He's usually working on a piece at the front of the store. Either way, he's not there today. He'll be back tomorrow."

"Seems like a really dedicated employee, considering he's just temporary."

"You sound...jealous."

"Why would I be jealous?" he asked, his voice devoid of any tone at all now.

When he took a sip of his tea, she could see the truth in his eyes. Ironic, considering she'd just been feeling the same way a second ago. "I'm free to date, you're free to date. That's what divorced means."

"I don't want to date, Margaret." He put the cup down on the desk and picked up a manila folder that was sitting beside his computer. He fiddled with it for a moment, as if debating whether he wanted to say something. "Ten years ago, I found the one woman I thought would be my forever. Turns out I was wrong. In more ways than one."

"What is with you?" He was in a weird mood today. First jealousy, now this coldness she'd never seen before.

He tapped the folder in his lap. "I swore I wasn't going to

mention this until we were at mediation. Neutral third party and all."

"What are you talking about?"

As he pulled the papers out of the folder, she could see the rows and numbers that marked bank statements. Their bank statements. She knew in an instant what was on those papers and what he'd seen. "Mike, that isn't what you think."

"It's not ten years of lies? Because that's what I see when I look at these."

"It's complicated." How was she supposed to explain this to him? To tell him what she had done?

Mike cursed. "When did you decide to start lying to me? Before you married me or after? Or was that the plan all along? Marry someone with a nine-to-five and steady paycheck and then funnel money from your joint account every month to do God knows what."

"Do you seriously think I *embezzled* from you?"

"Did you, Margaret? Because these bank statements make a pretty convincing case."

Her phone pinged with a text message. She glanced at it, then back up at Mike. "Can we talk about this later? I have to call someone."

"Why? Is Barrett having a tough time putting a sapphire in a setting?"

She blew her bangs out of her face. "No. This isn't about him, and there isn't anything going on with him. Not that it's any of your business. This is..." She dropped her gaze to the phone, weighing the wisdom of telling him that she was looking at a text from Richard. "It's a personal thing."

All the anger drained from his face, replaced by a hurt deeper than any she'd ever seen in his eyes. "Has there been someone else? Is that who you were paying? Does his name begin with *R*?" Mike held up a grainy image of a check with a single letter written on the memo line.

Margaret had covered her tracks in every possible way, or so she thought. Opening a separate account, never transferring the money directly, so that Mike couldn't trace the person in Zelle. She'd made one mistake, there in black and white, and the only way she could explain what she had done was by telling him the truth.

We've been giving money to the last man you'd expect for ten years.

Mike would never understand. Never. Better for him to think the worst of her than to tell him the truth. "It's not what you think," she said again.

He tossed the bank statements onto the desk. Papers skittered everywhere, some floating to the carpeted floor. "Does it really even matter now, Margaret?"

His voice cracked on the last couple of words with a deep sound of hurt. He turned back to the computer. Margaret hovered behind him for a moment, wanting to apologize, to explain, but she had no words. She reached out but drew her hand back before she touched him. He was right. It didn't matter anymore.

❧ ❧ ❧

After a few more days of enforced rest at the behest of everyone in her family, Eleanor decided it was time she started cooking again. She baked Harry some cookies and made him a pot roast, which brought a smile to his face. He still had a few weeks of healing before he could even think about physical therapy, but he was in good spirits and had mastered moving about in his wheelchair. They were both feeling considerably better and had settled into a nice routine where Harry came over early in the morning and Chad wheeled him back to his house after they watched a rerun or two of *Jeopardy!* after dinner.

Which meant it was time for Eleanor to have a conversation with her eldest granddaughter. Something had happened the other day, something that had Mike gathering up his notes and his computer, saying he was going to work on the book at his house from now on, and he hoped Eleanor could understand. He'd called her a couple times since then to clarify something he read or ask her about a story, but he had avoided the house as if it were infested with termites.

Neither Margaret nor Mike had mentioned the other. The one time Eleanor tried to broach the subject of the divorce, Mike had said that he didn't want to talk about it. Ever. Margaret had given her a similar answer. She turned to the man sitting beside her. "It's bothering me, Harry."

He muted the television and swiveled his gaze in her direction. He'd been by her side every day since he was released from the hospital, often holding her hand. He'd been calm and patient and as helpful as he could be. She had gotten used to his presence, so used to it that she missed him fiercely when he went home at night to sleep in his own house.

"What's bothering you?" he asked.

"Margaret and Mike. It's not working out the way I hoped it would."

"Sometimes, my love, you have to let things sit and be patient. Like when you make your French onion soup. Those onions take hours and hours to cook. You've told me more than once not to touch them because it's only in the waiting that they turn into those perfect, sweet bites."

"This is different." Harry arched a brow as if to question her logic. He had a point. Forcing things along almost always made them backfire. The more she'd pushed at Margaret and Mike, the further they had retreated from each other. Maybe they were more like caramelizing onions than she wanted to admit. "Oh, I hate when you're right."

He cupped a hand around his ear. "Can you repeat that? Because I swear I just heard you say that I was right."

"I am not saying it a second time." She softened and covered their joined hands with her other one. "You drive me crazy in a hundred different ways, Harry Erlich."

"And you make me happy in a hundred different ways, Ella Bella. Ever since I got out of the hospital, you have worried about me and fretted over me so much I was a little scared I was on death's door."

"Why on earth would you think that?"

"When I moved in next door, you did your level best to keep me at arm's length for a year. Then we get in the accident, and you insist on spending every moment you can with me. I must be dying if you're being so nice all the time."

She thought of all the times she had rebuffed his attention, told him to get lost, or pretended she wasn't interested. "I wasn't mean *all* the time. Anyway, I've been extra nice because you were hurt."

"That's the only reason?" He leaned back in his chair and

studied her. "Are you ever going to admit to yourself that you love me?"

Her jaw dropped. The two of them had danced around that word for the last few months, but neither had spoken it aloud. Saying the word *love* meant taking things to another level, one that maybe involved a more permanent living arrangement than what they had now. Or at the very least, a bigger commitment.

Was she ready for that?

She looked at Harry's kind, wrinkled face, and thought yes, she did love him. She'd probably always loved him. She'd just been too stubborn to admit it. Not a surprise that all three of her granddaughters had had to be nudged—sometimes firmly—in the direction of love. They learned that reluctance from her. From her decades of holding a place for a man who would never have wanted her to do that. "I've been so afraid to love someone else," she admitted.

His eyes softened with understanding. "When my wife died, I thought I'd never love someone else like I had loved her. I even told my son I'd never get married again. Never fall in love again. He told me I would, if I stopped being so damned stubborn."

Eleanor laughed. "You, Harry, are the least stubborn person I know."

"Well, that's because I met you, and you gave me a reason to move forward again. You have been my best friend and my best supporter, even when it was against your will." He chuckled.

She smoothed the blanket over his leg where it had shifted, exposing the skin above his cast to the slight chill in the air. Maybe she should turn up the heat so he wasn't cold. "I was pretty difficult when we first met."

"Difficult?" Harry chuckled. "You were more like a porcupine wearing a barbed wire suit."

"Oh, I was not that bad." Well, maybe she had been. She was just so terrified of loss and of moving on that she denied her feelings for months. The truth was that her interest had been piqued the day her handsome neighbor looked over his hedges and commented on her garden. "I'm sorry, Harry. I should have been nicer."

"You were perfect, Ella Bella. You always have been. We both just needed to learn to stop being scared and open our hearts again." He leaned over and kissed her. "And doing that is the best thing I've ever done because I met a woman I love more than I ever thought possible."

"You love me?"

"Don't look so shocked. You know I do. And I know you love me too."

She felt her face heat. Was the man a mind reader? "How on earth do you know that?"

He reached into his pocket and pulled out the card that Eleanor had sent Gabby to buy that day in the hospital. "Because you wrote it, right here." He pointed at the four letters above her signature.

She wanted to protest, claim she was under the influence of painkillers, or pass it off as a joke, but what good would it do to keep running from her own heart? If she wanted her own granddaughters to trust their feelings and be vulnerable, then she'd better start doing that in her own life. She remembered telling Chad to send her love to Harry, a sentiment she echoed when she signed the card for him at the hospital. "I wrote that because . . . I meant it."

"About damned time. There. I'm glad that's settled." Harry sat back in his chair and reached for the remote.

"That's it? I admit I love you, and you're going back to *Law and Order?*"

He winked and put the remote back on the table. "I'm just giving you a taste of your own medicine, my dear. Because I know there are going to be plenty of opportunities for me to say," he leaned closer, his mouth inches from hers, "*I love you* in the future. Especially on our wedding day."

Had he just said what she thought he said? Wedding day? Was that some kind of proposal? "Harry Erlich—"

"Grandma, are you home?" Margaret called as she walked in through the back door. A gust of cold November air came with her but then quickly disappeared when the door shut behind her. "I brought a pizza so no one has to cook tonight."

"We will talk about what you just said later," Eleanor said. "Right now, I have to go talk to my granddaughter and see if I can shake some sense into her."

A look of disappointment flickered across Harry's features. "Of course."

"And I love you, too," she whispered as she placed a quick kiss on his temple and then hurried out of the room.

"I knew it!" Harry called after her.

Eleanor's smile was big enough to wrap around the whole planet. Her heart was light, her spirits high, and the future looked nothing but bright. Or it would, if her eldest granddaughter was finally happy.

Margaret had set the pizza on the counter and was pulling

three paper plates out of the cabinet. "I bought pepperoni. That's still your favorite?"

"Harry's too. Thank you, Margaret," Eleanor said. "But you really didn't have to do that. I was going to cook dinner tonight."

"Shouldn't you be taking it easy?" Margaret poured some water into the kettle and set it on the stove. The gas burner clicked until it lit.

Eleanor parked a fist on her hip. This had all gone on long enough. "Don't take this the wrong way, Margaret, but you have been here for weeks. I am all mended and fine, which means you can go home anytime."

Margaret planted her hands on the countertop and stared down at the teacups, her back to her grandmother, her shoulders hunched. "I don't want to," she said softly. "It's so...quiet there."

Oh, how Eleanor knew that roaring sound of silence. She'd had almost nine years of it between when her dear Russell died and the girls had come to live with her. She'd kept a radio or television on all the time, just to take the edge off the loneliness. She'd never imagined that her house would ever be filled with the lively sounds of laughter and love again. "Are you sure you're doing the right thing with the divorce?"

Margaret didn't say anything for a while. "No."

"Then why on earth are you going through with it?"

"Because I've done too much damage." Margaret turned around, putting her back to the countertop. The water in the teakettle started simmering. "There's something I never told Mike, and I think it's too late to try to explain."

"A secret, huh?" This family had too many secrets, Eleanor realized. Once she had thought they were a good thing, a way to protect the ones she loved, but it turned out that she was wrong. "Like me hiding the fact that I was writing the advice column all those years? How did it make you feel when you found out I'd been hiding that from you?"

"I was mad at first. I thought you would trust us girls with something like that, at the very least."

"And you would be right, my darling Margaret. I was the one who didn't believe in you girls enough. I thought you'd think I was a silly woman who was trying to meddle in people's lives."

A smile curved up one side of Margaret's face. "Well, the meddling part is true."

Also another thing someone else was right about. Harry did not need to hear that he was right twice in one day. That would just make him overly confident. "Once we cleared the air and talked about my little secret, didn't it bring us all closer together? Like when you girls were little?"

"Yeah, but this thing with Mike is not as simple as working for the newspaper."

"Perhaps. I don't know what this thing is, and I'm not going to ask. You can tell me if and when you feel ready. But I do know this..." The kettle started to whistle. Eleanor reached past Margaret and turned it off. She gently bumped Margaret out of the way and filled the cups with the hot water. "Mike loves you more than you realize. I watch how he looks at you, how he's always looked at you."

Margaret scoffed. "I don't think he looks at me like that anymore."

That was because Margaret clearly wasn't paying attention. "During family dinner a couple weeks ago, you were dishing up Scout's dinner, and I watched him watch you with her. He had this look in his eyes that was the same puppy-dog look he had all those years ago when you brought him home and told me you'd just married him."

Hope flickered on Margaret's face but then just as quickly disappeared. Oh, these two were not done, Eleanor thought. Not done at all.

"Grandma, we're getting divorced tomorrow. Even if what you say is true, it's too late."

"It's never too late…" Her gaze went down the hall to where Harry sat, waiting patiently for her as he had ever since she met him. "It's never too late for a second chance. You just have to be brave enough to take it."

CHAPTER 23

The divorce hearing was painful and short, a snippet of time that ended the ten years Mike had been married to Meg. They sat across from each other in a conference room with the judge at one end of the table and a court reporter in the corner, much like the day they got married but without the joy at the end. Since everything had been settled in mediation, Mike's lawyer told him the divorce hearing was a formality, so Mike had decided to go alone. Meg's cousin George had been waiting in the anteroom, but Meg told him she didn't need him in the hearing, which left just the two of them to head into the conference room.

In the end, Mike had let the money issue drop. He knew that legally he could have demanded she repay half of the money she had taken—and given to someone—as part of the divorce, but he didn't have the energy. Finding out that Meg had hidden something so big for so long had destroyed any hope Mike might have had for them to get back together. In the mediation a couple weeks ago, he couldn't even look at Meg. "Just divide it fairly," he'd said to Meg's cousin. "I don't care about any of the stuff or the house or the damned cars."

Then he'd walked out, leaving the lawyers to figure out the rest. Mike had gone back to his apartment, drawn the shades, and spent the rest of the day letting the TV play and not watching a damned thing. He'd done the same thing for the next few days, avoiding the pictures of turkeys and radio stations playing Black Friday commercials, hoping someday the holidays wouldn't be so damned painful.

During the divorce hearing, the judge asked them a few questions. Were these their legal names? Was the marriage irrevocably broken? Did they both still want a divorce?

Meg and Mike each answered with one-word answers and then it was over. The judge signed his name to the decree, stamped it with a county seal, and then handed the decree to the clerk to make copies. In five minutes, their marriage was dissolved. Over. Finito.

Forever.

The two of them walked out of the conference room and stood in the anteroom in an awkward silence, waiting for the clerk to come back with the copies. What was he supposed to say? *Thanks for not being argumentative? Glad that went smoothly?*

He glanced at Meg and could see tears brimming in her eyes. She looked broken and sad, and despite everything, Mike wanted to pull her into his arms and tell her it would all be okay. Then he thought about Barrett, the money, and all the water that had passed under the Brentwood bridge, and instead gave her a nod and turned away.

"Mike?"

He hated that his heart did a little leap when she spoke his name. He hated that he turned around so fast that he nearly lost his balance. He hated that his voice sounded high and excited. "Yeah?"

She waved at her cousin George to stay behind and then crossed the room until she was standing just a few feet away from Mike. She'd worn one of her dark blue suits to court today, but the curves from her pregnancy, now getting close to four months along, lessened the severe cut. Her eyes were watery, her cheeks red as if she'd been crying today.

She reached out, like she was about to take his hand, but then she seemed to change her mind and take a half step back. "I just want you to know that there was never anyone else, never. I was always yours and yours alone. The money wasn't for what you thought."

"Margaret, you don't owe me an explanation. You don't owe me anything." He was so tired of all of it. He just wanted to get out of this room and burrow into his misery for the next hundred years until he forgot Meg's smile, the touch of her hand, the sweetness of her kiss.

"I think I do. I think I owe everyone an explanation." She laced her fingers together and rested her hands against her stomach. He thought of the new life that was in there, the new beginning it could have been. "I should have trusted you more, talked to you more. Anyway, I know it's probably too late and that you hate me, but I want to ask a favor of you."

"A favor?" He snorted. "After you just divorced me and took away the life I used to know? Just before the holidays at that?" Okay, so maybe he was a little bitter. "I'm sorry. This just…hurts. A lot."

"I know. I'm sorry." She drew in a breath and raised her

gaze to his. "You were right, Mike. You were right about all of it. After...after we lost the baby, we never talked about it. We just went on as if life were normal. And it wasn't. It wasn't at all."

He could see the pain lingering in her eyes, a pain he still felt in his own heart. Two desperately sad people who had turned away from each other instead of toward each other. "I don't think we knew what to say."

"I know what I'd say now, but like we both said, it's too late." She toed at the floor. It was so unlike Meg to be unsure, almost shy. "I have one thing I do want to explain to you and my family. Can you come to dinner at my grandmother's house on Thanksgiving?"

"We can't keep doing family dinners like nothing happened, Meg. We are divorced. It's over. I'm not part of your family anymore." Simply saying those words was like severing his heart in half.

"Just this one more time." Her eyes brimmed with tears. "Please."

The clerk came rushing into the room, a sheaf of papers in each of her hands. "I'm so sorry. I know how awkward it is to stand here and wait. The copier was acting up. Here you go." She thrust a copy into Mike's hands and one into Meg's. "You two are free to go your separate ways now."

"That's the only good thing I've heard all day," Mike said. He tucked his copy of the decree under his arm and headed out of the room before he got caught in whatever Meg wanted to say. It was, after all, too late.

❦ ❦ ❦

Hands down, the hardest thing Margaret had ever done was go to therapy. She'd been through terrible, traumatic moments in her life, but in the chaos of those times, she'd always chosen to compartmentalize so she could plow through the hard parts without getting caught up in emotions. She'd stuff her thoughts on a shelf for later—knowing full well she had no intentions of revisiting any of them—so she could keep putting one foot in front of another.

Talking to a counselor, however, meant taking down all those carefully packaged and long-avoided memories, opening them up, and then dissecting them from one end to the other. In the six weeks she'd been coming to Ashley Gambrel, her therapist, Margaret had talked more about her feelings than she had in her entire life.

At first, she'd resisted, but as the words came out of her and her mind began to connect the dots between the things that happened and the choices Margaret made, she'd begun to feel an unburdening, a lightening, and now she looked forward to her weekly sessions as much as she dreaded them. Unpacking painful memories was never fun, but the results were worth every minute spent on that couch.

"So," Ashley said as she settled a yellow notepad on her knee and clicked her pen. She was seated in a velvet armchair across from Meg, who was perched on the edge of a dark cranberry leather sofa awash in pillows and comfy throws, maybe to make it feel more homey. "Let's start with how you're feeling this week."

"Physically? A little tired. But overall, great. Emotionally?" Margaret let out a wry laugh. "I'm all over the place. The divorce is final now and I thought I'd feel relieved, but I don't."

After that day in court, Margaret had gone back to the house with her copy of the decree on the passenger's seat of her car. She'd sat in the driveway for a long time, staring at the For Sale sign and the house it sat in front of, wishing she could turn back the clock. She'd dreaded going into that empty, echoey house and facing the heartbreaking chore of packing up her half of their lives so she could move on. None of it had felt like moving in anything other than the wrong direction.

"Why do you think you didn't feel relieved it was over?" Ashley asked.

"Maybe because it all seems so…unfinished, which is weird to say because the divorce puts a pretty final stamp on things." Margaret fiddled with the edge of her shirt, a white blouse that fit loosely and allowed her a little more room around her belly that was just beginning to show. "When I was at the courthouse, I decided I had to tell Mike the truth about where the money had been going. He deserves to know at least that and have some closure, instead of wondering for the rest of his life. So…I invited him to Thanksgiving dinner."

Ashley arched a brow. "Wow. That seems like a big step. This is the same dinner you've invited someone else to, isn't it?"

Margaret nodded. "Mike hasn't said whether he's coming and the whole thing could still backfire. I just feel like none of us—not Mike, not my family, and not me—can get past this unless we're dealing with the truth."

A smile crossed Ashley's face. "That's great, Margaret. I'm proud of you for taking that step."

Hearing *I'm proud of you* from her therapist was almost

like getting a pat on the head from her mother. It made Margaret feel like she was finally—maybe—getting a handle on this adulting thing. "Thank you. I appreciate you saying that."

"How about that other big step I asked you to take?" Ashley asked.

At her first meeting with her therapist, Margaret had shared that she hadn't gone inside the bedroom they'd set aside for a nursery for five years. She'd come close many times, but ultimately hadn't been able to turn that handle and walk into a room that had once held so much hope. "I finally did it this morning. I went into that room and stood there, just looking at what was and thinking about what will be. It wasn't as hard or as painful as I thought it would be. I should have done that a long time ago."

"We all grieve at our own pace and in our own way," Ashley said. "Don't beat yourself up for taking a while to get there. It was a devastating loss."

"True, but we both know I don't handle loss well at all. I just shut down and go all 'Margaret,' as my sisters would say." Even as Margaret said the words, she could think of a hundred times when she had fit those words to a T. No wonder her sisters and Mike sometimes used her first name like it was some kind of affliction. "I did it when I lost my mom and again when we lost the baby. I blocked out my feelings and all the people who cared about me, and got even more regimented about my job and my workouts."

"Sounds like you were doing whatever you could to avoid thinking about what happened."

That had pretty much been Margaret's modus operandi for most of her life, a choice that had brought her here, to a professional who could gently nudge her into dealing with all those thoughts. Being more open in this room and in her mind had led her to be more open with her family. She'd had girls' night with her sisters twice this month and spent more time at Grandma's than at her own house. She was slowly building a relationship with all of them that was more about having fun than anything else.

"I realized something else this morning." Margaret reached for the little notebook she'd started keeping with her. The tiny blue pad had become a place to jot down the thoughts that occurred to her and the emotions they evoked, a suggestion from Ashley that had helped Margaret recognize and confront her feelings more often. "Most of the bad things that happened in my life were completely out of my control. I couldn't stop my mother from driving in the rain; I couldn't stop the miscarriage from happening. But I could stop…" Her voice trailed off as a sob chased up her throat and thickened her words. "I could stop my marriage from falling apart."

"By yourself?"

Margaret shook her head and swiped away her tears. "I know it wasn't all my fault and it takes two to build or hurt a relationship. All I can do is own my mistakes in not telling Mike the truth or opening up about what I was going through. I should have trusted that he would be there for me when I needed him."

The sun streaming through Ashley's office windows cast slashes of bright light across the floor and the chair and then danced off the highlights in her blond hair. "Do you think you struggled with relying on him because you lost the one person who was supposed to be there forever when you were a little girl?"

"I think that's part of it, for sure." When her mother died, her father had retreated into his own grief, distancing himself emotionally and leaving the girls with their grandmother as their main support system. Dad had set a pattern that Margaret had unwittingly copied. "But I think I did the same thing to Mike."

"How so?"

She liked this, how Ashley would ask just the right question that opened Margaret's mind and made her come around to her own conclusions. As she sat there and let the conversation percolate, realization dawned in Margaret's mind and made her see everything that had happened from a slightly different angle. Maybe the end of her marriage wasn't as black and white as she'd thought. "I just realized that I wasn't there for Mike, either. He lost a child and was grieving that loss, just like I was. I selfishly didn't think of what he was going through or how painful that time must have been for him."

"To be fair, you were going through a lot yourself," Ashley said.

True. There'd been days when simply getting out of bed had seemed like a herculean task to Margaret. The pain of losing that baby had been deep and almost unbearable. "I was. But at some point, I should have stepped back and realized that not only did I need my husband during that awful time," she took in a breath and exhaled on a note of regret, "but he needed me, too."

"That's a great breakthrough, Margaret. Really great." Ashley made a couple notes on her pad. "The question is, what are you going to do now?"

CHAPTER 24

On Wednesday morning, Margaret lingered in bed, reading the pregnancy book she'd bought when she first found out she was pregnant. Every Wednesday, she turned to the chapter for that specific number of weeks and read the little snippet about how big the baby was and what it was doing now. Today marked sixteen weeks, not far enough along to alleviate all her fears but getting closer to where Margaret hoped maybe she'd be able to relax and stop worrying.

At sixteen weeks (four months along!) your baby is the size of an avocado! You're probably ready to start wearing maternity clothes as your baby keeps on growing. Sometime between sixteen and twenty-four weeks, you should be able to feel your baby kick.

"My little avocado, huh?" Margaret rubbed her belly and thought of how Mike would have made dorky jokes about fruits and vegetables if she told him that little factoid. And how much she missed those dorky jokes. "Don't kick yet, baby, okay? Save it for tonight."

Margaret climbed out of bed, got dressed, and headed into work. Tara didn't come in until eleven and Duane was off today, so Margaret opened the shop herself. She flipped the sign to Open, started up the register, and put out all the jewelry that they locked away at night. A little after ten, Barrett strode into the store. "Good morning, Margaret." He handed her the decaf coffee he picked up every morning on his way to work.

She set the cup on the counter and decided it was past time she dealt with whatever this was with Barrett. "Why do you do this? Bring me a coffee every day?"

"Because it makes you smile. And making you smile makes me smile."

"I hope you don't think this," she waved between the two of them, "is going anywhere."

"You are divorced now. A free woman." He gave her a smile that a month ago might have caused a flutter but now just annoyed her. "Free to date as well."

"I'm not interested, Barrett. I'm sorry. Besides, I might be divorced but I'm nowhere near ready to date. I have things I have to figure out about myself. Things I can't figure out if I'm dating someone just to stop the house from being so empty."

His brows knitted in confusion. "I don't understand."

"That's okay. You don't have to." He was a handsome man, there was no doubt about that. He just wasn't the kind of handsome she liked. She preferred men who were a little more...nerdy sometimes. "If you're still working here because you want to date me, then I'm going to kindly thank you for all you've done for my store and ask you to move on. If you're here because you love Harbor Cove, then by all means, stay. But don't wait for me. I'm never going to be available."

Barrett's jaw dropped, and he still wore that look of confusion, but Margaret didn't care. He wasn't her problem. Not anymore.

At five-thirty, Margaret stopped by Suzie's bakery to pick up three dozen rolls and an apple pie for Thanksgiving dinner at Grandma's. She and Suzie spent a few minutes marveling at her baby bump and the new loose-fitting jeans she'd found online, perfect for her slightly larger belly.

Margaret checked her phone several times on Wednesday and again on Thanksgiving afternoon, but Mike had not responded to her question about coming to dinner. All she could do was hope he would. But when she pulled up to Grandma's house and didn't see his car, it was impossible not to feel disappointed.

Margaret spent the next few minutes fluffing the pillows, rearranging the flowers, and making sure the silverware lined up perfectly with the plates. She flitted about Grandma's house, touching up this, fiddling with that. Scout had papered the windows and fridge with construction paper turkeys and cornucopias, giving the room a decidedly Thanksgiving-y air. Soon, the turkeys would be replaced by Christmas decorations, a change that Margaret dreaded. This would be her first holiday in a decade without Mike's Christmas morning pancakes—that he inevitably burned because cooking was not his strong suit—and the lit set of reindeers he liked to set up on the lawn. This year, she'd decided the decorations would stay on the shelf in the garage. She couldn't bear to decorate. Not this year. Not yet.

"You are as nervous as a bull in a china shop," Grandma said. "You need to sit down and take a deep breath."

"I just want it all to be perfect." That way, there'd be one less thing for people to get upset about, one less thing to upset the very delicate issue she was bringing into her family's life.

By four-thirty, her sisters and their spouses had arrived and were sitting down at the dining room table, which had an extra leaf in it tonight to fit everyone. Scout had already eaten, so she was in the living room watching a movie. Emma and Luke sat on one side of the dining room table, Gabby and Jake on the other, with space for three other people remaining. Harry sat at one end of the table and Grandma was sitting at the other, the two of them smiling at each other like they had a secret just between them. It was good to see Grandma so happy, even if that same joy made Margaret's heart ache.

A set of headlights swung into the driveway, and a small sedan parked behind Luke's truck. Margaret rushed to the front door, hoping to see Mike's car, but instead saw Richard's. She had a hundred doubts as she watched him park. Maybe she should have warned them all first, tested the waters a little. But if she had, would they have said yes?

Richard made his way up the front steps, clutching a bottle of wine and a bouquet of flowers. His normally friendly face was pale and tense, an echo of the nerves Margaret felt. For weeks, they'd talked about him coming to dinner to meet her family, to tell them in person what he'd wanted to say for decades. She'd kept putting it off, wanting to find the perfect time, until she realized there was no perfect time for such an event. And so she'd chosen Thanksgiving, the day of gratitude and community, and hoped her family understood why.

"Here, let me take those," Margaret said, relieving him of the wine and flowers. "Is Tabitha coming, too?"

"She's at her mother's today, but I told her I'd text her later. Maybe she could come for dessert. Assuming, of course, that this goes well."

"It's going to be fine. I promise." Except she didn't know that for sure. What happened today was out of her control, a position Margaret was gradually getting used to as part of her new, less rigid self.

She looped her other arm through Richard's and led him into the house and over to the dining room. Everyone swiveled toward the stranger as Margaret set the wine and flowers on the buffet table. "Grandma, Emma, Gabby, I want you to meet someone." She took a deep breath. "This is Richard Hargrave. He is—"

"The one who killed Penny," Grandma finished. Her face, usually so welcoming, went stony. Emma's gaze darted from Grandma to Margaret, and Gabby looked like she wanted to kill Margaret for upsetting everyone.

Margaret swallowed hard. Had she just made a massive mistake?

"I know I'm probably not who you expected to see, particularly on Thanksgiving. I hope you all know this is as hard of a meeting for me as it is for all of you." Richard released Margaret's arm and put up a hand, telling her he had it under control. "I appreciate Margaret inviting me to this dinner. I have wanted to meet you all for so many years, but I was afraid that it would be too difficult for you, too traumatizing."

"You have that right," Gabby muttered.

"Gabs, please," Margaret said. "Just listen to him."

He took a couple more steps toward the table, uneven steps that revealed a glint of metal every time he moved. Jake scrambled to his feet and pulled out a chair for Richard. "Thank you." Richard took the seat beside Jake while Margaret came around to sit beside Emma.

The tension in the air was thicker than snow piling up in a January nor'easter. No one said anything for a long moment. The grandfather clock in the hall ticked away the time. The oven dinged, but no one moved to grab the turkey.

"I want you all to know I have no expectations for this meeting, and if you want me to leave, just say the word and I'll go." Richard waited a beat, and when no one replied, he took in a deep breath and then went on. "For years, I've wanted to say how deeply sorry I am for what happened. I was a different man then, a man I am not proud of, and as much as that moment cost me, it cost all of you an unbearable price that I can't imagine paying." He looked at each of the Monroes in turn, facing them directly, not shying away from the pain in their faces or the history between them. Tears brimmed in his eyes and began to fall. Margaret wanted to reach out and hold his hand, make this easier somehow, but she knew this was a speech Richard needed to make on his own. "I have no excuse for what I did. Nothing to offer you except an apology that I mean from the deepest parts of my heart. If I could take it all back or if I could be the one inside that car, I would do it in a second. I never wanted to hurt your mother or anyone else. I am so, so sorry."

The front door opened, and Mike walked in, along with a quick gust of November air. He shut the door and held up what looked like a ream of paper. "Sorry I'm late. I wanted to print the finished draft of the book for you to read, El—" He glanced at the dining room table and any trace of friendliness disappeared. "DJ? What are you doing here?"

"Turns out Margaret invited the drunk driver who killed our mother to dinner," Gabby said with an acerbic tone. "Wait…how do you know him, Mike?"

"Richard Hargrave Jr., also known as DJ, for Dicky Jr. I didn't put it together when I saw your name in the folder Margaret kept about the accident." Mike glared at Richard for a second and then shifted his attention back to the table. "DJ was my father's best friend and drinking buddy. The same man who convinced my father that one more round was always a good idea."

Richard winced. "I deserve all your anger and more. I've made a lot of mistakes in my life, but none as bad as the decision to pick up that first drink and the thousands that came after it."

Margaret could see it all heading south at a fast clip. A simmering resentment was building in the room, the last thing she wanted. "Everyone, I know this is a lot to take in, but I hoped that on Thanksgiving at least, we could all try to be open-minded and hear what Richard has to say. Mike, you need to hear this, too, so I hope you'll stay." Margaret gestured to her ex-husband to take the seat across from Richard. Mike set the book on the credenza and then slowly lowered himself into a chair, his face stunned, confused, and angry.

"Let me back up a little and explain how we got here," she said to her silent family. "I was as angry as all of you about what happened to Momma. Spitting mad, as Grandma would say. So, when I got my driver's license, I looked up Richard and reached out to him. I wanted to tell him face-to-face how much he had ruined our lives."

She could have dropped a pin in the room and heard it bounce off the carpet. Margaret kept on talking, hoping if she put enough words out there, they would all understand. "Then Richard walked—well, rolled—into the coffee shop, and I realized we were not the only ones paying a hefty price for what happened that night."

The light dawned in Grandma's eyes first. The way he limped slightly. The metal that shone beneath his pants leg. "You lost a leg in the accident?"

"Yes, ma'am," Richard said. "Both of them."

A couple people gasped. "And then you spent a year in jail? In a wheelchair?" Emma said. "That must have been awful."

"It was nothing compared to what you all went through, so please don't spend a second feeling sorry for me. I got what I deserved, and I spent a long time hating myself for it. Killing someone, losing my legs, going to jail...none of it was enough to make me stop drinking. I was in a deep hole of misery and bad decisions that I didn't think I'd ever escape. Then my daughter was born, and I realized I needed to sober up for good, so that she could have a better life than I ever did." Richard shifted in the chair and looked over at Mike. "That's why I stopped hanging around with your father, Mike."

She had never seen Mike this quiet and still. He barely blinked. He seemed to be digesting Richard's words, weighing them, before he responded.

"I didn't know any of that initially," Margaret said to Mike. "I had no idea that he was connected to your father until a few years later when you and I got married and Richard told me he had been friends with your dad."

Mike's gaze flicked to her. "Why didn't you tell me then?"

For a hundred reasons, she thought. She was protecting Mike from one more reminder of what his father had done. She was avoiding a tough conversation. She was scared and unsure how her husband would take the news. "Because your father was dying and you were working all the time, trying to keep a roof over everyone's heads. You were so angry with your father then and with anyone who had been a part of his circle that I knew you'd never understand why I would help Richard out. Especially when you and I were barely making ends meet to begin with."

Mike leaned across the table, his brown eyes meeting hers. "Why, Margaret? Why would you give him money?"

"You gave this guy money?" Gabby said.

"I did. And I did it because it's what Mom would have done." Margaret smoothed the tablecloth in front of her, trying to find the words to explain her actions. When she'd sent that first envelope, she'd felt a sort of release inside herself that eased the anger and grief just a tiny bit. Over the years, as she saw Richard pick himself up and raise his daughter, it made her want to help even more. "I knew that Richard was struggling financially. He'd lost his license, spent a year in jail, and had a history as an alcoholic. No one would hire him. He showed me a picture of his little girl, and she looked just like you, Em. I thought that little girl didn't deserve to become a casualty of all this, too. We were given a beautiful life with Grandma, and it was only right to make sure Richard's daughter had the same."

So many of her reasons for helping Richard were tied up in that continual need to be responsible, Margaret knew. That was part of what she was dealing with in therapy, trying to find the line between supporting the people she loved but caring for herself, too.

"Every few weeks, I'd find an envelope with cash or a

cashier's check in my mailbox," Richard said. "It wasn't a ton of money, but for a single dad who could barely keep the lights on, that money made a huge difference. It took me years to figure out it was Margaret."

Her sisters and grandmother were listening, their eyes wide with surprise. Mike wasn't saying anything and still looked angry with her or the situation, it was hard to tell which. But no one was yelling. This was good, Margaret told herself. "I know it's hard to understand. When Momma said, 'Watch out for your sisters,' I guess I took that job pretty seriously."

"I think she meant making sure we didn't fall off the monkey bars, Meggy," Emma said.

"I was nine, and nine-year-olds are pretty literal." Margaret shrugged. "With Richard, it was more than that. I thought long and hard about what Mom would have done if the situation had been reversed. She wouldn't have wanted Richard's daughter to suffer because of what happened, and she wouldn't have wanted to carry bitterness in her heart. At first, I started out sending him money because I wanted to help his daughter, but over time, it became about much more than that. I saw that he was doing work that would help people who had been through what we had, and I wanted to do whatever I could to support that."

"What kind of work?" Gabby's anger had eased, replaced by genuine curiosity in her voice.

"I'm a family counselor at a rehab just outside of town," he said. "I work with families who have been affected by alcohol and substance abuse, particularly children who have been through traumatic situations."

Grandma sat back in her chair with a bittersweet smile. "Oh my. That's wonderful. That is exactly what Penny would have wanted. Her whole life was about making the world better for children, her own and others."

Just as Emma had done, continuing on their family legacy. And Gabby with re-creating Momma's favorite dresses. And Mike with the book, bringing Dear Amelia's advice about relationships to everyone in the world. Margaret glanced over at the picture of her mother that sat on the credenza and thought how proud she would be in this moment.

"So, how do you help the kids?" Emma asked. "It sounds like the kind of program that could help a lot of the women at my community center."

"I start with honesty, which can be tough, but it's necessary." Richard looked at Margaret, and then at each of her sisters, and finally, Mike. "Because you can't fix what you don't acknowledge."

The family began peppering Richard with questions. Margaret sat back and watched, no longer nervous because she knew the Monroe women, and if there was one thing they did well, it was accept and love other people. Then someone said, "Pass the potatoes," and it was as if a dam had broken, shifting them into a normal family dinner full of jokes and small talk and memories. Margaret retrieved the turkey and carved everyone a slice and the room filled with warmth.

Once everyone had finished eating, Margaret brought some of the dishes into the kitchen to make room for the pie she'd brought. The meeting had gone better than she expected, and she hoped that it would be as healing for her sisters as it had been for her. They'd all been through so much with the loss of their mother and hopefully seeing that there was some good coming from a tragedy would ease that loss for everyone.

When she turned around, Mike was there, standing in the doorway of the kitchen. "Can the pie wait? I'd like to talk to you."

"Sure." She set the plate and pie knife on the table, and tried not to fidget. She'd been nervous before, but now, alone with Mike, she was ten times more nervous. They hadn't spoken to or seen each other since the divorce was finalized. She'd thought of reaching out but had no idea what to say or how to open those lines of communication. It was quite possible that he hated her after everything that had happened and that all the realizations she'd had in therapy had come too late for them. "Thank you for coming. I'm sure it was difficult."

The words were so impersonal and chilly. She had played this moment in her mind a hundred times, determined not to withdraw and be Margaret, but to be Meg. So far, she was Margaret, through and through. Those old defense mechanisms kept rising to the occasion, keeping her from being vulnerable, from getting hurt.

"It was." He slipped his hands into his pockets, as if he was nervous, too, and unsure of what to do or how to stand in the same room as his ex-wife. "It's hard to see you, Meg."

"Margaret? Is dessert coming?" Grandma called from the dining room. "Scout says she's ready for pie."

Margaret glanced at the apple pie on the counter. The perfect excuse to avoid a difficult moment with Mike, and something she would have used as a reason to leave the room before. Where had that gotten her over the years? Certainly not where she wanted to be. Margaret had gathered her family, invited Richard to come, and encouraged Mike to be a part of this dinner because she no longer wanted to be the Margaret who lived as a solitary country and erected walls between herself and the people she loved. She left the pie on the counter and instead met Mike's gaze head-on. "She's an avocado now, you know."

He arched a brow. "Who is?"

Margaret took Mike's hand, half expecting him to yank it away. When he didn't, she gently pressed his palm against her belly. Touching him after so long apart was like...coming home. All she wanted was more of him, more of this connection, but she dared not push it. "Our little girl, or little boy. I'm four months along, and the book said that's when you can start feeling it kick."

"I don't think avocados can kick."

She laughed and he laughed and everything eased between them. "You still crack me up, Mike."

"I'm glad." He held her gaze for a long moment, and as foolish as it was, she hoped he would say the words she hadn't heard in months, maybe years, because they were beating so hard in her heart. Instead, Mike stepped back and leaned against the counter. "I wish you had told me about Richard earlier. I understand why you didn't, but we should have talked about it."

"I have a million should'ves, Mike." She sighed. "We did so many things wrong. We got married so quickly that we never had those conversations about our childhoods or what we were afraid of. Then your dad got sick, and we got hit with real life, and I think we didn't have enough of a foundation to know how to handle it. After we lost the baby, it was like the last straw for our marriage. We should have gone to see someone like Beverly back then."

"Instead, we shut the door. Literally."

She nodded and took a step closer to him. She tried to read his eyes but everything inside her was brimming with hope, making it impossible to be objective. "I'd really like to reopen that door, Mike. There's a can of paint sitting in that bedroom and three walls that need to be finished."

He sighed and glanced away. "We just got divorced, Margaret. What are we doing here?"

"Honestly, I don't know." She saw Emma poke her head into the kitchen. "We need a minute."

"Oh! Take all the minutes you need." Her sister darted back to the dining room.

"You're asking me to reopen a door," Mike said, "and it seems like you mean a door to more than just a nursery. Why did you go through with the divorce if you were going to turn around and change your mind?"

"Because I didn't think it was possible to rebuild what we had from where we were. By the time the court date came up, we were no longer talking, and I wasn't sure you'd want anything to do with me. I thought…" She bit her lip and blinked away the tears that threatened her eyes. "The only fair thing to do was let you go so you could make your own decisions, not feel obligated to stay with me just because of the baby or anything else."

He considered that for a moment. "So, you don't want to sell the house?"

"Not if we can find a way to make it work, financially. I

mean, we have two places and that costs a lot, so it may be impossible." How she wished they didn't live apart, that they had never let all these unspoken truths become a wedge in their marriage. "I'd really like to see our daughter—or son—grow up there, just like we dreamed years ago."

"That would be easier," he said, a grin toying with the edges of his mouth, whispering a tiny bit of hope, "because I do still have all my tools in the garage."

She laughed. "You are such a practical dork. I've always loved that." *I've always loved you*, she thought, but didn't speak.

Mike brushed her bangs off her forehead and let his hand remain against her cheek. The brown eyes she loved so much softened and his smile widened. "I thought you loved the motorcycle."

"I loved what the motorcycle represented." She took his other hand in hers. "But what I truly loved was that being with you gave me permission to stop being so responsible for a little while."

"Little did you know that I'd turn out to be just like you. We fell into a pattern, Meg. Protecting other people at the expense of ourselves. Putting their needs ahead of our own. Hell, you went through with the divorce because you thought it would make me happier, not because it would make *you* happier."

No wonder they had found each other and ended up together. Ironically, it was only by leaving Mike that she could see what being together had created. "Can we break those patterns?"

"I think anything can be fixed if you try hard enough." He cupped her jaw and met her gaze. "If you want to."

"I do. I never stopped, you know." She swallowed and whispered the words that made her most vulnerable, tearing down that last defensive wall between them. "I never stopped loving you, Mike."

A big smile spread across his face. "Oh, Meg, I have loved you from the minute I met you. I still do." He kissed her then, a sweet kiss that was as tender as their very first kiss and as precious as that kiss in the stairwell. His kiss told her everything was going to be all right, that he was right here, and all she had to do was let go, be the woman he saw in her, and trust him.

This time, Meg was going to do exactly that.

Mike drew back, and everything about him seemed to ease. "We were young and dumb when we got married. If we had waited until we were older, do you think we would have done it differently?"

"Maybe." She took his hands in hers and thought of all the issues neither of them had dealt with from their past. She'd finally started tackling them in therapy and she knew Mike was open to doing the same. "We're older now. Hopefully wiser. Do you think we should find out?"

He pulled her into his arms and kissed the top of her head. She inhaled the familiar scent of him, this man she had loved for so long, and hoped she never had to let go. "I think we absolutely should."

ONE YEAR LATER

Meg fidgeted at the back of the church, straightening her dress that had been retailored to fit the hourglass figure she'd developed over the last year, a big change from the lean runner's body she'd always had. Apparently, Mother Nature didn't care how many miles Meg ran before and after she became a new mother. She glanced at her reflection in the glass doors and had to admit she liked having these wider hips, a fuller chest, and a little more meat on her bones, as Grandma called it. "Does it look okay? I'm not as thin as you, Gabby."

Gabby fluffed the train, lifting it and letting it flutter back down to the maroon carpet. "You look perfect. And you have curves that I would kill to have."

"In a few more months, you'll have those curves, too." Meg grinned at her middle sister, who was just beginning to show. "You and Emma both."

Emma heaved herself out of the upholstered chair, a hand at her back. Meg's sisters didn't know yet, but soon there would be four Monroe babies, all around the same age. Family dinners were never going to be the same—or quiet—ever again.

"That assumes I don't roll out into the street," Emma said. "This baby is as big as a house. Therefore, I am as big as a house."

Scout dashed over to Emma and hugged her belly, something she did every chance she got. She still fit into her pink dress from Gabby's wedding, which made pink-fan Scout ecstatic. "I can't wait to meet you, little baby."

Emma laughed and patted Scout's head. "Me too, kiddo. Only a couple more weeks."

A few feet away, Suzie was swaying back and forth, cooing to the baby in her arms. A little girl named Penny, dressed in head-to-toe pink, who always had a smile for every person she met. Penny was just like her namesake, a happy addition to everyone's lives. "This little girl can't wait for her cousins to come along and keep her company."

Meg leaned over and pressed a kiss to her daughter's temple, inhaling that baby scent that still struck Meg as a miracle every single time. "She's so beautiful when she's sleeping."

"She's so beautiful because she's wearing pink," Emma said.

"The color is growing on me, but only because you put it on my adorable little girl." Meg tapped Penny on the nose. She did look cute in pink, but if Meg told Emma that, there'd be an explosion of pink clothes for Penny under the Christmas tree next weekend.

The violinist started playing, and all three Monroe women perked up. "I think it's time," Meg said.

"Not yet. You need one more thing." Gabby reached in her pocket and pulled out a necklace. A simple silver pendant with intertwined birthstones that glinted in the overhead lights. "I borrowed this from you, and now, I think it's time to return it."

Meg put a hand over the necklace and fought back the tears that were brimming in her eyes. She'd just done her makeup, for Pete's sake. She was determined not to cry over a simple piece of jewelry that had been the beginning of the first time she married Mike and the little something borrowed when Gabby married Jake. It was a necklace that would always symbolize to Meg new beginnings and, hopefully, perfect second chances. "Don't make me cry before the pictures."

"It's okay to cry. You're the bride." Gabby gave her sister a quick, gentle hug. "Okay, it's showtime."

The sisters wandered out to the foyer of the church, taking their places behind the rest of the wedding party. Her whole family, together again for another happily-ever-after. It seemed fitting, after all she and her sisters had gone through, that love had made their bonds grow exponentially. Grandma was going to need a bigger dining room table, that was for sure.

Harry walked Eleanor down the aisle first, the two of them giggling like schoolchildren—or more like newlyweds. They'd come back from their honeymoon last weekend and had been inseparable ever since.

After Margaret's father and his wife headed down and took their seats, Suzie began walking down the aisle, pushing Penny in a carriage that had been bedecked with pink bows and even a pink balloon on the handle—added by Emma at the last minute. Emma followed behind in a pale pink maxi dress that swished around her ankles. Gabby was next in a paler pink dress she'd fashioned partly from an old dress of Momma's that she'd found in the attic.

Meg drew in a deep breath and then started walking down the aisle in the same wedding gown Gabby and their mother had once worn, clutching her bouquet so tightly that she was sure the stems would snap in half. Nerves fluttered in her stomach. Well, nerves and...

A secret she was keeping from her not-yet husband, for a tiny bit longer.

And then she saw him at the end of the aisle, standing beside Jake and Luke, his brothers-in-law and brothers-in-life. Mike had let his hair grow out a little, making him look a bit more like the motorcycle-riding guy she'd met more than a decade ago and the author he now was. Grandma's book had sold well, resulting in the publisher asking for a follow-up book that Mike was currently working on between clients. He enjoyed working from home, partly in accounting and partly in creative pursuits, and spending a lot of time with his new daughter. He shifted his weight as the music swelled—clearly just as nervous as she was—until Meg closed the gap and stood beside him.

They'd spent a year apart, working on themselves, dealing with their childhood issues, and most of all, getting to know each other again. Mike had met with Richard a few times, trading stories about his dad and getting to know the man he had been before the alcohol changed his life. There'd been family dinners every Wednesday night with Mike at the table every week, because, after all, he'd never really stopped being a part of the family.

Slowly, gradually, Meg and Mike had come back together. They'd talked every night, whether in person or on the phone, sometimes for hours. They talked about all the things they had set aside over the years, and when those were talked out, they talked about their dreams for the future.

"You look stunning," Mike whispered to her, his eyes filled with so much love that it emanated from him like heat from a radiator. Gabby took the flowers from her, but Meg barely noticed. All of her attention was on Mike, on those deep brown eyes that she'd fallen for in the middle of a party and never quite stopped loving.

"Let's do this right this time," he said, and she knew he meant more than just their wedding.

"We might have a little bit more of a challenge this time around," she said, and then she leaned forward and whispered something in Mike's ear. His eyes widened and a grin bigger than the state of Massachusetts spread across his face.

"That's going to be a lot," he said. "Two kids? Are you sure we can handle it?"

She leaned in again and whispered softly, "I dare you."

YOUR BOOK CLUB RESOURCE

READING GROUP GUIDE

AUTHOR'S NOTE

Dear Reader,

As I wrote the last book in the Monroe Girls trilogy, I definitely felt a little sad. It's been a great ride with the Monroe family, and I will definitely miss them!

A lot of readers have asked me where I get the inspiration for the sisters in my family-centric books. I'm the oldest of four—with one sister and two brothers—and have been through all those sibling squabbles about toys and who gets the bigger bedroom. Now we're all adults, so the squabble days are long behind us, and we have a totally different, grown-up relationship.

My second husband has three daughters of his own, so with my two, that makes five kids between us. We just took our young adults on a family vacation to a mountainside cabin in Georgia and did all the kitschy family things—tie-dyeing T-shirts, making friendship bracelets, and playing games. But most of all, we talked and built those all-important family bonds.

It's been wonderful to sit back as a parent and watch them all create a connection. Most of my Monroe Girl inspiration has come from the loving relationship our kids seemed to instinctively find the minute they first met.

I hope you get to do some kitschy things with your family this year, no matter if that family is related by blood or by love. Feel free to write to me at shirley@shirleyjump.com if you come up with a really cool idea, because we plan on taking lots more family vacations so we can strengthen those bonds even more.

Thanks for being a part of the Monroe Girls family with me. I hope you loved them as much as I do!

DISCUSSION QUESTIONS

1. This novel explores a marriage on the brink of divorce. What were the turning points in the story? How and when did Margaret and Mike change and grow? Who changed the most?

2. Are Margaret's motivations for ending her marriage believable to you? She struggles to share these feelings with her family and with her husband. She tells herself it's because she's a private person, but what do you think is the real reason she keeps her emotions buried?

3. How does Mike avoid difficult subjects? How does that impact his relationship with Margaret and lead to their separation? Have you ever missed warning signs in your own personal relationships?

4. Margaret and Mike try one appointment with a marriage counselor. Do you think that they were open enough with the counselor to make a difference in that meeting? Has counseling helped you? How?

5. Mike's self-esteem takes a serious hit when he is laid off, but he manages to build a much happier work life for himself. Are you satisfied with your work life? What does your

intuition tell you that you should do? If you were to make a change, do you think that you would be proven right to have listened to your gut or should you play it safe and stick with the job that you have?

6. Margaret kept a big secret from Mike. Do good intentions ever make up for a deception? Have secrets over money ever affected one of your relationships?

7. What wounds do you think Mike brought to their relationship? How are Margaret's wounds both different from and similar to Mike's? How are her issues different from and similar to those of her sisters, Gabby and Emma, even though they each experienced the death of their mother?

8. How do Margaret's sisters try to help her as she goes through this difficult time? Who in your extended family provides the best support for you in times of crisis?

9. Shirley Jump is often praised for writing stories that elicit readers' emotions. Discuss the moments of the story that were the most emotional for you. What moments made you cry? What moments made you laugh?

10. Margaret is scared and overjoyed when she finds out she's pregnant, but she doesn't tell Mike about the baby until she is rushed into the emergency room. Do you think she was wrong to keep that information from him? Do you think having a baby can help repair a troubled marriage?

11. Eleanor and Harry decide to meddle in Margaret and Mike's relationship by bringing them together to write a book. Do you think that helped or hurt the situation?

12. Eleanor is clearly the heart of her family. Who is the heart of your family?

13. Margaret thinks of herself as Margaret, and everyone around her calls her Margaret, but Mike sees her as Meg, the fun-loving girl he met all those years ago. By the end of the book, Margaret has shifted to seeing herself as Meg, too. How has she changed over the course of the story?

14. Do you know of any real-life couples who have remarried? Do you believe this is a sign that a relationship is meant to be?

15. The sisters have started a tradition by wearing the aquamarine and diamond necklace that will hopefully extend to the weddings of their daughters. What are the meaningful traditions in your family? If you started a new one, what would it be?

ABOUT THE AUTHOR

When she's not writing books, *New York Times* and *USA Today* bestselling author Shirley Jump works on perfecting her baking skills—and then runs several miles a day to work off all those dessert calories. She's published more than eighty books in twenty-four languages, although she's too geographically challenged to find any of those countries on a map.